LOIS LANE™

FALLOUT

SWITCH
PRESS
a capstone imprint

CHAPTER 1

"Remember the plan," I muttered.

I sped up as the school came into view, a telltale yellow bus lumbering away from the curb. The soles of my knee-high boots clicked against the concrete sidewalk.

Fit in. Don't make waves.

A small herd of stragglers were still dragging their feet toward the three-story, pristine brick structure of East Metropolis High. I'd made it before first bell, then—barely. A slouchy boy in a baggy T-shirt held the door for me. That must mean my carefully selected ensemble of a plaid mini, black tights, and sweater with a small, cute skull-and-crossbones motif was okay. I'd been to enough new schools to know that people didn't hold doors if they thought you were dressed too weirdly.

"Where's the office?" I asked the first studious-looking girl I saw.

She shyly pointed up the hall, and I set off as the bell rang.

This was a bigger school than I was used to, more people roaming the halls, the classrooms fuller and in greater number. The school colors were blue and red, and walking down the hall felt a little like being inside an American flag. My Army general dad would love it.

I spotted a sign hanging up ahead that read "Principal and Administrative Office." But when I got closer to the glassed-in area, I hesitated. There was a line.

Six boys—no, wait, a couple of them were girls—stood in silence a few feet away from the door. They were dressed in all black, and obviously together, facing each other in rows of three. How they stared at each other tempted me to joke, *Get a classroom*. Except on second look, it wasn't moony-eyed-in-love staring. It was more intense than that.

"So . . ." I said when they didn't budge. Or speak. "Are you waiting?"

"Yes," a boy with brown hair said.

"But not for you," another added, in a flat tone creepily similar to the first.

The second bell rang. We became the only people left in the hallway.

"I didn't think you were," I said, in a nice way. "It's my first day here."

None of them spoke.

Oh-kay.

"Thanks for the warm welcome." I went wide around them to the door. "I'll just cut the line now."

Inside, the layout was simple: a reception area with a few chairs and a desk positioned to serve as gatekeeper. Behind it, the first few feet of a carpeted beige hallway were visible, leading, no doubt, back to the principal's office.

No one was at the desk, so I sat down to wait. Patiently. As patiently as possible when I was already late on my first day at a brand-new school, anyway.

I hoped they hadn't pulled up my transcripts, seen my dreaded permanent record, and decided not to admit me. *If* permanent records even existed, which I wasn't sure about.

Then again, nothing in my life had ever been permanent. I might be biased.

I took a deep breath, crossing my fingers that the rude group in the hallway wasn't an omen. Things had to be different here. *I* had to be different here.

"Don't screw this up, Lane," I whispered.

Then I heard voices. Overheard, actually. They were coming from up that bland beige hall. And they were arguing.

No one had showed up to help me, and the creepy group outside wasn't loitering where they could see in the windows. So it wasn't like there was anyone to notice when I got up and moved a little closer to the gatekeeper's desk to better hear what the argument was about . . . And a little closer . . . And right on past the desk . . . *There.*

I stopped at the edge of the hall, still technically in the front office. But now I could hear what they were saying.

"Principal Butler, please." The girl speaking had a quiet voice, but it was raised and wavering. "You know I would never inconvenience you without justification. I know how it sounds, but the Warheads are annihilating my sanity. Or endeavoring to. I swear to you, they're . . . *doing* something to me. To my *mind*. Cognitive assault. Psychological coercion. Those are the closest terms I can find, though they are not precisely correct."

That was some SAT-worthy vocabulary. Impressive.

I started to edge closer, into the hallway, but I forced myself to stop. I needed to stay out of view, under the radar. I did not need to be caught trespassing in admin offices.

That didn't stop me from listening hard.

"Anavi," a smooth, older man's voice said, "I can see something is bothering you, but now isn't the best time. Don't you play some computer game together? Is this a crush gone bad on one of them, maybe?"

"No." The girl held firm. "They wouldn't permit me to complete my computer science homework this morning. I kept . . . transcribing incorrect answers. It was almost like they were forcing me to write the mistakes. Please, Principal Butler, if you'll just make them stop—"

"I'm busy with the school's guest speaker this morning," the older man—Principal Butler—said. "But Anavi, I want you to think about what you're saying. I'm tempted to send you for a psych eval, questioning your own sanity like this, but I know how your parents would react. You and your gaming group need to work this out."

"But I'm not part of their group. I have not a single iota of interest in it. I just want to be left alone."

The girl sounded like she was out of options. But the smooth-tongued principal wasn't completely wrong. What she was saying *did* sound crazy.

Which was what interested me.

Without meaning to, I was walking up the hallway, just to get a look at the people in the conversation. I peered around a corner.

"If that's true," the principal said, "then making wild accusations is probably not the best way to keep a low profile. I'm confident you can work this out on your own."

There were three of them, standing outside a closed office door. A man in his mid-thirties in a hip, knock-off suit was staying quiet, but watching the exchange. The girl was medium height, wearing glasses and an expression closing in on panic. No doubt her reaction to being dismissed by the third, a slickly dressed man who must be the principal.

He started, "Now, I need to escort Mr.—"

The quiet man gave a slight shake of his head as if to say *Don't mind me.* "No rush."

"Please, you have to listen," the girl said. "I don't want to get anyone in trouble. But you know that in order to claim my scholarship winnings I must maintain a spotless academic record. They're disrupting my mental capacity, inside the game and outside it. You have to stop them."

"Calm down, or the psych eval is a possibility," the principal said, as if it pained him.

I recognized his type. The veneer of niceness didn't fool me. His gray suit and silver hair made me think of a shark. Only he wasn't predator king of the sea, but entitled emperor of this school. He didn't seem to want to help the girl with her problem. Instead he seemed inclined to protect the gamers who were bullying her.

I cleared my throat and took a few more steps toward them, joining the conversation. "Excuse me," I said. "I couldn't help overhearing. I have to agree with—Anavi, right?—that an administrator should take a bullying complaint seriously and do what he can to stop it. I'm assuming the school does have a policy?" I waited for a response.

The slick principal blinked at me. The other man tried to hide his amusement. Meek Anavi braced as if for an explosion.

"Who are *you*?" the principal asked with a note of disbelief.

I'd forgotten about the plan. *Stay quiet. Keep my head down.*

"Um. Lois Lane," I said.

"Oh," the principal said, "yes, I remember your permanent record. It was . . . lengthy. Your father called me. Said to keep an eye on you."

So they are *real. Also, thanks, Dad.*

"This is a big school. You can't see everything," I said. And, mentally kicking myself, I added, "It's my first day."

"Auspicious beginning," the other man said.

"I know you're enjoying this," the principal said to him. He returned his attention to me. "Since it *is* your first day, shouldn't you have arranged to be here on time? And did you really turn your seventh grade class into a 'gambling den'?"

I ignored the first question. "I taught some girls how to play poker at a sleepover," I said, a little defensively. "Now, why wouldn't you send her for evaluation? By a professional or a counselor? What she's saying would merit that if you took it seriously."

"No, that's okay," Anavi said, with a betrayed expression. "I shouldn't have reported the Warheads' behavior. I should have stayed circumspect."

"Glad to hear you're rethinking," Principal Butler said. "Ms. Lane, I can tell this wasn't true at your previous schools, but here, we guide our students. Sometimes my job is to protect them from themselves. Like Anavi here. A grand-prize winner of the Galaxy Spelling Bee. I'm positive she's capable of handling the situation on her own."

That explained the girl's twenty-dollar word choices—and meant she could spell them too. I read constantly. Magazines, newspapers, biographies. Reading was a good way to pass travel time. But I still considered auto spellcheck one of humanity's greatest inventions.

The principal gestured toward the hallway, and the gray fabric of his jacket didn't crease with the movement. That was one expensive suit. "You two are late for first period now, and so are we. Might I suggest, Ms. Lane, that you watch and listen until you understand your new school? Wait to pitch in with your . . . knowledge. Do that, and I know you'll be very happy here. Most of our students are."

"Like the one standing right across from you," I said, nodding to Anavi.

I gave myself another mental kick. *Remember the plan.*

But Principal Butler ignored me, turning to the amused man in the suit. "We should go. Ready to give your talk?"

The man hesitated. He pulled a business card out of his suit pocket. "I'm Perry White, an editor at the *Daily Planet*. I'm overseeing a new online start-up the paper is doing for teens. For students who want to be real journalists, all from this school to start. I've got a small staff already, but we have room for one more." He extended the card to me. "Would you be interested in a job as a reporter?"

I accepted the card. Scanning it, I took in twin logos. The first was the familiar globe with thick lettering across it that said *Daily Planet*, but the other was a smaller, more stylized globe with a slash of sleek lettering that read *Daily Scoop*.

I looked back to the man who'd offered me a job. Maybe even a dream job.

"No background check necessary," he said, fighting a grin. "Your permanent record shouldn't be an issue."

I instantly liked the idea of being a reporter. Able to ask all the questions I wanted, without anyone scolding me *or* scribbling in my file. The ability to look into things that were wrong and tell lots of people about them. This was my chance to find a place here.

"Yes," I said. "I'll take it, Mr. White."

"Great, but don't call me mister," he said. "Perry's fine. Come by after school. We have a staff meeting on Mondays at four. I think you'll fit right in."

See, that was part of the plan, the fitting-in part. I hadn't screwed up after all.

Principal Butler said, "Remember what I told you."

Well, hadn't screwed up *everything*.

"How could I forget?" I asked under my breath.

Butler swept out, and Perry White followed. I trailed behind them with Anavi. I wanted to talk to her, find out more about these so-called Warheads who were bothering her to the point of fraying sanity. But as soon as we left the front office, that creepy group peeled away from their spot and came toward us. Principal Butler steered the editor around them and up the hall. Leaving me to wait with Anavi for the group to pass by us.

There was something so *alike* about them. Down to their black clothes and the mocking expressions they wore, even the liquid way they moved.

A tall one at the front of the pack said, "Got your," and another finished, "homework done," a third adding, "Anavi?"

Aha. These must be the infamous Warheads.

They'd been waiting for *her*.

"Are they gamers or a performance art group?" I asked, frowning.

But she didn't answer. She was busy bolting at the speed of light in the opposite direction. They kept moving, and I watched them until they were gone.

I'd track her down again later.

I had a job to do now.

CHAPTER 2

I might have a job, but I was still without a schedule. So I returned to the front office and sat in the waiting area, studying the *Daily Scoop* logo on the business card like it would disappear if I stopped. But it didn't.

It was real.

I put the card in my messenger bag and took out my phone. After a second's hesitation, I signed into the secure messenger app that I only used with one person, my one long-distance friend. I wanted to tell someone about this.

All right, I wanted to tell *him*.

I tapped out the message, and it popped up alongside my screen name.

SkepticGirl1: *Guess what?*

I waited, not sure if he'd be signed in or able to respond. He was probably in class.

SmallvilleGuy: *You got kicked out of school already, setting a world record?*

SkepticGirl1: *Ha-ha. Nope.*

SkepticGirl1: *I got a job.*

The door opened and a blond twenty-something in a pastel flower-print dress rushed in clutching a tall latte with the word "Skinny" scrawled on the cup.

I texted: *Tell you all tonight.* And re-stashed my phone.

The woman made for the hallway to the principal's office.

"He's off taking Perry White somewhere," I said.

Her shoulders slumped and she turned. She set the latte down on the desk. "My life is over."

I nodded at the coffee. "That was for him?"

She exhaled, blowing a fringe of bangs out of her eyes. "There was a huge line, and—"

"Then he should have been there to wait in it himself."

Her eyes widened.

"Yes, he should have," she said, low, as if he might overhear us. She shot me a smile that was the equivalent of a bright sunrise. "Ronda. What can I help you with?"

"I need a class schedule, locker assignment, the good stuff."

"Name?" She was still smiling.

"Lane. Lois Lane."

Her eyes widened again, and her smile dimmed. "Did you

really doxx an art teacher who was living under an assumed identity?"

"No. I sent the cops some publicly available documents."

Ronda raised her eyebrows and flipped through some files on her desk. I resisted the urge to ask to see mine. It sounded like it was full of details woefully devoid of context.

She wrote down a locker number at the bottom of a sheet of paper with a list of classes. "You need someone to show you around?" she asked.

It wasn't like this was my first new school. Or my fifth, for that matter. "I'll manage," I said, taking the sheet. "You should drink the coffee."

"Maybe I will," she said as I left the office.

Schools usually felt the same to me. At the others, I'd never minded being asked by the teachers in every class where I was from and having to say, "Nowhere." Or, sometimes to mix things up, "Everywhere." My first two class periods at East Metropolis went exactly that way, except this time I had to hide how nervous I was.

My third-period AP lit teacher, Mrs. Garret, herded us to the library to do critical research on a poem before she remembered to ask the inevitable first-day question. I was settled behind a flat-screen computer to search the article database, like everyone else. "Lois," she said, her updo held in place with chopsticks that could have served as a weapon in a pinch, "before we get started, tell us where you're from."

The rest of the morning had gone pretty well, give or take. So I went off script. "Here. Now I'm from here."

The odd round of looks reminded me why you were supposed to stay on script when you were new.

But then I never had been much good at supposed-tos.

"A philosopher, I see," she said.

"And a lady," I quipped.

Stay under the radar.

No goofy jokes.

Mrs. Garret left to go chat with the librarian, and instead of starting on the assignment I pulled up a browser window. I typed: Journalism, history of.

But I hesitated before I hit enter. The history of women in any field was often separated out and I wanted that part of the story too. I changed the search terms to: Journalism, history, women in.

I glanced around and caught the girl in the seat next to mine taking in my screen. Her otherwise blond chin-length hair was streaked with bold crimson around her face.

She didn't shrink away at being busted. "You should look up Nellie Bly," she said.

Could she be friend material? Because making a friend here was part of the plan too.

I slid my notebook over. "Can you write it down? I'm one of the top five worst spellers you'll ever meet."

With a laugh, she took the notebook and wrote the words. The T-shirt she had on was for a band—Guerilla Bore. I'd never heard of them.

"I'm Maddy," she said, and we both noticed that Mrs. Garret was watching us chat. Maddy pushed my notebook back.

"And I'm letting you work on the assignment so you don't get in trouble," I said. "Thank you."

I typed in the new search term.

*

After school, I flagged over a taxi driver and flashed him the business card Perry White had given me.

"I need to get here," I told him as I got into the backseat.

"So you will," he said, adjusting the collar of his white tracksuit as he checked the rearview mirror. The car lurched into traffic.

I'd intended to track down Anavi and try for some observation of the Warheads during lunch, but after third period Ronda had been waiting outside the library to take me back to the office to fill out paperwork we'd neglected to do that morning. I ate from the vending machine, and my afternoon classes seemed to crawl by in slow motion. Because I could hardly wait for this—going to my first staff meeting at the *Scoop*.

I fidgeted, antsy to get there, and watched Metropolis speed by outside the window.

Most of the places where my decorated Army general dad got stationed—and our family then moved to, careful not to put down too many roots—were military towns. Places with wire fences around bunker-like buildings and clusters of three-bedroom homes that all had the same floor plan. The cities and schools were usually small, a low sprawl surrounded by desert or woods or strip malls.

Metropolis, so far, was all tall, shiny buildings and sleek, crowded subways, with the *Daily Planet* sold at every corner newsstand. I'd never lived anywhere like this before. Metropolis was different. It was *supposed* to be different. My plan was intended to make sure that it would be.

It wasn't like I had *wanted* to not fit in at my other schools, to never come out of them with true friends . . . but I'd always been able to pretend that it didn't matter. Soon enough we'd be headed somewhere else, and fewer goodbyes to say made leaving easier. My problem was that I had bad luck. And I spoke up when I saw something wrong. I did it because I could, without having to worry about the fallout lasting years. And yes, there was always fallout.

But this time, we weren't leaving. We were here to stay. And I had a job. And a plan. The plan consisted of four things:

1. Pretend it's a tea party. Be on time, polite, and go by the schedule without protest. (In other words, not like what happened in Iowa . . . or Kentucky . . . or Minnesota.)

2. Don't swim with sharks. No need to make enemies right off the bat. (Even if they're jerks, and you're just standing up for someone they're tormenting, like in California. And Germany. And Michigan.)

3. Make like an invisible girl. Stay on the right side of the teachers and the principal. (And the best is if they barely notice that you exist. Again, even if they're jerks, or wrong about something, or completely unfair . . . like in New Mexico, Arizona, and Alabama.)

4. Make a friend.

As the shiny, hectic blur of the city passed outside the taxi window, I spun a whole scenario of life here: a perfect set of non-jerk friends chasing down stories together, vanquishing the villainous, and then heading to the movies, where we'd crack in-jokes and share popcorn coated in delicious, chemical-filled faux butter.

The taxi pulled up at the curb of the Daily Planet Building. I'd seen pictures of it on TV and in magazines re-covering stories the *Planet* had gotten to first. It had always struck me as larger than life, but here it was.

"You have to pay me and get out before you can go in there, you know," the cab driver said, not unkindly.

"Right." I passed him some money and climbed out. My eyes traveled up and up the many, many floors and landed on the globe at the top.

I looked down at the card in my hand again. And that was when it hit me—I was going to be working at the *Daily Planet*. I added to my fantasy: me and my friends staring out over the city from high in the skyscraper, drinking coffee and rubbing elbows with real reporters, people who pressed politicians and mobsters and people like my dad for answers.

Before I even realized I'd started walking, I was at the bank of revolving doors and then inside one, my fingertips pressed to the glass panel like I could make it turn faster, until I spilled out into the lobby. The buzz of conversation echoed off the marble floor, people clicking across on their way in or out, in the middle of no-doubt important conversations with each other or on their phones.

A fresh-faced, freckled security guard waited behind a desk. I approached, the card still in my palm.

"I'm Lois Lane. Here for Perry White," I said.

My heart was beating embarrassingly fast, but he couldn't know that from looking at me. He gave me a sweep of the eyes up and down like he could, though. "For the *Scoop*, I take it?"

"Which floor do I go up to?" I asked.

He shook his head. "You'll need the service elevator. Go past the main ones there, and then take it *down* to level B."

"B as in 'Baby, this view is to die for'?" I asked hopefully.

The guard raised an eyebrow. "B as in 'basement,'" he said.

So: not exactly my fantasy. But, like a good soldier, I marched past the nice elevators, the trademark globe traced in white like icing across their fronts. I stopped at a set of narrow, grim, gray elevator doors.

Turning, I saw the guard watching me. He nodded.

I pressed the call button, and the service elevator doors creaked open so slowly I was tempted to help them out. I admit it. I was a little bummed that the *Scoop* offices weren't far above the city streets with a great view through the gleaming windows. But even the basement at the *Planet* must be pretty awesome, right?

Not so much to look at, I discovered. I exited into an even grimmer sub-level, the walls painted a dismal gray. My boots echoed on dingy tile as I passed tall frames that held yellowed front pages, their headlines shouting about murders and corruption, stock market crashes and deadly fires. The sound of muffled voices, hollow and indistinct, came from the same general direction as a dim glow at the end of the long, dark hall.

Past the bend in the dark hall was an open door. As soon as I went inside, I recalled my fantasy vision of working here and pressed the mental self-destruct button to erase it.

There were three staffers my age, a girl and two boys, all of them frowning at Perry White, whose back was to me.

The girl was Maddy from my English class, so at least that was an excellent sign for the making-a-friend part of the plan. She and one of the two guys sat at big slabs of desks—not unlike coffins—which housed computers that appeared to be the only things in the room that weren't holdovers from history. The ancient variety, recorded in lost decades of decaying newsprint. The third staffer was a preppy boy perched on the corner of his coffin slab.

A fourth desk was empty.

The three noticed me at the same time, aiming their frowns past Perry to where I stood.

"Lois!" Perry turned and greeted me with a suspicious level of enthusiasm. "Welcome to the Morgue!"

I frowned, and he added, "This room still has all the last old editions that haven't been turned into pictures and ones and zeros. And the ones that are too rare to throw out."

Around the walls of the long room were cabinets that went all the way to the low ceiling. They did in fact look like every line of morgue drawers I'd seen in movies or cop shows.

"You're sure there are no bodies?" I asked.

"Bodies? Nah, the obits were the first things we digitized,

don't worry," he said. "This place is part of history. That's why we thought it was perfect for the *Scoop*, you know? A past-meets-future kind of thing."

The cabinets appeared to be labeled with dates instead of names or random numbers. So the odds were good that he was telling the truth about the place being corpse-free. Still, when I raised my eyebrows, he admitted, "And we were out of space upstairs. Come on over and meet everyone. I was just telling them about you."

Uh-oh. The other three were frowning, and he'd been talking about me?

"Go on," Perry said, "introduce yourselves."

He gave a pointed look to Maddy. She'd added a layer of dark eyeliner and bright pink lipstick since class.

"Lois and I already met," she said. "I'm style editor. Not by choice. Mr. White here thought a girl would be better at style than these two. I wanted to be the music critic."

"Perry," he corrected her. "I told you to call me Perry. And you're . . . stylish."

Maddy regarded him.

Nice try, Perry. "Hi again," I said.

"Too bad your sister wasn't interested," said a lanky boy in a crisp button down. He was the one on the edge of his desk rather than sitting in the chair behind it. He had a glossy crown of brown hair and blinding white teeth, like he'd been bred for them.

"I needed a job; the perfect one didn't," Maddy said. "Sorry to disappoint you."

Aha.

The preppy boy with the posh enunciation might think Maddy was being sarcastic, but she wasn't. The makeup she'd added before work was one giveaway, but so was the complete sincerity of her tone and how she looked at him when she said it, waiting for him to look back. He didn't.

Maddy truly *was* disappointed—that the boy would rather work side by side with her sister than her.

"Maddy has a twin sister," the guy said to me. "You'd never know they were identical."

There probably were things worse than the guy you had a crush on saying that kind of thing about your sister, but not many. Maddy could do way better than teeth-and-hair guy.

Teeth-and-Hair extended his hand, and I had no choice but to take it.

"James Worthington," he said. "News writer."

Over the years, my dad had dragged the family unit to tons of social functions, and I had met enough silver-spoon scions in tow of their politician parents that I could easily spot a seriously rich boy. And all of the seriously rich boys were dead ringers for James.

"Charmed, I'm sure," I said. His name was familiar. "Your dad's a . . . state senator?"

James released my hand and his frown returned. "No!" He sounded like I'd implied he worshipped Satan by the light of a full moon or, worse, was from new money. "He's—he *was* the mayor. He's . . . taking a break. To decide what his next move is."

The remaining staffer, a cute boy with a short afro and an air of casual cool, failed to hide a low snort. His desk had two giant monitors and several other gadgets scattered on it.

James was scowling. Yet somehow he managed to throw off an "I'm superior" vibe while doing it.

"Remember, Lois is new to town," Perry put in dryly.

"Your dad is *that* James Worthington?" I asked, before I could think better of it. I'd read about the charges against the ex-mayor of Metropolis. Multiple charges, including embezzlement. He'd gone to jail, but the family fortune supposedly remained. Why would his son work *here*, especially if he didn't have to work, period? "Didn't the *Planet* cover the scandal?"

The boy who'd snorted before spoke up. "Perry here was nominated for a Pulitzer for breaking the story."

James gritted his teeth as he answered. "Dad was editor of the *Crimson* in college. Wants me to follow in his footsteps."

"Probably not *exactly*. Not all of them," I said. "He's James Worthington Jr., right? So that makes you the Third?"

He shrugged one shoulder. "Yes."

But he'd held on to his manners, more or less, which I couldn't help but respect. Even if he was a "the Third."

"I'm Devin, master of all things computronic," the last staffer said. "Also on the news staff, and web designer. James will let us know when his dad's back in office." He added a word silently, mouthing to me: NEVER.

"People come back from worse all the time," Maddy said.

"Thanks," James the Third said to Maddy. Who soaked in the millisecond of attention he gave her like it was sunlight.

"So," Perry said, "now that you've all met, you can stop bickering about disgraced politicians—sorry, James—and take a lesson from Lois. I asked her to join the staff because I could see right away that she has the instinct. The *killer* instinct. The nose for news. The thing that makes you ask questions and not stop until someone answers them. That makes you chase the great stories. Lois didn't even know who I was, but she jumped right into a conversation, not afraid to challenge the principal with a tough question or two, even though it was her first day. If you watch Lois, you might learn how to do what you haven't so far: report actual news that matters to your audience." He looked at the staff and shook his head. "You were all the top of the applicant pool, but it's time for this experiment to yield some results. Soon. I'll leave you to it."

I gaped at his back as he left. Did he not realize that he'd practically guaranteed they would hate me? Guess I had my answer about whether my plan for our new city was going to work.

I shifted my attention from the door back to the others.

Maddy narrowed her eyes. James lifted his brows, skeptical. Devin shook his head, like he was almost sorry for me. Almost.

"Are you going to let him talk to you like that?" I asked, unwilling to concede. I *would* make this work. "Are you going to let him be right?"

"He is right," James said. "But he won't help us."

Devin sighed. "He keeps telling us that we should be able to find stories without being assigned them. That we're, and I quote, destroying his faith in the next generation."

"You agree with them that you guys suck?" I asked Maddy, hoping it wasn't too blunt.

"Well . . . we haven't been doing many stories," she said. "No news noses or whatever."

I went to the fourth giant hunk of desk and leaned against it. "Okay. I do think I might have a story for us."

"Of course you do," James said.

"Let's hear her out," Maddy said.

James's mouth opened to say something else, but Devin said, "All right with me."

Buoyed by the vote of semi-confidence, and not wanting James to have time to object, I pressed on. "We all go to East Metropolis?"

They nodded with varying degrees of reluctance.

"What do you know about the Warheads? I think they might play some kind of video game."

"They're those creeps, right? The black shirts?" Maddy asked.

Devin leaned forward and picked up one of the techy gadgets that littered his desk. It was a small black shell, curved to fit over an ear. Holosets were the biggest thing in gaming. They'd been rolled out two years ago, state-of-the-art reality-simulation tech and a handful of multi-player games to go along.

"They're into *Worlds War Three*," he said. That was the first game that had been released for holosets, and still the most popular. "I have second period comp sci with them, and I've seen them in there. The kind of players we call cannibals."

"Cannibals?" I asked.

"They seem like they'd eat not only each other but their young. Tight unit lately, though. Racking up lots of kills."

I reached out for the holoset, and Devin hesitated. "You want to try it?" he asked.

"You mind?"

After another moment, he stood and handed it to me. I slipped it over my ear. I understood how holosets worked in theory, but had never used one myself.

I asked, "Now what?"

He mimicked touching a spot at the top of the shell, and I pressed the button I found there. The office faded from view and a 3D holo-scape took its place, right in front of my face. It didn't blot out the entire world around, not exactly, but it was impossible to look anywhere else. It felt like I was inside it.

I saw a landscape with a red sky and smoke and fire, human forms picking their way through it. Someone was riding a big scaly dragon, but there was a round metal spaceship cruising above too.

Devin was speaking, and it took effort to focus on his words instead of the ambient sounds from within the scene. "The worlds warring are ours, plus alien and fantasy ones. Elves and monsters. Rayguns and Martians. You can play solo or in teams like the Warheads. It's multi-player, live action. Anyone you see is playing right now."

A missile fired from beneath the dragon's right wing, racing toward me. Coming straight at me, actually, a blazing streak—

I reached up and hit the off button, handed the holoset back to Devin. I shook my head to clear the scene from it. It took a few seconds.

"You called them creeps," I said, turning to Maddy. "Have they done something creepy that you know about?"

"Not really," Maddy said. "It's just the way they are. Always in a pack together."

"I ran into them at school," I said, "and yeah, they're creeps. And they're bullying this girl named Anavi. I think in the game first, and it sounds like outside it now too. She must be in your class, Devin. Former spelling bee champion of the world or something?"

"I know her," Devin said. "Solid player, and scary smart in class."

"The thing is, Principal Butler didn't do anything when she reported it to him. Except tell her to get over it. I don't like it. Not with stories about bullying all over the place. No principal should be waving it off, not for some great student like Anavi. That's our first story."

If the messing with the inside of her head part was true, then it might be an even bigger story. The whole thing might fall under the heading of Strange Phenomena. More and more things did these days, even if no one would admit it. The trick to seeing things other people missed was to look for them.

But the bullying angle was enough for now. No need to make these guys think of me as some nutty conspiracy theorist. I waited for the verdict.

James sniffed and crossed his arms in front of his chest. "You're not the editor."

"Neither are you," Devin pointed out. "We're just news staff. Same as Lois."

"Technically, I'm the only person in this room who's an editor," Maddy said. She smiled. "Look, it's a better idea than we've had yet. May as well try to get a story out of it and get Perry off our backs."

"Which means you're outvoted, the Third," I said, and hopped off the desk. Time to get out while I was ahead. "I have to go home. See you in class tomorrow, Devin."

"But you're not in it," he said.

I winked. "Maybe not," I said, "but I will be by then."

CHAPTER 3

When I breezed through the front door of our new apartment, the whole place smelled like from-scratch tomato sauce. In other words: heaven. If heaven was full of unpacked boxes, anyway. We'd arrived ahead of the Army-hired movers the Friday before and had only unpacked stuff we needed immediately over the weekend.

The new place was nice if still a work-in-unpacking-progress, a two-story brownstone in a good neighborhood, a couple of blocks from a subway station. We might not have James the Third money, but generals got paid well enough.

Especially when they were as beloved as my dad.

Speaking of, he poked his prematurely gray head around the kitchen doorframe and waved me over. "Come tell me about this gainful employment you've supposedly found."

He sounded like he approved of the idea. I wasn't so sure he'd be happy when he heard *where* I was working. The military liked its secrets, and part of my dad's job was keeping them. He definitely seemed to be doing more and more of it since two years ago and that night in Kansas when the two of us had seen . . . whatever it was we'd seen.

I walked to the kitchen, choosing the right words as I went. But when I reached the doorframe I realized too late that Dad had summoned me into a trap. A second later, a small knee swooped in behind mine, dropping me half to the ground. My little sister, Lucy, erupted into giggles, and then let me up.

"No fair." I cuffed the pink-cheeked, blond-ponytailed brat on the shoulder. Everyone always said Lucy and Mom looked just alike, blond and fine-featured, while I took after Dad with my dark hair and sharper angles. "I was distracted."

Lucy crinkled her nose up, her hair swinging back and forth as she shook her head. "I don't think you're supposed to admit that. Not in front of Dad."

"She might be taking the self-defense lessons a little too seriously, Sam," Mom said from the stove. But she couldn't have been that concerned, because without even looking over to check out the scuffle, she kept stirring.

I knew Dad had gone to the office today, but he'd been home long enough to change out of his dress uniform with its medals and ribbons. In a crisp polo, the lack of heroic bling left him only a shade less intimidating.

"So, what's this job you texted about? Do you know if you got it?" he asked.

General Sam Lane cowed lesser mortals—at least those who weren't his daughters. But the first lesson I ever learned? *Never show fear.*

I steeled myself in case he fought me on this. He was not a fan of the media, and regularly spent breakfast grumbling over the "slant" of stories in the morning paper.

"It was the luckiest thing," I said, going over to pick up a wooden spoon and steal a taste of the tomato sauce. "There was a guest speaker at school recruiting people for a new, um, online magazine that the *Daily Planet*'s doing. For teenagers. I figured, since we'll be here a while, it'd be a good way to meet new people. Put down roots." The things he'd said he wanted me to do.

I stole another spoonful of sauce to hide my nervousness.

"The *Daily Planet*, hmm?" he said.

"It's called the *Daily Scoop*," I said.

He and Mom exchanged a look. A long one.

"All right, I guess," he said, finally. "Sounds like it might keep you out of trouble."

"That's what I thought too." I put down the spoon and started backing out of the room. "Me and trouble are no longer on speaking terms."

Lucy whined, "Lois gets to do everything fun."

I stuck my tongue out at her. "Your turn will come."

I'd spend some quality time with Lucy later.

She had a holoset—it hadn't come with the game she'd asked for, but she played it enough despite that. I wanted to try it out, learn more about how the tech worked in prep for taking on the Warheads. But first, I had a more pressing engagement.

"Dinner's in twenty minutes," Mom said as I turned and bounded up the stairs to my room. I closed the door and waited a second with my ear to it to make sure no one was following, including Lucy practicing her stealth skills. Then I turned the lock.

Sure, it was probably overkill. But my friend claimed it was too dangerous for us to talk on the phone, let alone use Skype. He wouldn't tell me his real name, or let me see his face or hear his voice. He said it was too much of a risk for him—and for me, too, by extension. He wasn't willing to chance it. He wouldn't say more about why. I suspected it had something to do with his parents, though he claimed they were just farmers.

But I always locked my door to prevent having to explain to *my* parents or kid sister what I was doing, since any of them were capable of barging in without warning. My friend and I were also careful about passwords. We only communicated using a hyper-secure chat service. He had an online techie developer friend who was paranoid about spyware and had created the app we used on our phones and the more elaborate software installed on my laptop. Secrecy when we met up was a ritual now too, like locking the door. Habit.

He was my secret and I would keep it faithfully. Yes, it was irritating that he wouldn't trust my word and refused to tell me who he was. But, well, it wasn't irritating enough for me to give up on our . . . friendship. He had his reasons and I had to believe that they were good ones.

Someday maybe he'd tell me what they were. Or I'd figure them out on my own.

For tonight, I hoped he was there.

I opened the silver lid of my laptop and typed in my secret fourteen-character alphanumeric password. After it was accepted, I opened the chat window and put in the next code.

He *was* there waiting, or at least it looked like he was. The second I logged on to my chat account, invisible to anyone else, I saw his handle. Before I could type a greeting, he did.

SmallvilleGuy: *I expected to see you on the news, the first girl ever kicked out of a Metropolis high school on her first day. I was going to tell you I was impressed. But a job?*

I grinned. Rolled my eyes a little, and laughed. I typed out several messages in a row, not letting him get a word in edgewise—he was used to that from me, he always teased—about school, my new job, and the fact that even my dad had seemed to approve.

Sorry to disappoint you, I typed last, *but I told you it's going to be different here. I'm making a change, onto the straight and narrow.*

I waited, the cursor blinking, until a line of text popped up that told me he was typing a response.

Those seconds when I was waiting to see what he'd say next, sometimes they were the longest moments of my life. The pure anticipation made my heart race.

I could admit it to myself, because no one else would ever see it. Even he would never know how silly and vulnerable I was while I waited.

I—also known as SkepticGirl1—had first met SmallvilleGuy

two years earlier on Strange Skies, a message board where the slightly-less-lunatic fringe tracked reports of phenomena or sightings or events that couldn't be easily explained away, no matter how dedicated the local cops and the military and anyone else who got asked about them were to downplaying and denying.

I wasn't dumb—especially when he said he couldn't tell me his name, I was aware he might be some middle-aged creep pretending to be my age, and so I demanded proof that he wasn't.

After a few minutes, he'd sent me a message with an image attached. It was a photo he'd taken with his phone of his learner's permit, his thumbs covering up his name and his face. The age and locations were right, though, and it had only been issued a few days before.

Then fourteen, he was too young for a regular driver's license, but had been able to get a permit early because of his parents' farm. His willingness to provide proof (and his personality and my gut feeling) had convinced me.

Before, I never really had anyone I could talk to. No one who was interested in things the way I was.

Before, there was no one I could count on talking to about my day at the end of it.

He was *still* typing. But when he finally stopped and the words appeared, I suspected he'd typed something else first and deleted it. The message was way too short for the time it had taken.

I knew it wasn't fair, because I liked that he wasn't able to see me blush or snort laugh or scoot up to the edge of my chair during our chats. But I did consider it a downside that *I* couldn't see *him*.

SmallvilleGuy: *I hope you love it there, but you don't need to change. You said Perry saw you arguing with someone. Who was the someone?*

SkepticGirl1: *Um . . . it might have been the principal?*

SkepticGirl1: *Shut up.*

SmallvilleGuy: *Yes, clearly the straight and narrow.*

SmallvilleGuy: *(But I mean it. Don't change.)*

SkepticGirl1: *Anyway, sap, I did want to tell you about that part. I think it might be like something off the boards. Maybe. This girl's claiming a group of gamers have been messing with her head. Literally. At least according to her.*

I called him sap, pretending it was a joke. But it wasn't. He was never afraid to be openly sincere, something I had a tougher time with. "Don't change"—who besides a counselor would be brave enough to say that to someone and emphasize that they meant it? Not me.

I told him the rest of the story about Anavi and her pleas to the principal.

SmallvilleGuy: *Definitely weird. I'll see what I can dig up. It could just be stress from them targeting her. I have a feeling they'll regret it, now that you're on the case. Promise me you'll do something, though?*

SkepticGirl1: *Kick them in the face?*

SmallvilleGuy: *Be careful, at least until you know what the deal is.*

SkepticGirl1: *Sounds boring.*

SmallvilleGuy: *Ha. You know, I wasn't that far off. So what if you're not on the news . . . you're going to be writing it. And you'll be great.*

I grinned. Then typed: *So, how was your day?*

He might not be willing to tell me his real identity, but we told each other just about everything else.

SmallvilleGuy: *Same old mostly. Got a B on my* Macbeth *paper, even though the teacher hated it. All her comments were about how I was focusing too much on my own reactions.*

SkepticGirl1: *Or maybe she just likes the play. Didn't you make it a big discussion of how terrible all the people in it are?*

SmallvilleGuy: *It's not a good sign when the witches are the most sympathetic characters, that's all I'm saying. And maybe she has a crush on the Thane of Cawdor.*

SkepticGirl1: *A B's not so bad. Don't complain too much. Anything else?*

SmallvilleGuy: *Bess the Cow (your favorite) finally gave birth.*

SkepticGirl1: *And you didn't lead with that?!*

Bess was the subject of many hilarious farm boy anecdotes.

SmallvilleGuy: *Sorry. I'll take a cute calf picture for tomorrow.*

SkepticGirl1: *Then I'll forgive you. Did you name it yet? Boy or girl?*

SmallvilleGuy: *Girl. Why?*

Because I had a crazy thought about what he should name it, thanks to Maddy.

SkepticGirl1: *I did some research at the library during English, on famous women journalists.*

SmallvilleGuy: *Of course you did.*

I smiled and stuck my tongue out at the screen.

SkepticGirl1: *Anyway, I think you should name her Nellie Bly—she was one of the first investigative reporters. She did all kinds of amazing things like infiltrating an asylum to expose what was going on there and setting a world record by circumnavigating the globe in 72 days.*

SkepticGirl1: *What do you think?*

SmallvilleGuy: *That my dad will think I'm crazy. But okay. Nellie Bly it is. Speaking of, I have to go check on Nellie now. Make sure she's doing okay.*

SkepticGirl1: *Okay, sap, because I have to go eat dinner. Spaghetti. You ready to tell me who you are IRL yet?*

I always asked, though I didn't expect an answer anymore.

"Lois!" Dad called out for me, but I waited.

SmallvilleGuy: *I wish I could. You know I do.*

SkepticGirl1: *But you can't. Even though . . .*

Today had been a good day and there was going to be a baby cow named Nellie Bly in the world, a tribute to my new hero. Maybe I could risk being brave with SmallvilleGuy too.

SkepticGirl1: *Even though if you did, then we could see each other. For real.*

I closed my eyes, only opening one to see his response. It wasn't there yet, but then the words popped up.

SmallvilleGuy: *Now I really wish I could. More than you know.*

I sighed, and if my fingertips touched the screen and those words for a second before I typed my response, it didn't matter to anyone but me. No one else would ever know that I could also be a sap.

SkepticGirl1: *I'll keep it in mind. Later, mystery boy.*

"Lo, dinnertime!" Lucy shouted from right outside the bedroom door, trying the knob.

I clicked to sign off. But not before I saw one last message from him.

SmallvilleGuy: *The Warheads really do sound like they could be bad news. Be safe.*

I closed the laptop.

The night I "met" SmallvilleGuy online, two years ago, I had gone to the Strange Skies site for a reason. I'd seen something a week earlier that I didn't understand and couldn't let go.

It happened during the overnight drive portion of our then-latest move. My dad and I had been the only ones awake. Kansas was flat and boring, but I was staring out the window all the same. "Stop," I'd told him as we were passing a field, and he'd pulled the SUV over, probably thinking I needed to go to the bathroom.

But that wasn't it. There were a few spotlights from the city we'd just driven through playing out over the fields, and one of them had illuminated a large . . . tower . . . made of giant stones, piled one on top of the other. I had the door open as soon as we stopped.

"Lois, wait," Dad said, but I kept moving. He jogged to catch me, saying, "Stay behind me," so he either wanted a closer look too or knew I wouldn't stop until I got one. He never said which.

The structure was eerie, almost teetering, the hunks of stone stretching precariously high into the air above us. We approached it together, both too drawn to the weirdness of it to be cautious, when something slammed into the top, and the rocks flew out into the air, hurtling as if they were going to rain down on me and my dad. I screamed so loud that my throat ached remembering it. Dad threw himself over me, knocking us both to the ground—

But then nothing. No impact. Nothing but the impression of movement and wind around us, the rocks flying around and around and then up and up, until we couldn't see the stones anymore. Until it was as if the rock tower had never existed. I could swear—would swear, if anyone ever asked me, even though Dad had been clear I was never to speak of it again—that I saw a form, a body, a person directing those rocks, then streaking away into the sky. But it was dark, and whatever I'd seen had been moving *fast*. Too fast to be sure about.

There were posters on Strange Skies who reported things that weren't so far from what I'd witnessed. Things that should have been impossible.

So I created my SkepticGirl1 account and shared my eyewitness report.

Posted by **SkepticGirl1** *at 11:13 p.m.*: I know how this story will sound, but it seems like if anyone will understand or believe me or have an explanation, then it might be someone here. Driving outside Kansas City last night with my family, I think I saw someone who could fly. No, that might give the wrong impression. Crazy as it is, I believe that I saw someone flying. Through the air. Actually flying . . .

I told the whole story, including everything except details

that would identify my father. His security clearance alone would have the posters at Strange Skies swooning, and this wasn't about him. It was about what we'd seen. What I now knew might exist out there in the world, not talked about in the open. I ended my post with: So, am I crazy or did this happen to me? Did I really see this?

SmallvilleGuy had reached out to me right away via private message on the boards, almost as soon as I had posted, and said he went to high school in a small town in Kansas and that he knew I was telling the truth. Because he was confirming what I'd seen, he also said he couldn't tell me exactly how he knew or who he was. There were others on the boards who made nonsense claims about aliens in the middle of the night and spaceship experiments. I didn't buy into those. Of course. That was why I'd chosen the username I had.

But SmallvilleGuy's reassurance and other reports on the boards seemed legit. I was convinced: the reason Dad didn't want me to talk about what we'd experienced to Mom or Lucy or *anyone* (even him) had nothing to do with keeping people from thinking we were crazy.

It was because we had seen something real, something we weren't supposed to.

And my dad—even with his top secret clearance—hadn't known how to explain it either.

CHAPTER 4

I went to breakfast with a mission the next morning. After dinner the night before, Lucy had blown me off, so determined to spend the evening playing on her holoset that she'd already done her homework. That equaled no love for letting me see it.

But today, the curved shell was, as usual, sitting beside her plate of toast and turkey bacon. It was hot pink. When she'd unwrapped the present at Christmas last year, she'd seen the color and done her trademark nose wrinkle. She'd wanted *Worlds War Three*; my parents had been steered to *Unicorn University* as a more appropriate game for a young girl. After some justified ranting and raving, she calmed down enough to try it out. Based on how much she used it, the galaxy of unicorns was apparently more interesting than she'd thought.

I put toast on my plate with one hand, then reached out and snagged the holoset as I sat down across from her.

"Lois!" she protested.

"I just want to see it, Luce. Will you please tell me how to work it?"

"Fine," Lucy huffed. But she didn't snatch it out of my hands. Which made me remember that we needed to have a sister movie night sometime soon.

I hooked the holoset over my ear like I'd done with Devin's, though the fit was a little snugger, and she nodded. "Then you push the button to turn it on." When I lifted my hand, she jumped up.

"Wait!"

"Yes?" I said, my finger poised on top of the button.

Lucy came around the table to the chair beside mine. She whispered, "You won't tell Mom and Dad, will you?"

Our parents weren't around. Dad had already left for work, and Mom was upstairs changing so she could take Lucy to school.

"Tell them what?"

"On me, how I use it."

"Now I can't wait to see," I said, and hit the button.

I blinked in confusion. I was inside the game world, but I wasn't sure what I was seeing.

Just as the day before, a scene popped into being in front of me. The way holosets worked meant the details of the 3D holo projection were visible in detail only to the gamer, who felt like they were inside the game world, which felt so vivid it almost replaced the real one. But to someone looking on it was just a small blur of light and movement sprayed from the earpiece in front of the user's face.

This was definitely different than the *Worlds War Three* landscape. It was all pastels and bright colors and nothing was on fire. The grass was princess pink.

"Trippy," I said, attempting to get my bearings.

"Try not to talk. People in the game can hear you." Lucy's hand clutched my arm. "The holoset tracks your pupil movements and that's how you'll move."

But I didn't want to move, because I noticed the unicorns standing around me.

The biggest one neighed and trotted in front of me, batting enormous sea-green eyes. She was trailed by three others who each had dangerously sharp-looking horns.

"Hey, Deathmetal," said the unicorn who stopped in front of me. A black ribbon was wound around the right foreleg it lifted to high-five me. Or high-foot me. Whatever you called it when a unicorn did that.

I glanced down. My own unicorn leg was wrapped in the same renegade style, as were the others'. One even had a black bandana knotted around its pearl gray horn. They might have once been delicate pristine versions of the imaginary creatures who represented the players doing word mini-games and running races and visiting castles as part of mastering *Unicorn University*. But these unicorns had gone bad.

"This feels so real, Luce," I said. "You can customize it, I take it?"

But even getting the words out was hard. It felt like what was in the game was realer, almost more than reality, than Lucy's hand on my arm. Or her voice near my ear.

"When you get enough points to graduate," she said, low and worried.

"What did you do with Deathmetal?" the first unicorn said, taking a menacing step closer.

Lucy ripped the holoset off my ear and put it onto hers. "That was my sister. You see what I mean, right? She's terrible. Gotta go." She took off the holoset slowly, but I was having trouble watching her. The kitchen swam in and out, the odd sensation of coming out of the game worse than the day before. It must be because I'd spent a little longer inside.

I'd done some reading on the manufacturer's website the night before. The more used to the real-sim tech your brain got, the easier it coped with entering the game—and the more careful you had to be when leaving. Some critics questioned whether it meant the technology might be dangerous, capable of making unintended changes in the brain's neural pathways.

The kitchen stopped swimming after a few moments, and Lucy didn't seem to be suffering any ill effects. *Because she took her time removing it.*

Lucy didn't say a word, staring down at the holoset as she turned it over in her hands.

When she finally looked up, I'd recovered completely. I crunched a bite of toast and raised my eyebrows. "Lucy," I said, "are you a killer unicorn?"

"You promised you wouldn't tell."

"I wouldn't dream of it." I set the toast back on my plate. "Who are those unicorns?"

"They're from all over," she said. "They didn't want to play stupid unicorns either."

"So you formed a gang." I was glad she'd made friends in there. Our many moves hadn't been easy for her either. "Why Deathmetal?"

She shrugged, sheepish. "It was the least unicorn-y name I could come up with." She bit her lip, and then blurted, "You're not really terrible, Lois."

"Thanks for that, sis. Neither are you."

*

Thirty-five minutes into first period, I breezed into the admin office. The blond assistant was behind her desk, wearing another flowered ensemble and appearing far less frazzled than she had been yesterday.

"Ronda, it's so nice to see you," I said. "Is the principal around?"

"In a meeting," she said, and I breathed easier. Without batting a mascara-coated eyelash, she asked, "Shouldn't you be in class?"

"On shore leave." I waved the yellow hall pass my geometry teacher had given me after he finished lecturing and told us to do practice problems for the rest of the time. "I want to make a change in my schedule. I'd like to switch bio for computer science—I already checked and there's a class that will fit second period."

She waited—for what, I wasn't sure. Then she said, "I guess it's okay. Since you're not asking to transfer to chemistry." She paused. "Did you really create a noxious cloud that caused the evacuation of your school in Ohio?"

"Of course not." I waved my hand dismissively.

"Good," she said, typing something into her computer. I hoped that meant she was getting me where I needed to be next hour, if I was lucky. Which I wasn't usually, but today might be the day.

"It was a few harmless chemicals mixed into an equally harmless cloud. Not noxious so much as big," I said. "It was a distraction to help this girl, Sophie, who really needed an A. Her partner messed up their lab on purpose, because she broke up with him."

"Huh," she said, and gifted me a skeptical side-eye as she hit enter. She reached over and plucked a fresh document from the printer beside her desk. "Just don't . . . hack the mainframe or whatever in your new class."

"I solemnly swear," I said. After all, there probably wasn't even a mainframe *to* hack.

I crossed my fingers it would go just as easily when I came back and asked to transfer out of comp sci. I didn't want to stay in the class any longer than I had to, not if the Warheads were also in it. Computers were more SmallvilleGuy's thing.

When I reached the classroom, Devin had saved me a seat next to him, along one of several rows of tables with tricked-out computer workstations that could have come straight from a Coast City high-tech start-up that also helped design futuristic movie sets. This school appeared to be way more flush with cash than most of my previous ones.

No doubt due to Principal Butler's semi-convincing layer of charm.

"Morning," I said, slipping into the seat beside Devin. I wasn't used to having someone to sit next to. Not that I was convinced the other *Scoop* staffers wouldn't go hungry zombie and turn on me yet, but maybe. Maybe the plan and the job would work out.

And it was impossible not to notice that Devin was cute.

"Do you even know anything about coding?" Devin asked.

"I know how to use computers," I said, frowning down at a keyboard that included a few rows of symbols that might as well have been hieroglyphics.

"This is an advanced class," he countered, "grasshopper."

"So I gathered. I'm here to learn."

I gave up on the keyboard and surveyed the classroom. A few other students were playing around on their computers, screens scrolling with lines of code. Anavi came in, slouching into a chair directly across from us, without even looking up. She must sit there all the time.

Well done, Devin.

Once at her workstation, Anavi glanced around, like she knew she was being hunted but couldn't tell where the predators were hiding.

None of the Warheads were there, though. Not yet.

Before I could say anything to Anavi to lay the groundwork for interviewing her later, the teacher—Ms. Johnson, according to my revised schedule—showed up. She wore a boxy, skirted suit, and her black hair was swept back in a bun so tight that it must give her a headache by the end of the day. She primly carried a stack of papers.

As she went to shut the door, a hand pressed it back open. The Warheads had arrived—in pack formation.

"Pop quiz," Ms. Johnson said to the owner of the hand, "and you almost missed it." But her voice was timid, and she'd come close to dropping the papers.

Annoyance would have been the response I would have gone with, not being obviously unnerved. But, hey, I wasn't the teacher.

The Warheads were dressed in black again. They also wore the same slightly mocking expressions. Half-smirks, like full ones required too much effort.

They glided in one after the other, moving like they were cogs in a well-oiled machine or individual bones in the skeleton of some large animal. Fanning out, they took seats down both sides of the table directly behind Anavi, who seemed already to be freaking out—even more—as a result.

And the choice to sit there had to be on purpose, because Anavi really did look like she might lose her breakfast, lunch, and dinner on the keyboard in front of her. They must have known that she wouldn't be able to forget that they were behind her. But she also didn't give them the satisfaction of looking.

Or, I thought, it might have been an attempt not to provoke them.

Anavi flinched and rolled her head from one side to the other with an odd jerk.

I leaned forward and spoke low. "Anavi, try to breathe. They can't do anything to you here, not with all of us around."

Anavi squinted at me through her glasses. "Who are you?" But she must have recognized me from the day before quickly enough. "You . . ." She spoke in little more than a whisper. "I entreat you not to talk to me. They might ascertain that I spoke to someone."

Her eyes widened, like she'd realized they might *hear* as well as *see* her. She made that same weird flinching motion again, her head shaking from side to side—like she heard voices the rest of us couldn't and wanted them out of her head.

"Um," I said, "yes, because you're speaking to me right now. They might ascertain that. But I've got your back."

I looked over at Devin.

"I've never seen her act like this," he said, quiet enough so only I would hear. "She's usually low-key. Model student, smart game player . . . "

"And them?" I asked. "Is this casual jerkery the norm?"

"Yeah, I have seen them be like that before. And worse in *Worlds*."

The tightly wound Ms. Johnson cleared her throat from right behind us. Devin stopped talking and reached up to accept the papers she held out to pass along the row. She moved on to the next one.

I scanned the wording of the quiz questions and understood some of it, mostly from conversations with SmallvilleGuy about security and encryption protocols. He was into secrets. Protecting them, and obtaining them. But I wouldn't be able to answer anything on this quiz with any confidence.

At least you don't have to take a spelling test.

The teacher returned and stood over me. "Since you're new, we'll use your quiz to gauge what kind of catch-up you'll need."

Like that was a reassuring thought.

Finally, almost as if she'd been putting it off, the teacher took the remaining papers to the Warheads' table. A boy took the sheets and then they all mechanically passed the sheets down the row in a way that was so synced, each person's movement exactly the same, that it looked the opposite of natural.

"You'll have five minutes for this," Ms. Johnson announced, and if the Warheads' arrival had rattled her prim groove she had it back now. She set an egg timer that *tick-tick-tick*ed at the front of the room.

I pretended to fill out some answers, and then skipped ahead to circle a few random multiple-choice responses. I'd have tried to get some help from Devin, but becoming an expert in comp sci wasn't why I was here. I wanted to see how the Warheads treated Anavi.

The overly-loud-for-stealth whispers came first. "What do you think?" said one, and another, "I think she should study harder."

"Or try harder."

"Now, now, it's so hard when you just can't remember."

"What should she put for number two? A big word?"

Anavi shifted in her seat, uncomfortable. She twitched, moving her head like she heard voices again—but only *after* they'd stopped talking. Sweat ran down her cheek and, behind the lenses of her glasses, her eyes were squeezed nearly closed. She was gripping her pen so hard that I worried it might break.

Her head turned from side to side yet again, and she raised her free hand to brush by one of her ears.

I thought of how she'd described what they were doing to her to Butler the day before. She'd said it was like they were inside her head messing with her, on top of the whispers and harassment visible to everyone else in the class.

Including the teacher, who wasn't doing anything.

Another round of whispers started up from the Warheads.

"It's hard to concentrate with all the noise," I said, loud enough that Ms. Johnson couldn't pretend she didn't catch it. "I didn't realize we were allowed to talk during a test."

The whispers ceased, but that didn't mean silence won. The Warheads switched to low, offended laughter. Anavi shook her head and made her best attempt to return to the sheet in front of her. Her hand still clutched the pen.

"You're not." Ms. Johnson did step in, finally, focusing on the pack of offenders.

Took you long enough.

"You should stop disturbing the others," she told them. She finally showed some irritation. "Hydra doesn't mean you can act however you want. Not in my class."

Now *that* was interesting. I made a mental note to find out what "Hydra" was, and why a teacher would bring it up to them. That couldn't be a coincidence.

"I'm disturbed," said one of the Warheads.

"Aren't you?" another said.

"Anavi, Anavi, Anavi," several of them chanted her name in a near sing-song, "are you disturbed?"

Anavi's hand trembled around the pen, and I couldn't imagine that what she was producing on the quiz was legible. But she was trying to take it, trying not to give in. That, I admired.

I scribbled down a few more answers, guessing the whole way and mostly paying attention to Anavi and the whispers. When the egg timer dinged, Anavi jolted in her seat in shock, triggering another round of sarcastic laughter. The girl had completely lost her cool.

While I clung to my spellcheck, I'd seen spelling competitions like the one Anavi had been in. The night before, after my game research, I'd looked up Anavi's winning year and found a video of the last few rounds.

Some of the participants' composure had melted away as they got closer to the finish line. But not Anavi's. She stayed completely cool, calm, and alphabetically collected, right up to the end. Even when she won, the most extreme part of her reaction had been to crack a big smile and pump one fist in the air before walking over and hugging her proud parents.

But here she was, about to pass out over a pop quiz in a subject she usually made A's in. I wanted to know how she'd done this time.

So I reached over to take her paper to pass it up front, then subtly leaned in when I handed it to Devin. "Give it a quick look," I told him.

Even if I hadn't witnessed how Anavi's pen shook, the quality of the marks on the sheet made it plain. Devin skimmed the page and murmured, "This is weird."

"What?"

But Ms. Johnson hovered over us, her hand outstretched. Devin accepted my quiz and added his own, handing them to her.

Once she walked away, he said, "They were wrong. All of them. Nothing even close to right. Like I said, Anavi was acing this class. She's as good at this stuff as anyone in here."

The Warheads stared over at us.

And there it was. I had earned the full smirk. From all of them.

That was better than them being focused on Anavi. So I accepted it and sent back a look of challenge of my own, proud.

Until I glanced over and caught the expression on Anavi's face. It was even more pained than it had been before.

For the rest of the class period, she sat folded in on herself, with only an occasional movement.

Every time, it was that same unnatural jerk, a flinch like an invisible fist had just punched her or a voice was hissing insults in her ear.

If there was one thing I hated, it was bullies.

CHAPTER 5

Finding Anavi in the crowded cafeteria at lunch was harder than I expected. But eventually I ferreted out her near-hidden spot in one of the back corners. Alone, which wasn't a surprise. After what I'd witnessed in class, I felt sorry for her. I'd have to ask Devin if her being a loner was new behavior.

"You mind?" I scooted the chair opposite Anavi out with my boot and gingerly put down my lunch tray. I didn't want to spook her.

The pizza on my plate was the sad-slice variety, staple of food courts and gas stations everywhere. But it was still pizza, and more recognizable than most of the other cafeteria offerings. And I was starving.

Meanwhile, Anavi was busy staring at me, wide-eyed. "Um, sincere apologies, but—"

"I'm sorry that you do mind. But I'm staying. Don't worry, I'm not offended that you don't want me to. My feelings don't bruise easily." Or at least I was good at pretending they didn't. I sat down, putting my bag on the table beside me. "You should know I'm going to help you. Bullies like the Warheads don't work like adults usually say. It's not that they're all talk and you just have to stand up to them. It's that talk can be bad enough, but usually they're more than willing to act too. And from what I saw earlier, it's pretty clear these guys are not shy about acting."

Anavi didn't interrupt, which I took as a positive sign. I went on.

"Whatever those creepy Warheads creeps are doing to you, it's wrong. I know there's more to it than whispers." Here it was. I was going to talk about things most people would call crazy with someone besides SmallvilleGuy. I didn't see any other way to convince Anavi that I was on her side. "What you told the principal? After this morning, I believe you. I'm not going to leave you to deal with them by yourself."

Anavi swallowed, but she didn't speak.

I gave her time while I took a bite of pizza. Definitely sad, but, again, still pizza.

"Why?" Anavi asked finally, the question forcing its way out.

"Because they're jerks of the highest magnitude," I said, trying to speak the girl's language. "The principal shouldn't be letting them get away with tormenting you, or anything else. I didn't like the way the teacher acted around them either.

Like she was intimidated, afraid to put them in their place. Something's definitely wrong here."

I set down the sad pizza slice, puzzled again by how willing the adults were to indulge the Warheads' behavior.

"No," Anavi blurted. "It's just . . . that's not what I . . . Why do you believe me? About the rest."

"Oh." I had fallen into my old habit of barreling ahead and leaving whoever I was talking to behind by accident. I back-tracked. "You mean about them messing with your head? This isn't my first school. It's not even my tenth. I've been a lot of places, and I've seen a lot of things. I can tell when things are . . . off. I also know that sometimes the explanations aren't the obvious ones or ones that even seem possible."

"But . . . " Anavi hesitated.

"Go on. I'm on your side."

"But I'm becoming more convinced that I am . . . losing my sanity." Anavi looked away, into the corner. There was nowhere else to look if she didn't want to meet my eyes.

Reaching into my messenger bag, I found a notebook and pen. I inched my tray back to make room to take notes.

"You're not," I said. "I won't let you. How long have you been playing *Worlds*?"

Anavi looked at me then, which was progress. And she didn't balk at the notebook, though she raised her eyebrows at it. "I've only been playing since I aged out of the bee. I had all that time to fill. No more flashcards and word lists and sessions with my coach. Studying for school doesn't take as long. My neighbor, Will, was into it, and he taught me how to play."

More progress.

"Tell me when it started. Them acting like this toward you. Were they always so mean?"

"In the game?" Anavi asked.

I thought back to what Devin had told me. "I heard that they're cannibals in it."

"I disagree," Anavi said. "They were, they used to be. They used to turn on each other. I've been in there while they were fighting amongst the team, hurling each other into four-story monsters or into alien-probe traps."

Alien-probe traps? "Yikes."

Anavi went on. "But then they turned more . . . socio, serial. A couple of months ago."

"What does that mean?"

"Sociopaths, serial killers."

You don't say. "Psychos. I got that part. What does it mean in the game?"

"It means they stopped griefing each other and started in on others. They began acting as a unit, no in fighting. They weren't cannibals anymore, not within the group. They were socios, serials, psychos . . . that means they go after other players together, no mercy. Rampaging."

"Those other players included you?"

Anavi leaned forward. "No, not at first. My friend Will . . . He used to be my friend. My neighbor. They went after him. I should have helped him. But I was afraid they would come after me. The definition of absurdity, isn't it?"

"What happened to him?"

"He's one of them now. I could try to describe him, but . . ."

"*But* they all dress alike, and so I wouldn't know who you meant," I said.

"Yes. He has been assimilated."

In addition to her fear, she sounded like she was carrying a load of guilt around. I tapped my pen on the table. "You think this is revenge. That Will's having them target you because you didn't help him out. Is that why Butler thought one of them had a crush on you?"

"No, that's just because I'm a girl. Isn't that what adults always think when you complain about treatment by boys?" She considered the other question before she answered. "I did wonder at first, if the crush was part of it. But now I don't think so. He's just one of them. He's not orchestrating anything. He used to be able to recite chapter and verse about soccer, every score, always streaming it when we weren't in the game. He had an obsession with this UK team. The last time I went over to his house, he had taken down all his posters and I tried to make conversation about them, be normal, but he said he didn't care about it anymore. That he had more important things to do. He wasn't acting like himself."

"And neither were you, this morning in class."

"Correct," she said. "They didn't just mess up Will in the game. Before he started hanging out with them all the time, in the game and real life, he failed several tests. He couldn't generate the right responses."

"Again, like you this morning."

Her nod was more like a wince.

"Sorry," I said. The last thing I wanted was to make her feel worse about all this.

"If I forfeit my scholarship . . . My parents are going to slaughter me."

"No, they're not." I clicked my pen closed. "You're not losing anything."

Anavi's eyes met mine. She didn't look convinced. "What if they force me to assimilate, like they did Will? I don't want to be one of them."

"I'm helping you, remember?" And I wanted to know who was conducting the bully orchestra, if not Anavi's former pal. Both in the hallway and in class the group had been in such sync, no one had stood out as mouthpiece or mastermind. "Who do you think is the leader?"

"That's another unlikely thing. You would assume there would be one commander. But it feels like they all are the leader, or none of them is." Her glasses had slipped down her nose, and she pushed them back into place. "I haven't been back in *Worlds* in days. But it doesn't seem to matter. In there, I can hold my own. It's just bad play. But out here . . . When they're near me and they want to . . . the only way I can describe it is that they disrupt my mind. Like they're *in* my head, wearing jackboots and stomping around. Or not that, not precisely. It's closer to a feeling of very fine control, like I'm a computer and they're writing a piece of code that makes me perform however they want. An invading army, executing a coup in my mind."

That was new. "So, they have to be close by for you to feel this way?"

"I think so. It only happens when they're physically proximate. This morning in class, I *knew* the correct answers. They were at the forefront of my mind, but I couldn't transcribe them. What I wrote was wrong, and I *knew* it was." She lowered her voice. "But I could not stop. You know Occam's razor? It's a scientific principle that says the simplest explanation is usually the correct one. By that logic, the simplest explanation for this particular situation would be that I am absolutely losing my sanity. It defies any other explanation. Why else would I be telling you this?"

"Because I'm helping you." Maybe I would regret not sending her straight to the counselor's office. But my instincts said not to. "Give me a few days."

"I should've known better than to bother reporting them to Principal Butler. He has always been kind to me, but his adoration for the Warheads this year is unparalleled. He allows them afternoons free. They get to leave campus."

I clicked my pen again, noted that detail, and added a question mark.

Then I remembered the other question I had for Anavi. "Does the word 'Hydra' mean anything to you?"

"A mythological monster. The root's Greek. There's one in the game." She shrugged. "Mid-level boss. Not that hard to defeat. You know what's almost comical?"

"Nothing about any of this," I said.

"I think in language roots, still, after all those years studying them. I notice them, the components of words. I don't think I will ever stop. That term I mentioned the other day, the one I found that was closest to what's happening . . . psychological coercion?"

I scribbled it into my notes too. "I didn't remember it before, but I do now. What's it mean?"

"The root, *psyche*, is Greek. It means breath, life, soul. Roots often have a certain poetry about them. Psychological coercion, it's an elaborate way of saying that they're stealing my soul. My breath. My life. That's what my mind is to me."

I couldn't let that happen. "I can't believe I'm asking you this, but would you be willing to go into the game again? Tonight? I'll arrange to be there, too. I need to witness what they're doing there so I can make the case that they're targeting you. Don't worry. I won't talk about the inside-your-head stuff. Only what others can see."

Suddenly, Anavi's head ducked and she examined the boring plastic pattern of fake wood grain on the tabletop. I turned, expecting to see the Warheads lurking behind me.

But it was Maddy, standing at my shoulder. Her T-shirt today was another band that I hadn't heard of: Danger Dames.

"Join us," I said. "We're almost done. Do you two know each other? Maddy, this is Anavi."

"Hippopotamus," Maddy said, sliding out the chair and scooting into it. She tilted her head at Anavi. "Come on, I can never remember how many P's. Or U's."

I protested, "She's not a trick pony—"

But Anavi rattled off the perfectly spelled—so I

assumed—word. Maddy grinned. Anavi smiled back, the first time I'd seen any lightness in her.

I *had* to make sure that her breath, life, and soul stayed intact.

"So, tonight? Ten o'clock in the game?" I asked. "We're on?"

"What article?" Anavi asked instead of agreeing, her forehead creasing in concern. "You mentioned something about an article."

"Maddy and I work for the *Daily Scoop*. We're going to do a piece about bullying, in game and out, using you as a case study."

"But I don't want anyone else to know it's me."

I understood. "I promised I'd help, right? Trust me. I'll figure out a way to not use your name."

"All right," Anavi said. "I will be present at ten, but I make no commitment for how long I will remain if they're in attendance."

"You probably know the exact location of the Warheads at this very second, don't you?" I asked.

"Always. How else can I avoid them effectively?"

"Point us in their direction. I want to officially meet them."

Anavi lifted her finger, which trembled only a little. "Next to the doors. They linger. I'm always late for my first period after lunch . . . I wait them out."

"Not today. Today they'll be leaving early." I stood and waved for Maddy to join me. "They have their methods of attack. I have mine."

CHAPTER 6

Maddy stayed by my side as we navigated the cafeteria with its walls of good old patriotic red and blue.

I had discovered that the school mascot was the Generals. Dad really *would* love that. It might even be why my parents had picked this school.

There were a few obvious groups in the cafeteria, but school cliques were never as clear-cut as they were on TV or in the movies. Jocks, preps, nerds—there was too much overlap to pretend it was that simple these days. But I did recognize some discrete factions within this crowd, ones that had been at most of my previous schools.

The Nerdfighter contingent would have been identifiable by the fact that half of the table was reading (or more likely re-reading) one of their favorite author's books—alternately laughing or weeping, depending how far in they were—even if a few weren't also wearing T-shirts featuring him and his brother, along with tiny video cameras for making their next vlogs beside their trays.

And then there was the basketball team, always the tallest and cockiest of the sporty types, though here it seemed refreshingly like the girls' team was part of the same echelon, sharing the table in an assortment of practice T-shirts, a welcome change from the usual.

Maybe the relative equality was the influence of the debate clubbers at the next table over. Or they might just be combative arguers with green political concerns; it was hard to say based on their heated discussions and environmentally friendly water bottles and lunch containers.

"What's your plan?" Maddy asked. "You're not going to confront the creeps face-to-face, are you? In front of everyone?"

We passed by a table housing a handful of drama club members, spottable by large gestures and supreme enunciation that gave way to a song more rehearsed than impromptu, complete with harmonizing. Maddy shivered in disgust at the singing, the crimson streak in her hair hiding her grimace from the table that was in full-blown a capella Broadway mode. Her expression reminded me of Lucy's when she disapproved of something.

"Not a musical fan?" I asked, instead of answering Maddy's question about what I had in mind.

"I cringe because that hurts me," Maddy said. "My ears. My taste. I can't."

"Got it," I said. "You'll have to make me a playlist. I never seem to find good music on my own."

"Sure," Maddy agreed, smiling.

SmallvilleGuy was the source of most of my music, not that I was about to tell Maddy that. Not yet. It would be nice to have a friend to talk to in person, and especially about the weirdness of my relationship with *him*, somewhere between friends and maybe-more-than-friends. I thought we were, anyway. Sometimes. Like last night when he'd said how much he *wanted* to tell me.

But, then again, defining where exactly on that spectrum we fell didn't matter *that* much, since we were stuck there, in whatever uncertain spot it was. Because I literally didn't know who he was and he'd made it clear that he wasn't going to change his mind and reveal all anytime soon.

Maddy's pleased surprise at being consulted on music faded fast, and she started to plod along. She slowed with every step.

I saw why.

The Warheads were dead ahead, sitting around a table near the doors, as Anavi had said they would be. At every school I'd attended, holosets and portable game consoles—and sometimes even phones—were prohibited during school hours. Not here. At least not for these particular students.

They were all playing, focused in on scenes impenetrable from outside their own holoset views, but glowing right in front of their eyes. Other than darting pupils, and the occasional low-spoken command, they remained frighteningly motionless.

Something told me they were all in the same gaming scene, and not having harmless bad unicorn fun either.

"Where does James sit at lunch?" I asked.

"Why would I know that?" Maddy returned.

When I gave her a pointed look, complete with raised eyebrows, Maddy sighed and said, "At my sister's table."

I followed her gaze. James was at a nearby table, grinning at a couple of other Richie Rich polo-shirt types, all of them involved in teasing a few well-coiffed girls. The girls were tolerating it—maybe even enjoying it. Then I froze.

Maddy and her sister were majorly identical twins, so much so that James was an idiot—or blind—if he couldn't see the resemblance. I also suspected based on yesterday that Maddy would be expecting me to react like I couldn't believe they were related either. Her sister was like a make-up ad, all soft luminous smiles and no edge. She was probably perfectly nice. But given Maddy's crimson-streaked hair and band fascinations, she was undoubtedly used to being lost in her glowing sister's shadow.

No way was I going along with that.

"James was right. You and your sister don't seem at all alike," I said. Before she could be hurt, I added, "You're the interesting one. I can see that from a mile away."

Maddy soaked up the compliment like she had the crumbs of James's notice at the office. People should pay more attention to her. She *was* interesting.

I had managed to keep her occupied long enough to reach the Warheads' table. There was an empty chair at the next one over, and I hooked it with my hand and dragged it over to the corner of the gamers' paradise.

Maddy hung back as I sat down and cleared my throat.

None of the six Warheads reacted, staring ahead into their fantasy landscapes. Remembering how rattled Anavi had been describing the way they'd treated her, I felt no urge to be subtle. Or nice.

I thought back to that morning when Lucy had ripped the holoset off me, and the warnings from the manufacturer that hard interruptions of the game could cause disorientation and maybe worse for regular users. The list of possible side effects had been long and I'd only skimmed it.

Seemed like a winning strategy.

So I took out my notebook, lifted it in my hands, and brought it down with a loud *slap* onto the top of the table.

Heads around the table shook, annoyed or dazed or both. Hands reached up to switch off holosets, killing the glowing gameplay. Each Warhead frowned at first in general and then, as they recovered, at me—still with that slight hint of mockery.

I smiled at them, like I hadn't made a loud noise to force them out of the game. "Hi," I said, and flipped open the notebook to the last page of my notes. "I wanted to ask you guys a few questions. I'm new and trying to get a feel for the atmosphere here at the school." I cast a glance over my shoulder. Maddy was hanging out, if not exactly leaping in. "All the little weird subcultures. You guys definitely seem like one. It's for a style piece at the *Daily Scoop*."

Not a single game continued to run by then, every holoset

switched off. The whole table looked at me with a force and focus that almost made me regret getting their attention.

Almost.

"Now," I went on, "what do you think is the most important thing for me to know about the social scene here, from the gamer perspective?"

"You have got to be . . . " a boy said, and a girl finished for him, "joking."

"Yes, that right there is what made me notice you." I couldn't help wondering which one was Anavi's former friend Will. Assimilated was a good way to describe them. "I've never met people like you in real life, let alone high school. You know what I mean . . . " I snapped my fingers, let my smile die when I finished, "The mind meld thing."

None of them reacted to that, not right away, but then one of the guys nearest me tilted his head. "What?"

"The way you finish each other's sentences," I explained. "You just seem to know each other so well. Like you're practically the same person. How did you meet? Was it in the game? What is it again—Wuss War Three?"

The remaining gamers' heads tilted, in mirror to the first guy, as they supplied:

"*Worlds . . .*"

"*War . . .*"

"*Three.*"

"Right," I said, "my mistake. I hear there's something called griefing in that, cyberbullying. Have you guys ever witnessed players being targeted? What would you do if you did?"

A snort, but I didn't catch who it came from.

A couple of them wore slow smiles, and I was glad all of them didn't. I'd never admit it out loud, but they were disconcerting in a way that went far beyond the typical creep. Part of me wished I'd approached them from a slightly less head-on angle.

Too late now.

"Well . . ." said one, and another jumped in, "We'd probably base that decision . . ."

And another, "On whether the player was weak. We like strong players on our team."

"It's a war," one more jumped in. "Things happen. Especially to those who get in the way of a strong team. We do—"

". . . like to recruit those with potential," another interrupted. "The bigger we get, the stronger we are."

Anavi was right. There was no clear leader. Or, rather, they all seemed to be leaders, in turn, but not different enough for the change in who was speaking to matter. Something very weird was definitely going on with them. I just didn't know what.

I hid my unease the same way I did when I was trying to win an argument with my dad. By keeping my voice level and my shoulders squared. "So, you're saying there's no problem with ganging up on weaker players? That you do it?"

No one said a word.

The answer came as a sensation—like the push of an invisible hand slamming into my mind, hard enough that my head went back as I jerked to my feet. My chair scraped the floor behind me, and Maddy's hand catching it was all that kept it from hitting the floor.

The pressure had been undeniable. It hadn't lasted long. Only for a moment.

That didn't mean I wanted to feel it again. I was breathing hard, but I did my best to hide my fear.

No one at the table gave a hint of any change, of having done anything. They were talking again, in that overlapping way:

"Maybe you should do a different story."

"And forget this."

"Forget us."

Then they were getting up, one by one, and leaving the cafeteria.

"Lois?" The look on Maddy's face made what she was asking clear. She wanted to know if I was all right.

I steadied myself with a hand on the table. "Finally," I said, "we're getting somewhere."

CHAPTER 7

After school, I crossed the Daily Planet Building lobby with a speed and purpose that came from having a noble cause paired with less-than-worthy opponents. Which meant I didn't spot James waiting for the service elevator in time to avoid him.

As I reached the elevator bank, the dull gray doors crawled their way open. *My luck is in rare form today*, I thought, giving him a tight smile. *After everything else, I'm reaching the* Scoop *office at the same time as the Third?*

I wasn't going to be ridiculous about it, though. I couldn't afford a delay, and who knew how long the decrepit elevator would take to come back again? There were important preparations to make for tonight. I had to be on time for my rendezvous with Anavi and the Warheads. And I had another invitation to make, too—one I was nervous about.

Poor Anavi. This was to help her, so my nerves didn't matter.

"You first," James said, holding the aged door open with his arm.

I didn't know why his being polite bugged me, but it did. I climbed on.

"Heard you did some interviews during lunch," he said as the elevator car creakily made its way to the basement.

"From?" I asked suspiciously.

"Maddy and I have last period together. She said the Warheads weren't what you'd call cooperative."

I shrugged one shoulder. "If they were, then I'd know I didn't have a story. They as much as admitted to ganging up on people in the game, and I saw them bothering Anavi this morning outside it. That's all I need." Before he could speak, I corrected myself. "Well, almost. I want a little more flavor, and I need to get Principal Butler in too."

Disbelief colored James's expression at the mention of the principal. I tried not to grin.

"Look," I said, "I know you're just here to follow in Daddy's footsteps. But you can still learn a thing or two."

The elevator stopped, the doors inching open. I pushed into the hall as soon as there was enough room. The dingy, dim length of it was less despair-inducing today. That was because I knew where I was going. And why.

Striding into the Morgue, aka the *Scoop* office, felt, well, right.

I *would* get Principal Shark to incriminate himself. I'd figure out what was up with that mental shove too, and before Anavi lost any more of her self or sanity. The memory of the press against my mind in the cafeteria made my stomach turn with discomfort.

No. That would mean I was afraid of them. I was probably just hungry.

When I walked into the office, Devin and Maddy were already there talking. She was standing at his desk, and I could guess from how they looked over when I came in that Maddy was relating the story of my daring lunchtime newsgathering again.

I was flattered.

"You're really going after Butler?" James asked, finally having recovered his power of speech.

I'd almost forgotten he was with me. I slid into the squeaky old chair behind my crypt-sized desk before I answered. "Him not helping Anavi, looking the other way . . . *that's* more of a story than boys—and girls—behaving badly. He has a responsibility to protect the students. He isn't doing that for some reason. I don't think this part will be hard."

I slipped out my laptop and opened it. There was a computer on my desk here, but even if I was set up on it already, it wouldn't have the uber-security required. I'd decided to cart mine with me in case I needed to phone a friend. So to speak.

Logging on and choosing a network, I frowned. Even if I *did* need to call him, I couldn't, not as things stood. We could only talk over chat. I'd brought my laptop because he claimed the app on our phones wasn't quite as secure.

"What is it?" Devin said. "I have a little sister, and whenever she looks like that I know she either skipped lunch or is mad at me for something I didn't even realize I did."

"Neither," I said. "Though I could use a snack."

Maddy rummaged in a desk drawer, then tossed me a bag of pita chips.

I caught them. They'd do in a pinch. "Thank you. My neurons go on strike when I'm hungry."

At their desks, the others went back to work. And after I unrolled the top and crunched a couple chips, I felt better. I remembered that I had an adorable baby cow picture coming later. Though I was frustrated by all the things I didn't yet know about the Warheads.

Thinking out loud, I said, "I wish I could see the Warheads' schedules. Anavi said something when I interviewed her about Butler giving them afternoons 'free' off campus. Do any of you have classes with them after lunch? Or know where they might go?"

Devin shook his head. "No, which is weird, because I actually do have an advanced design class that usually goes along with advanced comp sci. Electives that most people tend to elect together."

He hesitated. I put down the bag of chips and entered my passwords, but when I looked up, Devin was still hovering on the cusp of saying something. "What is it?"

"I could . . . I could get you in. To the schedules. I'm pretty sure. The school's firewall . . . A class I was in last year helped build it."

"That seems wise of the school," James said.

"They didn't tell us that's what it was," Devin said, clicking around to open some windows on one of his giant monitors as he talked. "But I figured it out by the questions they asked us, and how they made this big deal about destroying the code and all our work at the end of the semester. You want to see their schedules that bad?"

I stood and walked over to Devin. Maddy got up and followed me over. "Of course I do," I said. "Do it."

James was scowling again as he joined us. No surprise there. "You can't do that," he said. "I don't think Perry would approve."

"Perry's not here," I said. "Maddy, did Anavi seem like she needed us to help her make this go away?"

Maddy didn't want to disagree with James. She fidgeted, her eyes fixed on the floor. "Yes," she said. "She did."

James started to protest again, but then his face turned smug as Perry strolled through the door. He took us in, gathered around Devin's desk.

"I can already tell this is going better. I won't stay and get in your way." But he did come a little closer. "What are you working on?"

James gave me a superior look, but before he could open his big mouth and spoil things, I spoke up. Trying to keep my voice light, as if playing around, I said, "Devin's just hacking into the school's mainframe so we can check out some schedules for a few students. They're up to no good, and Principal Butler's in on it."

Perry snorted. "Good one. Whatever you're doing, carry on." With a wave, he was gone, out the way he'd come.

"He didn't think you were serious," James said, back to disbelieving.

I would need to make a list of his expressions: disapproving, disbelieving, dis . . . something else. I shrugged. "I didn't lie."

"Got it," Devin said. He stopped typing for a second, raising his hand to direct us to the screens on his giant monitors.

We watched as he opened several smaller windows on them, each one with a name and ID number at the top, followed by a class schedule and current grades for each class. The schedules shared something in common. There were no afternoon classes, nothing except the words:

Independent Study — Project Hydra

"That definitely looks like dirt to me," I said. "The incriminating kind."

Devin grinned.

He *was* cute, and he had hacking skills he wasn't afraid to use. I grinned back.

Then promptly thought of SmallvilleGuy and felt a twinge of guilt.

And though this Hydra mention on the Warheads' schedules was an undeniably positive development, evidence that there was *more* going on here, it bugged me. I wanted to know what it meant. What the more was.

"This isn't the first time I've heard the word Hydra today," I said. "Our comp sci teacher said it to them in second period. I thought it might be something in the game. But when I asked Anavi, she said even though it's in the game, it's nothing much."

"Yeah," Devin said. "Anavi's right about that. Easy to slay. I beat it the first month I started. And it says it's an independent study thing. They wouldn't get credit just to play the game."

That reminded me I needed Devin to set me up for that night's planned visit to *Worlds War Three*. But I wasn't ready to broach that topic yet. I was hoping I could arrange for SmallvilleGuy to be my backup, though it was possible he'd have no way to get a holoset. He had to save for extras, and as far as I knew he wasn't into gaming. But maybe he could borrow one, like I planned to. Lucy's only had access to *Unicorn University*, and I didn't have enough spending cash saved up to buy a *Worlds War Three* one.

Maddy interrupted my train of thought. "What is a Hydra, anyway?" she asked.

"Huh," I said. "I don't know."

James chimed in. "The Lernaean Hydra was a mythological monster, a sea serpent with many heads and poison breath and blood. If you cut one of the heads off, it grew two more. It wasn't so easily defeated in the myths. In Greek mythology, Hera raised it to kill Hercules, and he had no luck fighting it at first. He had to get his nephew to help out, cauterize the stumps before the heads could grow back after Hercules cut them off. Once it was down to one, that made it no longer invulnerable, and he was able to kill it for good."

We all gaped at James. It was hard not to.

"I guess the filthy rich do still get educated in the classics," I said. "Even the gruesome parts. Thanks for everything but the nightmares that will give me, the Third."

Devin had been clicking around during James's disturbing monologue, and he started to shut the windows. "I looked up all the Warheads whose names I know. Every single one has that same study project."

I went back to my own computer and chair. "I love it when a plan comes together," I said. "Dev, can you get me into the game tonight? Loan me your holoset again?"

He hesitated. "Probably. We'll figure it out in a few."

But he said it evasively, and crooked his head in James's general direction. James had gone back to his desk and wasn't paying attention to us. Maybe Devin was worried about him overhearing anyway. Why would James care about me going into the game?

Devin knew him better than I did, and I already had my own issues there. So I nodded, then signed into chat to ping SmallvilleGuy. If he couldn't join me in the game, I'd have to figure out a new plan or go it alone.

His name popped up a few seconds later.

I held in a sigh of relief.

Sometimes he was unreachable right after school, busy with all the farm chores his parents made him do to earn his allowance. When he'd first sent me the photo of his learner's permit, I'd done some sleuthing and confirmed farming was a common-enough occupation in Smallville that knowing his family had a farm didn't give me any actual intel about the reason for his secrecy.

SkepticGirl1: *You busy tonight?*

SmallvilleGuy: *Depends on how much trouble you're in.*

SmallvilleGuy: *Oh, wait, forgot you're on the straight and narrow. Forget I said anything.*

I had to bite my lip to keep from smiling. I'd never chatted with him when other people were around, except to exchange a few brief messages via the phone app. I didn't want anyone to notice if I made an inadvertently goofy expression.

SkepticGirl1: *Funny. You have any ability at all to play Worlds War Three?*

SmallvilleGuy: *Somehow I knew this was going to happen. So I spent a chunk of the money I was saving up for a new laptop today and got a holoset.*

SkepticGirl1: *Oh no!*

SkepticGirl1: *I mean thank you, but I know how long you've been saving that money.*

SmallvilleGuy: *It's okay. I was able to buy a used set off someone at school who doesn't use theirs anymore. It only cost three months of chore money. I'll earn it back. And I've always been curious to figure out how they work. Do you have one?*

SkepticGirl1: *Not yet, but I'm borrowing one from someone here. And really, thank you, because however much trouble I'm in, I'm about to get into more. Be nice to have you there to back me up. Ten?*

SmallvilleGuy: *I'll be there, your trusty sidekick.*

SkepticGirl1: *Ha. Right. Did you remember?*

His next message popped up before I could clarify.

SmallvilleGuy: *Remember to take a picture of Nellie Bly? Of course.*

His next message contained only an image—of the most adorable black-and-white patchwork calf face possible.

I laughed, and when I noticed the others looking at me in question, I shrugged. So what if I was chatting with someone? That was normal.

No need for them to know about the abnormal secrecy and conspiracy theory enthusiast parts.

SkepticGirl1: *Look at that face! I love her.*

SmallvilleGuy: *Good. Because my dad did think Nellie Bly was an odd name for a cow.*

SmallvilleGuy: *BTW, when you scam your friend's holoset off him, ask for the coordinates where I should meet you in the game and send them to me. See you later.*

He signed off and so did I.

Then I googled the word *Hydra* and confirmed that James's account of the Lernaean baddie had been accurate. I looked at a fearsome illustration of it, with its many snapping, fanged, monstrous heads, and then doodled in the margins of my notebook while I reviewed my notes from my interviews with Anavi and the Warheads.

Maddy had a pair of fancy headphones on, and the tinny sound of music emanated from them. She was in charge of posting a music review on the *Scoop* daily, and from the squinting and typing she was doing, she must be in the process of writing the latest.

At least a million years seemed to creep past before James the Third got up and went out to the hall, presumably to hit the bathroom. But when I glanced over at the Morgue's ancient Roman-numeraled clock, it had been less than ten minutes. "And we're clear," I said, keeping my voice low. "Now, what's the plan?"

Devin put a finger to his lips for me to not just be quiet, but silent. He typed something into his keyboard, and I nearly jumped out of my chair when the *Scoop* computer on my desk made a beep. I hadn't touched it yet, but I moved my laptop aside and squinted at the IM box that had popped up on the other computer's screen.

DevTheMighty: *Stay put. I can't let you have mine.*

I hit the reply button and my username popped up. It was apparently tied to my *Scoop* email account, which I was just discovering I had. And so my username was the boringly straightforward **LoisLane**. Why did Devin get a cool name?

Right. Because he's an expert with computers.

LoisLane: *But . . .*

That was all I got out of my intended attempt to tell Devin that he *had* to loan me his, that there was no other way, before he wheeled his chair away from his desk. He pedaled over to James's, checking to make sure Maddy didn't look up. She didn't.

Devin pulled out James's side desk drawer and lifted a holoset out of it. He shut the drawer gently and wheeled toward me. "You lost me a life the other day. I don't go around losing lives in there."

Maddy remained absorbed, the tinny music a soundtrack to this cloak-and-dagger.

"James won't loan that to me," I whispered.

"Plan B. I set this up for James the first week we were working here. I think it's something his dad taught him, find out what new people you meet are good at, and ask them for a favor. They'll say yes and like you more for needing them. Pretty sure he does it with everyone."

"Not me."

"Even James isn't dense enough to think he can *make* you like him." Devin slid his chair close to mine, hooking James's holoset over his ear. "Don't worry about it. It's good for him to run up against someone who isn't falling all over him. He'll never even notice this is gone—he hasn't used it since I set it up for him. Or even taken it back out of his desk."

"You don't seem at all pissed that he wasted your time," I said.

Devin shrugged and hit a couple of buttons. No holo appeared in front of him. He said, "I'm in the audio menu, setting your character up on here. I created it online." Then he muttered a few things that did in fact sound like menu selections. He took off the holoset and pressed it into my hand. He didn't move back right away.

"What?" I asked.

"James has had a rough couple of years. I know how that sucks. I figure we understand each other enough that I don't need to rub it in. And look how handy this is coming in. Maybe cut him a break?"

"I'll consider it," I told him.

Devin was more like me than the others. I liked him as

much as I did Maddy. Another genuine friend possibility.

Metropolis was all right.

"You should be good to go," he said. "It'll spit you out near my territory in the game . . . which is also a place Anavi and the Warheads hang out. I play solo, like she does now. They're in a team, and so a lot stronger than you'll be as a solo newbie. I gave your character an alliance that should help." Devin hesitated again. Then, "Do you want me to meet you in there? For backup?"

It was a generous offer, and if I hadn't already had an ally on tap, one that I would have taken.

"Not necessary," I said. "I have a friend inside already. He said to get the coordinates from you. And we might need you later since you're better at the game and all the computer stuff. Better for you not to get in their faces yet. Keep you in reserve."

Getting the same kind of target on Devin's back—or mind—that Anavi had was the last thing I wanted. I didn't know how dangerous the Warheads might be, but I did know they had a pattern of targeting people who played *Worlds War Three*.

I wasn't going to tell him that, though. Boys didn't like being protected—at least not when they knew about it.

"Let me know if you change your mind. Now or later," he said.

James came back into the room, but Devin still didn't move away yet. I jammed the borrowed holoset in my bag. Not that it sounded like James would have recognized it.

"Whatever you do," Devin whispered, "try not to leave the game in crisis. Go out calm. Otherwise, you can get hurt for real. And that's the other thing: it will feel real. Be prepared for that." He raised his voice, "And that's how your *Scoop* account works."

With that, he wheeled away, back to his own desk, more nonchalantly than I could have managed. Like he hadn't been up to anything but showing me how to work my office computer.

I wondered if his cautionary notes were overblown. Sure, I'd been a little woozy that morning when Lucy took her holoset off me, and there were all those warnings online. But even if the holoset was a revolutionary innovation, *Worlds War Three* and the rest were only games, and ones that millions of people played voluntarily. How dangerous could they be?

Not nearly as dangerous as the Warheads when they were outside it, from what I'd seen. Games couldn't make people doubt their own sanity. And it didn't matter.

The Warheads' reign of terror, Hydra or no Hydra, was about to come to an end.

CHAPTER 8

I settled down on my bed at the appointed hour of ten o'clock. After locking the door. My parents had gone to bed, earlier than most people as always, a habit Dad claimed he'd picked up way back in boot camp.

I hooked the shell of the holoset over my ear. I was unusually jumpy, but I didn't want to dwell on whether that was because of my worry about what might happen between Anavi and the Warheads, or my anticipation of "seeing" SmallvilleGuy in a new context. Devin had said the game would seem like it was real.

It's not a date. Don't think of it as one.

That didn't mean it didn't *feel* like a date, though, at least a little. Not that I had been on many, but there'd been a few coffees (Tulsa, Birmingham) and even a movie (Louisville). The guys always drifted away afterward, which never came as that much of a surprise.

I knew I could be intense. And since we were always moving around, it wasn't like I could let anyone get too close. I'd learned that the hard way when I made a best friend in fourth grade, a girl named Rory who read as many magazines as I did and liked watching CNN. We met in the waiting room of a dentist's office, both of us trying to find an issue of *TIME* we hadn't already seen.

But it was too hard to keep up via postcards and email, after the move. I had kept looking for another friend like Rory. I'd missed her. For years.

And today SmallvilleGuy had spent his prized savings *just in case* he needed to join me in the game. It was hard not to feel like we were coming to mean something more to each other.

But I didn't know if he felt the same.

He *was* my friend. That was all I knew for sure.

So don't think of it as a date.

I took a deep breath and told myself that I'd settled my nerves, though my heart was beating as fast as if I really was heading into a battle.

People from all over the globe played *Worlds War Three* and could go to any area they chose. But if you let the settings default, it put you in the vicinity of people who were also close to your actual physical locale. I hoped SmallvilleGuy didn't have any trouble changing his settings to the coordinates I'd passed on from Devin.

I reached up to switch on the covertly borrowed holoset. In

an instant, the world around me fell away and the game landscape rose to meet me.

Without others around and ambient noise for distraction it was spooky how quickly the game replaced reality. And how real it felt.

My research on *Worlds* had confirmed that, just like it had worked in Lucy's game, I could give voice commands if I wanted, but the game was sophisticated at reading pupil cues and translating them into movement. You could also move your limbs, and it would read the motion and translate that into action, but people rarely played that way. Apparently it was because it was hard to keep track of what you were doing outside the game.

"Look around," I murmured.

Like that, I turned in a slow circle, taking in my surroundings.

Night, but not full dark yet. Or maybe it was and the two giant moons that hung over the landscape, one tinged red and the other pale white, made enough light that it never truly was dark. There was also a large alien spaceship, round and ringed with glowing lights that made a pattern almost like visual music. The ground beneath my feet was covered in overgrown grass, and it tickled the bare skin of my ankles and feet.

I looked down to check that. Yes, I was definitely barefoot.

In a war game? Thanks, Devin. I wonder if you actually are good at playing this.

My clothing was some sort of leather dress, not cut low enough to bare too much of my character's ample (sigh) cleavage—so I wouldn't have to kill him—but with a short skirt.

Despite not wearing shoes, my feet didn't feel the least bit tender. Weird.

My immediate area was less flame-riddled than the holoscape I'd seen the other day, though there were wild puffs of smoke streaking through the sky up ahead. There was also the far-away sound of heavy artillery, something I could easily identify—I'd heard it enough times in tests and training exercises on base. The eerie flashing light patterns on the silvery spaceship repeated in a loop.

I faced the opposite direction of how I'd come in. Above me was an enormous castle. A banner flew off a turreted tower, and if I wasn't mistaken . . . was that? . . . yes, it appeared to feature a silhouette of Devin himself as viewed from the side.

A red dragon landed on one of the castle's turrets, and I wondered if it was about to shoot another missile at me. Tense already, when a hand touched my shoulder, I jumped. In the game and, I was pretty sure, up off the bed in my room.

It was disconcerting how I couldn't be entirely certain whether I'd moved in here *and* out there. What was happening around me in the game felt *more* real at the moment than reality. Devin hadn't been exaggerating.

"Sorry," a deep male voice said, and I turned to see the hand's owner. SmallvilleGuy.

He was a character here, like I was. But I still recognized him somehow. My cheeks warmed, and I couldn't help thinking of this as a first meeting.

Of sorts.

"Hi," I said.

"Hi," he said, at almost the same time.

I squinted at him like the instructions online had said to and lines of text popped into being and hovered beside his head. They gave his name—the same one he used in chat—and the type of character he was: alien, friendly. There was nothing else. But what had I expected?

Still, he'd designed this character. That had to reveal something.

His appearance wasn't so alien, only a hint of a green tinge to his skin, and he'd chosen a tall, slender form rather than a muscle-bound one like those usually featured in the game's commercials. Short, wavy black hair, thick-framed glasses. A little nerdy, maybe? But more appealing than he had any right to be despite that.

I was definitely blushing, which was silly. It wasn't like he could read my thoughts. I reached up to smooth my hair back behind my long, pointy ears . . .

Wait a second. What long, pointy ears?

I looked down at the leather dress again, then reached up to touch the points. Of my ears. "What am I?" I asked.

He grinned at me.

I pretended my heart didn't leap in response.

We are characters in a game. That's all.

Get it together.

"How much trouble will your friend be in if I tell you?" he asked.

"What. Am. I?" I crossed my arms. "Tell me, and I'll probably let you *and* Devin live."

He laughed, and I wished I knew what his laugh sounded like in real life. If this was it. I sounded like myself *to* myself, so maybe it was. It was a good laugh.

Still smiling at me, he squinted to read my stats and answered my question. "You are an elvish princess named Lo, inhabitant of the Realm of Ye Old Troy, ruled over by . . . " His grin widened. I hadn't expected the character graphics to make reactions seem so real, either.

"You said your friend's name is Devin?" he asked.

I nodded.

"This is his castle, apparently," he said. "King Devin."

"I will try not to kill him, since he's royalty and all."

"He did make you a princess," SmallvilleGuy said. "Could be worse. You know they have harem girls and serving wenches in here."

"Okay, okay." I—or was it Princess Lo, elvish lady?—said. I rolled my eyes. "Did he give me any other ridiculous traits to go with the bare feet?"

SmallvilleGuy's head tilted to one side. "I don't know if it's ridiculous, but your eyes are bright purple. Probably not out there, huh?"

I blinked, self-consciously wanting to close my eyes to hide them. As far as I knew, he'd never seen a photo of me, and certainly not a close-up. "Um, actually, they're violet out there too. I know it's crazy, like some color in a bad novel."

If he was surprised, he hid it. "They're *beautiful* bright purple, I should have said. The sovereign king made your character accurate—except for the ears."

"And the wardrobe. But I guess I'll give him a pass, as long as he's a benevolent ruler. Why'd you choose to be an alien?"

"That's what I feel like most of the time," he said, and I almost melted. But then he added, "*Or*, it was first on the list."

"Where do you think we should go from here?"

"We're looking for Anavi, right?" he asked. Before I could answer, he grabbed my arm and towed me toward a broad-trunked tree. But we had to stop at the discovery it had a grimacing wooden face filled with disturbingly long teeth.

"Over there," he said. He pointed out past the shadow of the tree. It hardly concealed us from the squadron.

The Warheads.

They were military characters in the game. Steroid human physiques, dressed in all black gear, and armed to the teeth.

They didn't seem to have spotted SmallvilleGuy and me yet. So I squinted to see what the game would tell me about them, a second before SmallvilleGuy said, "Don't try to look at their stats or they'll—"

A hail of fiery bullets sprayed in our direction. I pulled him back toward the toothy side of the tree for cover.

"—know we're here?" I finished. "Oops."

The tree snapped at us, and we were forced to back away again. "We need to find Anavi."

"Will she come anywhere near them?" he asked.

"Hard to say. She knows I wanted to see them interact with her, but she didn't make any promises."

One of the soldiers in the Warhead pack called out to the others, "We can pursue the unknown elf—"

Another chimed in, calling out, "But we just found our real target. This way."

They hesitated briefly before heading in the opposite direction of us. SmallvilleGuy took my arm, and I swore I could feel the pressure of his fingers against my skin. It was . . . nice.

Clearly, elvish senses caused you to turn into a princess in the silliest possible sense of the word.

"It has to be her," I said. "Let's go."

He followed my cue as we loped along after the Warheads.

We didn't get too close, just near enough to keep them in sight. The squad was having a blast, calling out to each other in that creepy overlapping way, moving like they did at school, like they were all part of the same entity.

Or like a Hydra, a monster with many heads.

"See what I mean about them?" I asked.

"It is weird. Do you think they can do something to her mind outside the game? You talked to her today, didn't you?"

"I know they can," I said.

SmallvilleGuy stopped cold, his light green hand on my arm gently pulling me to a halt too. "Lois," he said, "did they do something to you?"

"It was no big deal." I shrugged. "But it confirmed what she's saying. It proved to me that it's true. They can do things they shouldn't be able to. I just can't figure out how or why. They're getting away, we should—"

"We'll catch up to them. What did they do to you?" he insisted.

"I felt them . . . push me. Away. My mind, not me," I

clarified. His alien expression darkened. "But I was fine. I am fine."

"Time for us to catch them," he said in response.

I wished I had a secret decoder ring that would explain his reaction. Was he mad they'd done something to me? Or concerned in general that they could act outside the game?

We caught up to the Warheads without any trouble, watching as they spread out in a silent circle around a girl grappling with what appeared to be a giant troll. The hunch-backed monster stood three times the girl's height, and when it shoved her with a hand nearly as big as she was, she backed off, as if to rethink her strategy.

She was a soldier too, though not like the Warheads. She had on camouflage instead of black, and wore a crisscrossing belt filled with grenades. I took a closer look—yes, the grenades had words printed on them. They curled around the sides of the weaponry. I could make out *nirvana* and *karma* and *viscera*.

"That's her," I said.

"She's holding her own," SmallvilleGuy said.

Unfortunately, the troll meant Anavi was too occupied to notice the Warheads. But if I called out to warn her, then the troll would almost certainly be able to best her. And the other thing that had started to worry me was how real everything in the game felt.

I didn't want to find out whether getting hurt would too.

But Anavi had decided she was tired of troll fighting. She backed up a few more steps—the Warheads behind her doing the same, again, so she wouldn't see them yet—and then took a running start before—

"Is she really . . ." I started, but left off, gaping.

"I did not see that coming," SmallvilleGuy said. "And neither did the troll."

He was right. Anavi was stabbing into the monster's clothing with some kind of tool for leverage, climbing right up its arm. When she reached his shoulder, she stood and yelled out: "*Sic semper tyrannis,* troll!"

And she jabbed the small tool she'd used on the way up there into the creature's massive neck.

"That was a tranq dart. Look out," SmallvilleGuy said and pulled me out of the way as the troll swayed and then fell forward like a tree crashing down in a forest.

It hit with enough force that the ground shook beneath our feet. I leaned into SmallvilleGuy, trying to make out what had happened to Anavi.

I spotted the proud warrior at the exact same moment as the Warheads did. And vice versa.

The three of them nearest Anavi, where she'd landed on the ground in a fearless warrior's crouch, began to clap, balancing machine guns and other heavy artillery against their chests.

"Well done . . ."

"We could use . . ."

"A fighter like you on our side . . ."

The ring of them advanced on her, so that even in their appreciation, the sinister intent was clear. They had her surrounded.

Which was the kind of thing I needed to witness for the story, but now that I had, that was enough.

"Yo, boys and girls," I said, striding away from SmallvilleGuy, "give the lady some space." Anavi's character was wide-eyed at having been cornered, but she visibly breathed easier at the sight of me. Ironic, because after watching her take down that beast, I didn't think Anavi needed much help in here.

"We're just recruiting," one of them said.

"But we have an opening for our next kill."

"You look like you'd be a good one, elf."

"I am not an elf," I said, standing my ground. "I'm a reporter."

Maybe it wasn't the thing to do. Rifles lifted around me. And, yes, I recognized what kinds of guns they were, all of them military grade and designed to kill.

Anavi took a few steps toward the squadron and said, "Don't. She's with me."

But that was the wrong thing to say too, because it signaled the end of nonviolent recruitment mode. Half the Warheads' guns swung around to point at Anavi, while the rest stayed trained on me. A chorus of low laughter was next. Then someone said, "I don't think you want to be doing this. Any of it."

SmallvilleGuy, obviously. He had jumped on top of the downed troll, so he stood higher than the rest of us. I wanted to tell him to get down from there, to ask what he thought he was doing, to tell him they might hurt him . . .

But I didn't want to give them the satisfaction of showing any worry.

"Don't bother. I'm fine, and so's Anavi," I said.

One of the Warheads decided that was the last straw. Or maybe he just had an itchy trigger finger.

As the bullet flew toward Anavi, she said to me, "Hope you got what you needed." And then she *poof*ed right out of existence.

She'd said she would turn off her holoset if things got too intense. So she had.

I tried to reground myself, find my body, in prep to do the same. But it was taking a moment, especially because I was still focused on SmallvilleGuy, and the fact that half the Warheads were heading toward him.

He smiled at them. "You guys give teamwork a bad name. And I heard you don't know when to quit, either."

Before they could shoot, a spray of red and green beams emanated from SmallvilleGuy's eyes through the glasses his character wore. His head moved in slow motion from side to side, the lasers swiveling as he did, knocking all the weapons to the ground in one pass. Some of them fell into separate pieces, even.

"Lo, get out of here," SmallvilleGuy said when the beams faded. "I'll meet you after."

A Warhead spoke up. "Friendly aliens aren't supposed to have laser vision."

But another one said, "Good thing . . ."

And another, ". . . we have lots of extra firepower."

Before I could figure out what they meant by that, my shoulder exploded in white-hot pain.

CHAPTER 9

The sharp flare of pain knocked me back into being able to tell the difference between my in-game form and real-world body. I watched as SmallvilleGuy leaped high into the air again, in a probably doomed attempt to avoid a hail of bullets. At the same time, I lifted my actual hand and switched off the holoset.

I put my hand to my shoulder, which smarted with the phantom pain. When that faded, I laid it over my pounding heart and looked around at the quiet safety of my not-yet-familiar room.

Convincing myself it *was* safe took a little while. How long, I couldn't have said.

Devin's cautionary echo of the manufacturer warning rang in my ears, and I was breathing hard. But eventually my racing heartbeat began to return to normal. The bed beneath me felt solid again, the world real again, and in the real world . . .

SmallvilleGuy must be freaking out. Assuming he made it out okay.

I was at my desk in a few shaky breaths, opening up my laptop and typing in the passwords. The moment I got into the chat screen, I saw his name. He pinged me with a message, and I sank into my chair. With something like relief, but I wouldn't have called it that.

Not exactly.

SmallvilleGuy: *Are you all right?*

I could have run a marathon now that I'd recovered, adrenaline surging through me.

SkepticGirl1: *No. I'm not.*

SmallvilleGuy: *Do you feel disoriented? Pulling yourself out of the game like that can be dangerous, especially when you're hurt. Maybe I should call and wake up your parents.*

My fingers were as shaky as my breath. But being hurt wasn't why. No one was calling anyone and definitely not my parents.

And what if *he* was hurt? I wouldn't have a clue who to tell or anyone to call.

SkepticGirl1: *Physically, I'm fine. Are you?*

SmallvilleGuy: *Fine, like you.*

The shakiness in my fingers transformed. They continued to tremble, but the cause shifted. It no longer came from feeling like I'd been shot and then tossed out of an airplane without a parachute.

SkepticGirl1: *I am not fine.*

SkepticGirl1: *I am too angry to be fine. If the Warheads think they're getting away with whatever they're up to, they have another thing coming.*

SmallvilleGuy: *Lois . . . Don't do anything rash.*

I almost typed back *Rash is my middle name*, but that would only worry him. Tonight's reminder that if he *had* needed my help in the game or outside it, I would have been powerless to do anything about it was not welcome. It wasn't like I could travel to Smallville and go around to all the farms trying to see which cute little calf answered to Nellie Bly. I wanted to be the kind of friend who was always there when needed, who always had the other person's back—and if I was being honest, I especially wanted to always have his.

I balled my fingers into frustrated fists, and then unclenched them. Tradition was tradition. I would end tonight the same way as usual, before I said something that would embarrass me later.

SkepticGirl1: *You going to tell me who you are?*

I waited.

The chat window told me that he was typing, then typing some more. I sighed.

SkepticGirl1: *It's okay. Chat with you tomorrow.*

I closed the laptop before I could see his next message.

"Good thing it wasn't a first date," I said quietly.

Because, if it had been, it would have been a complete and epic disaster.

He protected you. You wanted to protect him. Don't be too mad.

But I was. Just not at him.

I thought I would have trouble sleeping, but once the adrenaline faded, it came easily. For a few hours, anyway.

I woke up in the middle of the night from a bad dream featuring a circle of black-clad commandos who were pointing weapons at me as I lay prone on the ground.

But it wasn't the dream threat that worried me. I turned over, clutching a pillow against my stomach, obsessing over the abrupt way I'd left the chat with SmallvilleGuy. I shouldn't have shut the conversation down like that on him, angry and frustrated or not.

But I understood something suddenly. It hit me like a lightning strike, and I sat up in bed. I realized *why* I should have stuck it out, talked about what was bothering me with him. Why I was so sure that he would know exactly what I meant about never wanting to let someone else down.

The two of us were alike. We wouldn't stand by and watch, not when we could act instead.

*

But I was still angry the next morning, stalking through the halls on the way to second period. I wouldn't feel better until I got back at the jerky Warheads and figured out what they were up to and why they could do the odd things they could outside the game.

And until I helped Anavi like I'd promised. That was priority one.

Devin was waiting when I got to class, and had saved me a seat again. "How did it go last night?" he asked.

After considering several responses, I finally went with, "Doesn't his highness get a full report from the *Daily Dragon Planet* or something when the cock croweth in the Kingdom of Devin?"

"It's the Realm of Ye Old Troy," he said, studying the keyboard in front of him. "You should've let me go in with you."

"You do have a very nice castle. But we made it out without too much trouble."

Anavi walked into the classroom, and I immediately regretted what I had said. Her eyes were ringed with dark circles. She came directly to us, taking the seat beside me.

"I'm sorry I just left you there." Her hands were balled in her lap. "I shouldn't have."

"You did exactly what you said you would. I was hoping you got out without any pain or problems. What's wrong?"

Anavi was subdued. "It's not the game." She gave her head a little shake, like there was water in her ears.

Or bad guys in her head. They clearly weren't giving up. "They're bothering you again here?" I asked.

Anavi nodded absently and turned, her eyes locking on the door seconds before the Warheads came through it.

"It's getting worse," she said.

She turned back around and stared down at her hands, twisting them together on the tabletop. I wished I had her grenade belt or SmallvilleGuy's laser eyebeams to direct at the smirking Warheads.

They arrayed themselves at workstations along the other side of the table from me and Devin and Anavi, sitting down at the same time, like they were one person. Then they started their taunts, putting some sing-song into them.

"Hope no one's got . . ."

". . . heartburn."

"Or was it the shoulder?"

"We figured out . . ."

". . . that Anavi's only got one friend."

"Besides us."

"We'd be much better friends, Anavi."

"We can keep *her* from bothering *you*."

I didn't speak right away. Mostly, in truth, because I didn't want to feel that mental shove again. I didn't want the distraction of it. I knew that they could do things outside the game, too. The problem was, I wasn't sure what the limits were. I didn't know anything about the how, or how much. Not even why they were able to.

Project Hydra must be the key.

"Stop." The word slipped out from Anavi.

"You know . . ."

". . . how to make it stop . . ."

". . . it would be easy . . ."

". . . just as easy as it is for us to never stop."

I didn't have a way to go on the attack at this particular second, but I had a story. A story it was almost time to tell.

"Save the threats for someone who's scared of you," I said.

I put a hand on Anavi's arm and nodded at her, and she tried to nod back. But it was weak.

Definitely almost time to tell the story.

I stood, hoping Anavi would do the same.

"What are we doing?" Anavi asked, but she didn't fight, climbing to her feet when I tugged on her arm.

"Getting you out of here for now," I said.

Devin was frowning at the Warheads. "Go. I'll handle the teacher," he said.

"You're a prince, King," I told him under my breath.

I was relieved, and even more worried, when Anavi let me lead her out of the classroom doors without a single big-ticket vocabulary word of protest about risking her scholarship. Her eyes were nearly shut.

I steered her carefully, but quickly, up the hall. Once we were several classrooms away, Anavi's state changed, but it wasn't so much an improvement. She . . . wilted. Like a delicate flower in burning hot desert sun.

With those dark circles around her eyes, she looked exhausted. "I don't want my consciousness to be erased. But they said it would be easy to take it. Lois, it *feels* easy."

I had been guiding us in the direction of the cafeteria, gambling that it would be empty. I was right.

The Warheads' usual table was the closest to the door. She wouldn't want to sit there even with it vacant, so I kept going until we reached the next one. I eased Anavi into a chair, and then sat down beside her.

"In the game last night," I started, trying to decide on the most important answers I needed, "were they able to get in your head?"

Anavi hesitated. "It wasn't like it is out here. But . . . something is changing. It was different. Here, I can feel them pushing and pulling, I can almost hear their voices in my mind. They're getting clearer, pulling me closer, overtaking my own voice."

She paused, embarrassed, like she couldn't believe she'd said that out loud.

"I believe you. You can trust me."

"There were whispers last night. When I was in combat with the bridge troll, I was too busy to notice, but once that concluded . . . You know that sense of disconnection there is when you're inside the game? As if you've been split in two, cleaved, but the mind is the part that matters now and it has its own sense and sensation?"

I wouldn't have put it exactly that way, but then I didn't have Anavi's way with language.

"It feels more real inside than outside while you're there," I said.

"The only way I can explain it is, last night, you heard and saw them in the game, but I also heard them outside it. Whispers in my ears outside too, after I departed, like a . . . a strange hummed tune, almost." Anavi waited, but so did I. I didn't quite understand yet. She continued, "They are bringing together their talents within and without. They are strengthening, making me one of them. It would be easy to submit.

To be assimilated. In there and out here. I do not know if I can resist."

Light spilled in through the long windows at the far end of the cafeteria, and from the kitchen there were the sounds of that day's sad lunch being made.

"You're stronger than you think," I said.

"Maybe," Anavi said, and I could see she was only half convinced. Which was better than zero convinced, but not ideal.

I opened my mouth intending to reassure her, but before I said a word the PA speaker beside the cafeteria door crackled to life. Ronda's crisp voice came over it, saying, "Lois Lane, report to Principal Butler's office. Lois Lane, to Principal Butler's office, immediately."

CHAPTER 10

When the announcement ended, Anavi was shaking her head. "You don't have to put yourself in further jeopardy on my behalf."

"Please," I said. "They shot me in the shoulder. Now I'd do it just because." *Also, just because there's more going on here.* "Stay here and wait out comp sci. Avoid the jerk squad until I can find you."

I'd intended to approach Principal Butler again today, so in some ways, this was convenient. Despite how weirdly dismissive he'd been before, I believed confronting him now would box him in, make him take action against the Warheads and protect Anavi.

Which would mean my first story for the *Scoop* would be slightly less awesome, as the school administration wouldn't be completely inept in it. But it would also mean the plan—my plan for Metropolis—wasn't completely scrapped, either.

Being good did not come easy for me.

But I couldn't regret anything I was doing. This *was* a story, an important one, with a girl's mind in the balance, and I would tell it.

Still. Rash might be my middle name, but I'd promised my dad—and myself—that I'd *try* to be different here. No need to get into trouble Dad would hear about, something that might make him change his mind about the *Scoop*. No need to engage in *Worlds War Three* against General Lane. Not yet.

"Besides," I said, "I need to see Brown-nose Butler to get his official statement for my story." I got up, ready to go do just that.

"You might want to refrain from using that particular name with him."

Anavi had tried to make a joke, despite her wan face and dark-circled eyes. She gnawed at her bottom lip.

Something was still bugging her, even though she was safe here in cafeteria-land for the moment.

I hesitated. "What is it?"

"You're not planning to mention me by name in the article, correct?" Anavi asked, with a hint of discomfort.

I inhaled sharply. The question stung.

After what we'd been through together in the last twenty-four hours . . . I wanted to be trusted. I *was* trustworthy. But you had to know people to trust them, and I hardly ever got to know anyone because of how often we moved. It wasn't like

I thought Anavi and I were close already, but I'd believed her when no one else would. I not only wanted to help her, but I liked and even admired her, not just for the mystifying gift she had at spelling, but the way she'd felled that troll. The way she was fighting to hold on to herself.

But she didn't trust me.

SmallvilleGuy trusts you.

Yeah, and he probably also thinks I'm ticked off at him because of the way I signed off last night.

I sighed. "Look, I made you a promise. I'm helping you. Worry about staying away from the Warheads, but don't worry about my end of the deal. This will all be over soon enough."

The PA crackled and I was summoned again. Time to face the principal's obnoxiousness.

"Lois, that's not what I intended," Anavi stopped me. "I . . . I *want* you to use my name. It will lend more credence to the story. And I thank you."

I nodded, not quite able to speak. I'd misunderstood. She *was* trusting me.

As I left, I let the cafeteria door bang shut behind me, once again on a mission. There was no one in the empty hallway to notice the noise. I could not under any circumstances—whether it was attack by brain-stealing jerks or trollpocalypse—fail Anavi.

I didn't meet a soul until I arrived outside the office. When I was a few steps away from the door, it opened and who should come out but the one and only James the Third.

James the Third just happened to be in the principal's office when I was called to it? Uh-huh.

What if he'd ratted out the way we hacked into the school system to take a look at the Warheads' schedules? I didn't like silver spoon guy, but would he *do* something that vile? Betray his fellow staffers, even Devin who'd told me to cut him some slack? And, if he had told, could he prove it?

His expression was *almost* unreadable, but not quite. What I saw there was a hint of apology.

"What did you do, the Third?" I asked as I passed him.

He held the door, always with the polite manners. He said, "Nothing, but be careful with—"

But his suggestion was cut short by the appearance of Principal Butler. An oily smile oozed across his face. "Ms. Lane, it's about time you showed up. Ronda, when did you call for her, again?"

"Ten minutes ago, sir," she answered. Her voice squeaked on the final word.

Sometimes a first impression was wrong. Most of the time, it wasn't. I remembered just how much I had disliked Butler the other morning. By now, if anything, that amount had doubled. He might pretend to be nice, but you could always tell what kind of boss someone was by how their assistant acted around them. He had poor Ronda walking on eggshells, which must have been uncomfortable in high heels.

"See you at the office, old chum," I said to James, "and we'll catch up on tricks."

I said it so I wasn't hopping to Butler's command, *and*

so he'd know that James and I worked together. If he didn't already.

James would also get the message that I wouldn't let it go if he'd played the part of rat. Bonus.

Gratifyingly, the principal's disapproval—as evidenced by the disappearance of his fake smile—meant I scored a direct hit by not hurrying. I sauntered toward him, taking my sweet, sweet time.

"Funny, it doesn't take ten minutes to get here from anywhere in the building," he said as I neared. "Of course, since you decided to cut class this morning, maybe you weren't *in* the building."

So much for this place being different. I'd forgotten about the plan again, in the moment.

But I hadn't even done anything wrong. My story hadn't run yet.

The story. That's why you're here. Anavi needs your help.

I followed him up the hallway and into his over-decorated office. Taking a seat opposite the desk, I removed my notepad from my messenger bag, put it on my lap and clicked my pen. I looked up at Butler, who sat behind a big oak desk.

"You're not here to take dictation," he said.

"Good," I countered, "because I don't do that. I did want to ask you a few questions, though."

He didn't respond, and so I made a closer study of his décor to see what I could see.

Predictable. Everything reflected a false sort of opulence. He must spend a lot of money on those pricey suits. There were scrollwork appliqués on the wood paneling, and his desk was varnished to a high gloss. The shelves behind it were filled with leather books, spines perfect and uncracked, meaning they might or might not have been empty inside and only for show. The paintings were grim hunting scenes with lean hounds and fleeing foxes and gentlemen in puffy pants carrying long rifles. In other words, more like some estate in England than the city around us.

"You hunt foxes?" I asked, skeptical.

His way-too-high-backed chair creaked as he leaned back in it. "That's what you wanted to ask me?"

He was turning on the charm again.

"No, actually." I might as well go all in, shake his confidence by being blunt, if I wanted to get a reaction. "I wanted to talk to you about bullying."

Two well-groomed silver eyebrows shot up at that. "You're not still fixated on those claims you heard the other morning, are you? They're baseless."

"You *are* familiar with a group of students known as the Warheads, aren't you? You said as much to Anavi the other day."

He steepled his fingers. He probably got weekly manicures.

"I make it my business to know what our students are up to. Especially our brightest, which the Warheads are among. I know that you took pains to be transferred into their computer class, despite not having any of the prerequisites. Something Ronda should not have allowed. I also know that despite this great desire to be in the class, you skipped out this morning and took another of our best and brightest with you. Anavi Singh has never cut class in her life."

"I'll take that as a yes." I scribbled some nonsense in my notebook, so it would look like I was writing that down. When I finished, the amusement on his face was like grit in my shoe. "But you *would* agree that bullying isn't something the school tolerates?"

I was giving him an out, even though I didn't want to anymore.

I waited, as if poised to take down the answer. All he had to say was that of course the school frowned on it, of course he'd intervene.

"The world is a harsh place," Principal Butler said instead. "Our job is to prepare you to take part in it. We don't baby our students here. Real bullying is much rarer than these news reports make it out to be. Handling uncomfortable situations is a good life skill. Anavi is perfectly capable."

So much for him taking the out I'd offered.

"You're really saying that bullying builds character? What would you say if it was the Warheads being targeted, instead of Anavi?"

"I'd say the same thing: handle it on your own." Principal Butler's fingers made a dome on top of the leatherbound notebook dead center on his desk. "Lois, we got off on the wrong foot. Your dad is a decorated war hero. And Perry White . . . saw something in you, after all. He's an important person in this city. I want to make sure you settle in here successfully. I'll be transferring you *out* of computer science, and into phys ed. To be frank, I believe you need an outlet for all that excess energy."

Anything but the horrors of P.E. Volleyball, locker rooms, polyester gym shorts. Oh, he was low.

"But—"

"But you're welcome. The other thing you're going to do is leave the Warheads alone. They are good students, promising minds, which we support. They need room to blossom."

"Like mushroom clouds, maybe," I muttered.

Being kicked out of that class wasn't a big deal, since I hadn't wanted to stay in it anyway. And P.E. would rue the day Lois Lane was invited into its sweaty nightmare.

"I do have one more question," I said. "Well, two. The first is what was James the Third doing here?"

"Not that it's any of your business." Butler shifted in his throne. "But his father was a friend. I like to check in, make sure the kid's doing all right these days."

Figured they'd be besties, what with the power and the criminal proclivities of ex-Mayor James Jr.

"And there's one more." I gripped my pen harder and stared at him. I didn't want to miss any part of his reaction.

"Shoot," he said, pleased with our little chat. He probably assumed he'd set me straight.

"About Project Hydra . . . What's that? Why does it preempt the Warheads' afternoon class work? I hear they leave every day after lunch. Is that why you're protecting them despite clear allegations of bullying? I've witnessed it, by the way. In the game they play *and* in the halls of *your* school."

He was silent for a long moment, and then he pushed back from the desk.

"That's no business of yours. Nothing to do with the Warheads is, as I've made clear."

When I got up, assuming he was dismissing me, he said, "Just a second," and left.

Left me right there in his office. All alone, with no one around.

And he didn't return right away.

I got up, peeked out the door. He wasn't in the hall, but I could hear him talking to someone out front—presumably poor Ronda—in barking-orders mode. I'd flustered him enough that he'd dropped his cheap-satin-disguised-as-smooth-silk veneer.

I scurried over to his desk and poked around the contents. Beside his giant dinosaur of a computer was a small faux leather stand holding post-its. Because he wouldn't want anyone to think his post-its weren't classy.

They didn't seem to be used, at a glance. But I picked up the pad and flicked through, confirmed they were blank.

I eyed the leather notebook, in its place of pride. Picked it up and flipped through it, as well. Also empty, except . . . I stopped when I reached the final sheet. The only page with writing.

A series of scratched out words ran down it in columns. All at least six characters. All with at least one number and one capital letter.

The last word wasn't crossed out.

I looked over my shoulder, confirming he wasn't back yet, and took the top sticky to copy down the last in the list. Which I'd bet a ransom was his password.

You never knew. It might come in handy.

I closed the notebook, scooting it back to the position where I'd found it, and then headed back to my chair. Dropping into it, I reached down to tuck the post-it into my messenger bag, finishing as he returned.

He was still rattled, and he did a double take when he came back in. Like he'd forgotten I was there.

"You're still here," he said.

"There's only one way out of the office, so if you didn't see me leave . . . " I smiled innocently. "I wasn't dismissed. I figured I should wait."

"You are now. I think we've settled the matter of these claims. Baseless. Enjoy gym class."

He waited by the door, and so I picked up my bag, placing my notebook inside. The yellow of the post-it within winked at me.

"This has been very educational," I told him, and he motioned for me to head out.

I made it almost to the end of the beige hall, right before it met Ronda's guard desk area, before I ran smack into a cluster of four Warheads, coming in where I was going out. So my mention of Hydra had gotten them summoned. Interesting.

Not that I could tell if the four of them minded. I stopped, and they glided past me with that same coordinated movement, like they were part of a single-celled organism. The same smirks, the same overlapping whispers, as they headed to Butler's lair.

"Uh-oh . . ."

". . . called to the principal's office . . ."

"She can't stay out . . ."

". . . of trouble, can she?"

I flattened myself against the wall to let them pass. Peeking past into the outer office, I saw that the poor assistant Ronda was at her post, but she had her head buried in her arms, not paying attention to anything around her. No doubt Butler had reamed her out for something, or at least been rude about asking for his favorite sociopaths to be brought to him.

When I heard the principal's office door shut with a click, I turned to confirm the members of the Warheads were inside, and went back the way I'd come. Hearing what he said to them would be useful. It might help answer my remaining questions.

I pressed my ear to the door, like I did at night before my chats with SmallvilleGuy. All I could hear was the non-dulcet tones of a voice talking. Droning on and on. It was Butler, but I couldn't make out what he was saying.

I wanted to.

So I fished out my phone, scrolled to the recording app, pressed it on, and locked the screen to prevent a stray sound from giving me away. I plugged in the earbuds, keeping the ends tight in one hand, then bent and pressed the phone under the bottom of the door. The gap was plenty big enough, the carpet muffling its slide into position.

Have your private consult, principal, so long as I can listen.

I stayed there, my leg muscles shrieking bloody murder at being forced to hold the crouch. After minutes that felt like hours passed, the doorknob started to turn . . . but stopped at a harsh order, which must have been Butler telling them to hold up. I yanked on the earbuds, pulling the phone back out and into my hand.

And I bolted up the hall and out to the front. I paused in the front office and said to Ronda, "I hope you spit in his coffee."

From the way Ronda looked at me, shocked before she gave a pink smile, I figured Principal Butler was lucky if that was all that his assistant did to his morning cuppa these days.

Good for you.

I left, inspired by her example. I'd already cut one class. Why not another later this afternoon?

If Butler wouldn't tell me where the jerk squad went and what Project Hydra was, well, then I had no choice but to find out on my own.

CHAPTER 11

Maddy and I were keeping Anavi company during lunch in the back corner of exile again. Though we weren't doing that great a job of it.

Anavi wasn't behaving normally, even for harassed values of normalcy. She had only spoken to us when we pressed her, spaced out otherwise, and so we'd settled into an awkward silence.

"You're making me nervous with that," Maddy said.

And I realized I was drumming my fingers on the table in the staccato rhythm of impatience. "Oops. Sorry."

With effort, I stopped drumming and fidgeting. I was practically dead from how much I wanted lunch to end so that I could listen to the recording and make my next move toward uncovering the dirty secrets of Hydra.

But distraction came in the form of a semi-surprise, when Devin walked up and pulled out a chair to join us.

Maddy found this even more notable than I did. "Are you sure this is where you want to sit, or will you lose cool points?" she asked him.

Devin settled back into the seat across from Anavi. "Last time I checked, it was a free cafeteria."

He must usually hang with a more exclusive lunch crowd, which made it a nice gesture on his part. I couldn't help wondering if his non-*Scoop* friends knew about his giant castle and gaming kingdom.

I remembered the banner with his silhouette on it and decided probably not. It might mean that he was on his way to trusting me too, since he hadn't hidden it from me. And not only that, but he'd set up the game to send me there and given elf Lo an alliance.

He directed his next words to me. "You're not in detention, so I take it Butler let you off with some kind of warning?"

"An infuriating one." I could almost see the secret realm ruler in Devin peeking through in his manner, as if he was comfortable anywhere.

Devin accepted my answer, and started rattling away about the game. I got the distinct impression it was to give Anavi something to focus on. Not that it seemed to be working.

Her eyes flicked over to Devin, and then back to the table. She was distracted, like she had been during the entirety of lunch. Not shaking her head and wincing, but not herself either.

I considered asking Devin and Maddy whether they thought James would rat us out, but I held off. He was sitting with Maddy's sister again, and there was no need to remind her that she was pining for a boy who liked her identical twin. I'd confront James about his close ties with the loathsome Principal Butler later.

Loathsome? Anavi's vocabulary might be wearing off on me.

I checked to see what Maddy's T-shirt was today, having forgotten to look earlier. It was for another band, called Pink Hippopotamus.

Hadn't Maddy brought up hippos the other day and asked Anavi to spell the word, saying she could never remember how?

Maddy noticed me staring.

"I've never heard of them," I said. "What kind of music?"

"They're good," Maddy mumbled.

Anavi still hadn't tuned in to anything we were saying, and Devin stopped his game talk to pay attention to us.

Maddy seemed uncomfortable, so I changed topics. "Devin, why an elf?" I asked as he took a drink of soda. "And is that get-up what elves usually wear in the game? The bare feet seem like a really bad idea in a warzone. Not to mention the short skirt."

By all appearances, soda went up Devin's nose as he snorted. He continued to sputter while Maddy cracked up. I couldn't help doing the same.

Anavi shook her head back and forth, barely noticing.

Maddy got her giggles under control enough to speak and leaned forward, putting both hands on the cafeteria table like she needed the support. "Devin. Seriously. You made *Lois* an *elf*?"

When I looked questioningly at her, Maddy said, "He mentioned he lent you James's holoset last night." At whatever my expression showed, she added, "I didn't tell James."

"I knew she wouldn't," Devin said, composed again. "I was only being stealthy when I took it from his desk in case he came back before we were done. There wasn't time to explain to Maddy what was going on then."

I thought of the longing Maddy directed James's way. If Devin really hadn't spotted that, he made for a less-than-perceptive king.

It was also a reminder that they all knew each other way better than they knew me.

But Maddy and Devin were here, backing me up and pitching in with the battle on Anavi's behalf against the Warheads. They were becoming my friends too.

I hoped they couldn't see this sappy reaction reflected on my face, or they'd think I was a hopeless cause. I didn't want to scare them away.

"No," Anavi said, with force. *"No."*

That broke the moment, along with any lightness in the conversation. I exchanged glances with Devin and Maddy. Anavi still didn't seem tuned into our channel: reality, cafeteria, the here and now.

"Hippopotamus?" I tried.

Still nothing.

Maddy reached out and touched Anavi's shoulder. "Anavi?"

Anavi blinked. Once, twice, three times. "Sorry," she said, "sorry. Just distracted . . . I keep thinking of that fight in the game. Replaying it different ways. I never kill the big monsters, not unless I have to. I leave them alive . . ."

She trailed off, humming three weirdly tuneless notes before going quiet. We gave her a chance to pick back up, but she didn't.

Devin seemed to be the most skilled among us at keeping things on an even keel, so I was relieved when he tried to reach her.

"Smart," he said. "Means you can take whatever loot they have again, once the game reboots them. Finding the tranqs is almost as hard as taking them out anyway. That's one of the ways I amassed my wealth."

Maddy bit her lip against a laugh at his phrasing.

"I want to kill it," Anavi said, and Maddy sobered. We all did. "Isn't that strange as dysphoria or euphoria for no reason? I *want* to *slaughter* it. I want to prove that I can, to demonstrate my ability . . . "

The bell rang into the disquiet that Anavi's comments had created.

I didn't want to abandon Anavi when she was in such a strange headspace. But I needed to put an end to this. Anavi had been tired earlier, worn thin, but not like this. Not talking about a bloodthirsty urge to murder trolls.

I pulled out my phone and sent a text to a local taxi service.

"I have to go," I said.

Maddy and Devin exchanged a look with each other, then with me again. No doubt they were surprised I was taking off when Anavi was losing it.

I wanted to tell them why, but I couldn't. Not yet. And maybe not ever, if I was honest. Not if I really wanted to be friends with them. And I did.

Devin said, "Okay. I'll stick close to Anavi. Walk her to class."

Anavi gnawed her lip again, but if she was preoccupied with death and destruction she didn't share more about it. Devin was a game insider, so maybe he could find an entry point to try to pull her back from wherever she'd gone.

I scanned the cafeteria and found my quarry. The Warheads were already on their feet, the room emptying. Unfortunately, they were also staring directly at the back corner of the room. At Anavi.

That was it.

I headed toward them, dodging the few remaining people in the cafeteria.

The Warheads didn't act like they noticed me coming their way. And I had no idea what I was going to do to distract them, get their focus off Anavi. Drawing their attention might complicate my plan for the rest of the afternoon, but I had to do *something*—

To my relief, at the last second before they'd *have* to spot me, they turned away from Anavi and went out the doors. There was no sign they'd noticed me.

On one level, that was irritating. But it did make following them that much easier.

Anavi had said they left campus each day, and their schedules and Butler's telling me it was none of my business and subsequent freak-out indicated it was true. I wanted to know where they went, and so I was going to tail them. This was a road that could only lead to the increasingly sinister Project Hydra.

I stayed a distance behind them in the hall, close to the lockers, intending to whirl and pretend to be opening one if they turned around.

But they didn't even slow as they went down the emptying hallway and out the far doors. I counted to ten before I pressed open the door, hoping I hadn't lost them.

I almost had.

A van was parked at the curb, and the driver was putting it into gear. I jogged across the grass in the opposite direction, out to the street. A security guard called, "Hey!" But I sped up, and from the lack of more shouts, he didn't come after me.

Butler would probably get a report of my hasty departure, but I didn't care right now. There'd be plenty of time to care later, if he called my parents.

The van was in motion.

I was about to lose them. I *couldn't* lose them.

Whew. I caught a break. The taxi service I'd texted had a car waiting at the end of the block, right where I requested. Just far enough from school that they wouldn't refuse to drive me without permission.

I jerked open the door and slung myself in, brusquely ordering the driver, "Follow that van."

The van that was pulling far ahead on the street in front of us. If we were going to catch it, we needed to get going . . .

But the driver hesitated, gold chains around his neck and heavy rings clinking as he shifted to get a better look at me. "Shouldn't you be in school?"

"Look," I said, "I missed the van and I need to get to the extra credit assignment they're headed to."

When he didn't put the car in drive, the white of the van almost out of sight ahead, I said, "I'm a great tipper. Legendary."

"Why didn't you say so? Hold on."

He meant it literally, since he screeched away from the curb, flooring the gas like we were in a chase sequence. Which we were.

I clutched the grip on the door, but calmed when he caught back up to the van with a few weavings in and out of traffic. We had one advantage: the van's driver didn't know anyone was trying to catch it.

"Good work," I said.

Possibly the only thing that could have made me release my death grip on the door was my desire to hear what was on the recording from Butler's office.

I pulled out my earbuds and put them in, cued up the recording, keeping my eyes on the van in front of us while it started to play. We were heading into a canyon of skyscrapers, housing what seemed to be tech company upon tech company from the names emblazoned on the buildings. These weren't the start-ups of someplace like Coast City, but old, well established companies. Big business.

"Just *what* do you think you're doing?" Butler's voice said in my ears, with overly loud menace. I thumbed the volume down. "I am *not* happy about your recent activities and the project managers won't be either. You shouldn't be drawing so much attention to yourselves. This is supposed to be a simple research partnership to study your team play. You need to knock off the rest of it, now."

A moment of silence, broken by a chorus of low laughs I was becoming all too familiar with.

"That's funny . . ."

". . . it seems to us as long as we keep showing up and doing what's asked of us . . ."

". . . then we can do what we want the rest of the time."

"We're not always on the company clock."

"And if sometimes we feel like recruiting . . ."

". . . they'll approve."

The principal made a strangled sort of noise. "Stop that!" he barked, losing his cool. "I can end this experiment now. I was the one who approved the independent study, and I can stop it."

More whispery laughs in my ears as the van took a turn up ahead. The gold jewelry-bedecked driver glanced back at me and I waved for him to keep following.

"You can't do anything to us anymore, and we think you know it . . ."

". . . you made us go . . ."

"But we are not yours, not theirs. We are our own. We are too valuable to stop."

"Look, just be more discreet," Butler said. "And leave the girl alone."

"Which one?" a voice asked, and for once there was no overlapping commentary to go along.

"Both of them," the principal said.

"Anavi is one of ours . . ."

". . . so don't worry about her."

"No," I said, "she isn't."

"What?" the cabbie asked over his shoulder. "Looks like your school trip's stopping up ahead."

There might have been a slight flaw to the story I'd told him. He'd expect me to join them.

"Pull up behind them, but um, leave some space," I said.

"You're the boss, legendary tipper."

On the recording, Principal Butler said, "Wait right there. If what you say is true, then convince her participating is a good deal and do it fast. You need the other girl off your case. Low profile? Keep one."

That was when I had pulled the phone out from under the door. Static hissed and the voices stopped. I removed my earbuds as the taxi pulled up along the curb of a massive mirrored building, a tall column thrusting into the sky. Bold silver letters across the front proclaimed: Advanced Research Laboratories.

"Vague enough name," I murmured.

I was familiar with the type, had encountered enough

executives of what amounted to Acme Destruction Computer Genome Bioweapons, Incorporated, at chichi receptions over the years. Who knew what this one was into? Besides, apparently, running an experiment with a bunch of jerky gamers. An experiment that had gotten way out of hand.

But I still didn't know *what* the experiment was. Butler claimed this was intended to be a "simple research project," but it didn't strike me that way.

And the Warheads had said he made them go—yet they didn't seem like victims.

Maybe they were anyway.

I had a whole new round of questions, in other words. Somewhere inside this building, the answers were waiting.

I watched as the Warheads stepped one by one from the van, migrating in creep formation toward the doors. This was the kind of building that would have tight security, the kind I couldn't easily bluster my way through if I wanted them not to see me.

I needed more intel.

"You getting out?" the cabbie asked.

I also needed to get Anavi clear of them before I did anything else. "No," I said. "I changed my mind about the extra credit. I'll do it later." He opened his mouth to protest, and I said, "That tip is getting bigger by the second. Take me to the Daily Planet Building and your day is made."

He grumbled, but put the car in drive. Good thing I was frugal with my allowance for times like this.

I peered out the window as we passed the van. The driver

was Ms. Johnson, the tightly-wound-and-coiffed comp sci teacher.

So the school really *was* in this up to its eyeballs. Given how little Ms. Johnson had seemed to care for her charges, I assumed Butler's policy of "this is what I want, deal with it" was responsible for her presence.

I had more digging to do into the lab, but I had quotes enough to ensure that Butler and his fancypants suits were taken to the cleaners and hung out to dry on the front web-page of the *Scoop*. More than enough to make sure he'd have to order the Warheads to leave Anavi alone.

All I had to do now was write the story.

CHAPTER 12

I let the story unfurl from my fingertips, waiting for the others to arrive as I banged away at the keyboard of my laptop.

The red-headed guard at the front desk had given me a skeptical eyebrow raise when I claimed I was allowed to be here so early in the afternoon. Around me, the Morgue was quiet as a, well, morgue. The smell of old newspapers, with their musty dead print, was almost comforting as I wrote.

I included my trip into the game, and what I'd witnessed the Warheads doing there—it was a story of cyber-bullying bleeding back into the real world, of jerks targeting an excellent student, Anavi Singh, and making her unable to work or even focus when her whole future, in the form of her Galaxy spelling champ scholarship, was on the line. The story of a principal who claimed bullying was hardly ever a problem, was always overblown, and who refused to help his own stellar student, undeniably the target of harassment, at the end of fake automatic weapons and real-world insults and insinuations.

I left out any mention of possible mind control, of course. Or of SmallvilleGuy.

Tabbing over to the chat program, I checked to see if he was logged in. He hardly ever did during the day, but sometimes he would show if I pinged him.

As expected, he wasn't there. And I was too afraid to send him a message to join.

But I left the window open, staying logged in.

Typing up the story had helped me calm down some. That was when I started to worry more about how the two of us had left things the night before. How *I* had left them, closing my laptop without even really saying goodbye. He must have assumed I was mad at him. When all he'd done was have my back.

He couldn't be mad at me, could he? He had no reason to be. After all, he hadn't been shot in the shoulder. And I wasn't the one who kept so many secrets. He knew exactly who I was, and what I'd seen that night in Kansas. He'd never told me what happened to convince him the world was filled with impossible things, why he was so certain about it.

I tabbed back over to the chat screen.

Advanced Research Laboratories, I typed in. *What do you know about them?* and hit send. He should receive the message the next time he signed on.

I clicked over to the Strange Skies boards, where it had been a slow week. Not too many updates, and most of the stories I scanned through seemed like flights of freaky fancy:

Posted by **Conspirator13**, *3:30 a.m.*: The visitors returned last night. In fact, they just brought me home a little while ago. There were three Greys, the usual alien scouting party, and they appeared at my bedside at exactly 1:02 a.m.—I looked at the clock when I woke. They took me outside and into their ship and that's where the rest gets blurry . . . But they must be taking me for a reason. I am beginning to think I'm special.

Aliens would travel all the way to Planet Earth to take sleeping people onto their spaceships? Really? Next.

Oh, here was a better one.

Posted by **QueenofStrange**, *8:10 a.m.*: I was working at the diner last night and a woman who came in told me a story that may sound familiar to some of you here (SkepticGirl1, at least). She had pulled off the road driving at night and saw what she swore was a young man flying through the air. She only got a glimpse of him, a silhouette against the full moon. She was rattled and said she was only telling me about it because I was someone she'd never meet again. And as a waitress out here I must hear all kinds of stories. I told her not to be so sure her eyes were playing tricks . . .

This one might be real, and not just because she'd also seen a flying person.

There was a sense you developed, hanging out on the boards, for which reports were legitimate—or at least, which were made in good faith—and which were the product of someone who wanted to poke fun at the crazies who believed in conspiracies and aliens and fringe science. But the ones that felt like the truth, they gave me that shivery sense that I'd had in front of the rock tower that night with my dad, the knowledge that there was far more going on in the world than most people knew. And now I'd happened on what I was increasingly sure was an example, right here in real life, at my school.

Would the others at the *Scoop* think I was crazy if I told them that the bullying was only one part of the story?

Probably.

Probably they'd look at me differently, distantly.

I jumped at the *beep* of a chat and tabbed over to see SmallvilleGuy's name beside the cursor.

SmallvilleGuy: *I'm glad you wrote.*

SkepticGirl1: *Do you know something about that company?*

No immediate response, but then . . .

SmallvilleGuy: *Not that. I thought maybe you were too mad to want to talk.*

SkepticGirl1: *Oh.*

Part of me wanted to type "Well, I wasn't, sap," and play it off. But I made myself give a more honest response. My pulse raced like I was in the game being pursued by a missile-carrying dragon.

SkepticGirl1: *I wasn't mad at you. I was mad at them.*

SmallvilleGuy: *Oh.*

SmallvilleGuy: *I thought maybe it was because I didn't keep you from getting shot. I know that must have hurt.*

I laid my hands against my face, then lowered them to type.

SkepticGirl1: *Don't worry about that. You helped make sure Anavi got out okay. We're the same.*

SkepticGirl1: *You and me, I mean. We're the same.*

SmallvilleGuy: *How?*

It was what I'd realized in the middle of the night, when I woke up from that nightmare. I searched for the right words, and they came, as easily as the words to tell Anavi's story. Because they were the truth.

SkepticGirl1: *We protect people, see what other people miss. We don't need anyone to look after us.*

He didn't respond right away. I was blushing, like I had when I'd thought of the night before as a date.

Had this been our first fight?

We're just friends, I reminded myself.

But then he posted a new message. I put my hands over my heart.

It was another photo of baby cow Nellie Bly, who was even more adorable this time. Because this time, Nellie wasn't alone in making big eyes at the camera. There was a golden retriever snuggled up against her, the dog's grinning face right beside her moony calf one.

That message was the sweetest thing I'd ever seen.

SmallvilleGuy: *My way of saying sorry, anyway. Meet Shelby, wonder dog. He's taken a liking to Nellie Bly. And Bess likes Shelby better than anyone else in the world, so she lets him.*

I didn't know what to type. Nothing seemed right. He'd never mentioned that the farm had a dog before.

SkepticGirl1: *Shelby made my day.*

It was as close as I could get to telling him that *he'd* made it. By taking that picture. By being worried that we'd had a fight, just like I had been.

By caring at all.

SmallvilleGuy: *I'll do some digging on ARLabs, see if anyone's posted about them before on Skies or elsewhere. And I can also ask TheInventor, my techie friend from the boards, the one who made our software. He's unearthed dirt on lots of high tech companies behaving badly—and this one doesn't sound like the kind that can be up to anything good.*

I couldn't help being a little disappointed he hadn't responded to what I said. But I'd give him a break this time. Not ask him to tell me who he was, a way of saying thanks for being here.

SmallvilleGuy: *Lois . . .*

I waited, not typing anything. Not sure what to say.

SmallvilleGuy: *You're right. But that doesn't mean I don't want to protect you anyway.*

I smiled and sent a one-word response.

SkepticGirl1: *Barbarian.*

SmallvilleGuy: *No, I was an alien, remember?*

I rolled my eyes.

SkepticGirl1: *Funny. And if you call me an elf, I'll . . . do something.*

SmallvilleGuy: *Talk to you tonight, Princess.*

His name disappeared and I said, to the empty Morgue, "I hate it when he gets the last word."

"Who?" Devin asked. He and Maddy stood in the doorway, watching me like I was crazy.

I knew I was blushing, because my cheeks felt as hot as the scene of a five-alarm fire.

"Don't worry about it," I said, closing the chat window.

"You have got to know saying that kind of thing only makes

me want to know more," Maddy said. She shot a glance at Devin then back to me, as if maybe he was the reason I wasn't spilling the details. "We'll discuss later."

"Thank you for sparing me the gossip session," Devin said. "I guess this is where you rushed off to after lunch?"

I deflected. "How's Anavi?"

"Not herself," Devin said. "But you noticed that."

"Did Butler summon me again?" I asked, afraid of the answer.

"Not that we heard," Maddy said. She walked over to my desk and put a tiny MP3 player down on the edge. "It's that playlist." She backed away, toward her own desk.

"Oh," I said, snatching it up. "I can't wait to listen to it."

Maddy sat down and stared at her computer screen. Her shoulders were board-stiff.

Devin's gaze ping-ponged between us. "Maddy is giving you music," he said. "Maddy, whose taste is superior to all? You better hope you like it."

"Shut up," Maddy grumbled.

"I know I will. I asked her for it," I said, and Maddy's shoulders relaxed. "She always has the best band T-shirts. Never anyone I've heard of."

"She does," he said, before changing the subject. "Want to tell us where you really went when you cut?"

I did want to tell them—about the principal's office, and the Warheads, and about the lab and the fact I was becoming more and more convinced the gamers' odd behavior and their ability to get *into* Anavi's head had something to do with whatever their independent study really was, whatever was happening in the afternoons at Advanced Research Laboratories.

But I wasn't ready to spin out my still-developing crazy-mad-science theory for them. I liked having Maddy and Devin as partners in journalism, and I definitely wanted them to be my friends.

What I did not want was to drive them away before there was any way to prove something beyond the norm was going on. Even if I got something more solid, I'd have to think over the best way to share it. They didn't know the true extent of what was happening to Anavi.

"I've been here," I said. "I was ready to write my story. I got Butler on the record saying that bullying is no big thing."

Devin whistled, low. "No one will ever call you a coward, that's for sure."

I took a half bow at my desk. "I'm glad people will know. For Anavi's sake. She gave me permission to name her."

Devin said, "I don't know how to explain the way she's acting. Stress, sure, but it's weirder than that."

He had no idea how right he was.

"If only you could give her a healing potion," Maddy said. "A glowing orb of health or something."

Devin opened his mouth to respond, but then shut it and went to his desk.

"What?" Maddy asked.

"There are no healing potions in *Worlds*, and only one glowing orb," was all he said, slinging his bag onto his giant desk and himself into his seat in front of the enormous computer monitors. I was glad he'd been distracted from his line of thinking about Anavi, for now.

"So," I said, "I figured even though I'm writing the story, we should all get credit. I want to put that you guys also contributed to the report at the end."

They both attempted to play it casual, but their reactions were too happy.

"Ooh," Maddy said.

"Perry will have to eat his words, hm?" I asked, before remembering their reactions when Perry had told them they should learn from me. I'd put my foot in my mouth. Again.

"Sort of," Devin said, letting me off the hook. "But I'll get started on designing a splashy layout for the piece."

"The *Scoop*'s first scoop," I said, grinning.

James came in at that moment.

"The Third," I said, feeling my grin turn dark, "did you tell Butler anything you shouldn't have?"

James ignored my question, striding to his desk with a holier-than-thou-mere-mortals air.

I cleared my throat.

"First off," James said, "I don't care enough about getting you in trouble to do that. But more importantly, I believe in protecting sources, and in journalistic integrity. Not that I'm sure breaking into the school's backend system counts . . . "

"For a minute, I almost liked you," I joked.

"But, no, I did not say a word, even though Butler brought you up. He knows I work here. He's convinced that Dad will one day get his political muscle back and those tiny donations that my father doesn't even remember will buy him a seat at the big kids' table."

"Oh," I said.

Maddy sighed. Then sat up straighter in her chair again, as if noticing she might have done it out loud.

I needed to mend the moment. I had been unfair in assuming James had sold us out. Devin and Maddy both liked him. I should give him more of a chance—even if his perfect teeth and hair and the family moneybags that went with them did make it hard for me to trust him.

"So, James," I asked, "you want an 'also contributed' on this story? Or not?"

"No, because I haven't," he said.

Well, I had made an attempt. "Okay with me," I said, and went back to typing, letting my fingers fly across the keys.

I couldn't wait until the piece went live.

*

After I got home, I didn't really breathe until I outlasted dinner and got to head to my room for the night. I'd been waiting the whole time for my dad or mom to reveal dramatically that they'd received a call from the principal, nail me on cutting class, ground me, say there'd be no more job.

But it didn't happen.

Maybe Butler had been distracted that afternoon, afraid his not-so-little Project Hydra secret was too close to the surface. He'd waved off the bullying like it was nothing, but I knew he was wrong about that.

People didn't look too kindly on adults who turned a blind eye these days. For good reason. Butler might not believe it was a concern, but tell that to the parents of teens who went around miserable or even killed themselves because of it. There were far too many.

I softly called, "Night, Deathmetal," and got a return good night from Lucy, before I locked my door and went over to the laptop. Part of me wanted to clip the holoset on instead and return to the game, purely to prove I wasn't afraid to go back.

And also to *see* SmallvilleGuy again. Even if it didn't count as truly seeing him.

But I had zero interest in going in solo, with the risk of running into the Warheads. And I wanted to preserve the newly recovered balance between SmallvilleGuy and me.

The sweetness of our talk that afternoon, and that picture he'd sent me. He couldn't tell me who he was, but he was trying to show me more about his life. At least, that was what I wanted to believe. His inability to tell all might frustrate me, but I was positive he'd never lied to me. That meant something. So I signed into the secure chat.

SmallvilleGuy: *I found some things.*

SkepticGirl1: *That was quick. Dirt, please.*

SmallvilleGuy: *First, you have to promise you'll tell me what you're doing where these guys are concerned.*

SkepticGirl1: *The Warheads? I thought we covered that. I can handle them.*

In the real world. Mostly.

SmallvilleGuy: *I meant the lab, but I worry about both. What I've turned up so far are some old articles about ARL research into mind control and group consciousness, and some more recent ones on acquisitions in the past few years.*

SkepticGirl1: *Relevant to my interests. Keep typing.*

SmallvilleGuy: *They did some experiments back in the '60s and '70s that didn't turn out so well. The test subjects were vets, retired soldiers who'd been in the same units together. One involved trying to remotely control actions in combat to prevent mistakes. But they also wanted to see if it was possible to make a unit think as one, pursuing an objective together. Idea being they would have less fear for their personal safety, and make smarter decisions with increased brainpower focused on the same goal, fear-free. But none of their research on behalf of the military back then panned out. And when word leaked and the ethics got questioned, the research was shut down. They switched to a pure tech focus, developed some life-saving medicine, some gadgets. Pulled in the big money.*

SkepticGirl1: *Charitable souls, you're saying, after they got busted. Interested in the good of mankind.*

SmallvilleGuy: *If by that you mean possessed of a desire to create the means of wiping out any parts of it that their customers might want to as completely and efficiently as possible . . . maybe.*

SmallvilleGuy: *Now the more recent stuff. With all this money, a year ago they bought the company that created the technology behind the first real-sim holo game, and if you guessed it was Worlds War Three, you're right. The management of WorldsHQ, that company, is still separate, but obviously ARL has access to their tech. I'm still digging to see if I can find more about that, looking for any joint projects.*

SkepticGirl1: *You think they bought it for a reason besides raking in more cash-money, I take it?*

SmallvilleGuy: *I do. On the ARL side, there have always been whispers that the R&D department was up to other things. I found them mentioned on the boards here and there, links to articles that imply their CEO wants to woo customers with even deeper pockets. I bet they'd like the military* *back as a partner somehow, no doubt hoping they can break into the world of special ops projects again. I wouldn't discount the idea of them working with less official partners either though.*

SkepticGirl1: *Hmmm . . . The Warheads definitely are in sync, and obnoxiously fearless. They didn't care about Butler being on their cases at all. Or me. Do you think it's possible this is R&D combining old ideas with new tech to take some handpicked gamers for a spin?*

SmallvilleGuy: *Yeah, but why would they be messing around with human kids? It doesn't make sense. It's not like they could send them out into the field or combat. Plus, the Worlds connection. There's more to this.*

I frowned.

SkepticGirl1: *What do you mean, 'human kids'? What other kind is there?*

A moment of waiting, of the display telling me that he was typing.

SmallvilleGuy: *I was typing too fast. I don't know what I meant. Too much reading about aliens on the boards.*

SkepticGirl1: *Klutz. ;-)*

SkepticGirl1: *My story goes live at 7 a.m. tomorrow. Just about Anavi, and the way they bothered her, the way Butler said the school wouldn't help.*

SmallvilleGuy: *Good. I'll let you know if I hear anything useful from my friend, but maybe the whole thing will go away. I'd rather not see you get shot again.*

SkepticGirl1: *I'm Kevlar, you're glue . . . Or are you something else?*

Earlier I'd resolved to leave the "who are you?" question out for once. This wasn't exactly asking that. So it didn't count.

SmallvilleGuy: *Night, Kevlar.*

Of course it didn't count. He didn't answer.

CHAPTER 13

"From their earliest years, children are taught that if they have a problem that is too big for them to solve themselves, if they are in trouble or in danger, they should tell a trusted adult. Parents might give examples—police officers, soldiers, ministers, coaches, teachers, and, of course, principals. And so, to go back to our story, when 16-year-old Anavi Singh, excellent student and one of only 98 people to ever win the Galaxy Spelling Bee, was being targeted by this vicious group of gamers, who could blame her for trusting that her principal would help her?

"This reporter observed firsthand Principal Robert Butler treating Singh's plea for help and confidential complaint not with the care it deserved, or by meeting his responsibility as a trusted adult to help her, but with disdain. He brushed it off. He brushed her off, left her to fend for herself. As he himself stated, 'We don't baby our students here. Real bullying is much rarer than these news reports make it out to be.'

"They tell us a trusted adult will be on our side, but what about when those adults can't be trusted? What then? Then, we must protect each other and tell the truth." – *from "A Tale of Two Bullies" by Lois Lane (Devin Harris and Maddy Simpson also contributed)*

★

I was rarely early for anything. It wasn't my fault. Usually. Life threw too many distractions in my path, like videos of frolicking goats online or possible research lab conspiracies offline. But today, I arrived at school an entire ten minutes before the first bell. The red and blue halls were teeming, the hum and buzz of morning conversation a dull roar.

Could it be my imagination, or was there a brief silence as I passed people?

"She's the one who wrote it," a skaterish boy said to a girl rocking a fauxhawk.

The girl gave me a thumbs-up: "Way to stick it to Butler."

I beamed at her with the force of an exploding sunspot. "Thanks!" I said, continuing on with more confidence.

There were a few more thumbs-ups, points and smiles—and the expected grumbling from people I could only assume were jerks or bullies themselves, adding a nasty comment here and there. But they couldn't get me down, not when everyone else's reaction was the equivalent of yay with pom-poms and confetti cannons.

Or close enough.

Maddy rushed up and took my arm.

"Oh. My. God," she said. "Everyone read it. A couple of

people even read some of my music reviews and shared them. Unbelievable."

Devin materialized on my other side, holding up his palm, which I slapped. "We did it," he said. "This is almost better than finding a dire wolf cache or getting a dragon to come over to House Devin's side in *Worlds*."

"Almost?" I said with mock offense.

He shrugged. "Dragons. Dire wolves. Versus school?"

James the Third was coming up the hallway toward us, and I felt Maddy and Devin tense. He wore an honest-to-god sweater vest. I hardly expected him to even bother to greet us unless he planned to express his disapproval again.

But he slowed, waiting until we reached him, and gifted me with a grudging nod. "Good work."

I put my hand over my heart and gave Maddy a light elbow in the ribs. "You might need to catch me. I may faint here."

The Third rolled his eyes, but he held up his phone so we could see the screen. The browser was open to the *Scoop*—not my story, but a sidebar that had been Devin's idea. The teaser encouraged people to post their own bullying stories to demonstrate how common an occurrence it was.

I leaned in to get a better look at the glowing screen, and my mouth dropped open when I saw the number. "Is that a one-zero-zero? Already?"

James angled the screen toward himself, tapped it. "That's a one-zero-one, because someone just posted a new one. They teased your story on the *Daily Planet* homepage, so you got Perry's seal of approval too. Almost all of these are stories are not so different from Anavi's, thanking her for being willing to come forward. And the *Scoop* for running it."

I stepped back, overwhelmed. "Are they *all* from East Metropolis?"

"Not most," James said, "but more than I figured. There are even a few others who agree that Butler lets it happen by not doing anything."

"Anything about the Warheads?" I asked.

"Shhh," Maddy hissed, but it was too late. Because said Warheads were nearly on top of our small cluster of justice and truth and gutsy reporting. And they would not be mistaken for fans anytime soon.

Gone were the mocking leers and grins, replaced by stone-faces that were somehow worse. They radiated dislike, disapproval, discontent.

No discord, though. They remained too similar for that.

"Creepy," Maddy whispered.

"Looks like I made myself some enemies." I sniffed, to show it didn't bother me. "Not the first time."

Even though it was unsettling. *They* were unsettling.

I tried to exile the memories of that shove against my mind in the cafeteria, of the hot explosion in my shoulder in the game.

The Warheads' synchronized movements slowed, and then stopped, so they were standing in a strange, strained half-circle around us *Scoop* staffers. But I realized that wasn't it. There was something about how they positioned themselves. It was . . . tactical.

They were arrayed around all of us, sure, but if I wasn't mistaken, they were focused on Devin.

The hall had gone silent as an abandoned tomb, people quieting in anticipation of seeing some kind of showdown. I was never one to disappoint. Except maybe my parents.

"You guys didn't really strike me as big readers," I said, shifting over toward Devin. "I'm so honored. But, then, it was about you, and you *are* egomaniacal jerks, so maybe I'm giving you too much credit. What do you think?"

Devin coughed beside me, and when I looked over, he shook his head. Then he did it again, a quick shake, back and forth. Like something was bothering him. I'd seen Anavi do the same thing.

Forget standing tall in front of our audience *or* the Warheads. The actual scope of Project Hydra, whatever it was, remained a mystery. And so the important thing was to get Devin away from these losers. My story was supposed to stop the madness of targeting Anavi, and push them into giving up more clues about what was going on at the lab in the process—not get someone else put in their jerkhead sights.

Speaking of . . . where was Anavi, anyway?

Lucky for me, Principal Butler decided to put in an appearance. The bell rang and the hall began to clear, and he got a few raised eyebrows as students rushed past him.

He was rumpled, even though it was barely past eight. His suit was wrinkled and tie loosened. Like he'd taken a dozen complaining phone calls already and needed not to feel like he was wearing a noose.

"School board read it too?" I asked before I could stop myself.

Butler directed a furious look my way, but he must have been too angry to speak to me. He said, "My office now," to the gamers.

He'd be coming for me sooner or later. Probably when there weren't so many people watching. Even he wasn't bold enough to collar me here and now.

Though he did finally say, "I'll be checking your facts, Ms. Lane. You'd better hope they were confirmed," before herding the gamer Hydra back up the hall toward his office.

Their many heads swiveled to give me . . . and then Devin . . . one last round of unsettlingly similar hard looks.

Devin was still being quiet in a way that I didn't care for.

"Dev, you in there? I'm out here stealing your dire wolves," I said.

For a second, there was no hint of a response from him, and even James and Maddy seemed vaguely alarmed.

But he shook his head once more, and then said, "In your elf dreams." If his voice was flatter than normal, the others pretended not to notice.

I wasn't always as good at pretending as I wanted to be, not in front of people who mattered to me, and so I towed him in the opposite direction of the principal and the Warheads.

The hall was mostly empty, and I waved away Maddy and James.

"Go on to class, you two," I said. "I want to ask Devin something."

They left, but not so happily—until James distracted Maddy by speaking to her.

Maddy's playlist. I couldn't forget to listen to it. I wanted to be able to tell her genuinely how much I liked it. I could at least stick to one part of my plan, even if the rest was kaput. The part where I made a friend here.

But right now, there were more pressing matters.

I stared at Devin, knowing that rumors would be flying if anyone saw us, me peering up into his face with my hands on his arms.

"Dev," I said, "did they do anything to you?"

He looked down at my hands, and then back up, probably noticing the same thing I had about the two of us standing so close. He struck me as in control of his faculties again.

Especially when a half smile crossed his face, and he said, "Why haven't I asked you if you have a boyfriend? Lois, are you single?"

"Um," I said. "I think I am."

He mulled that over, considering me. "That sounds like there's a guy in the picture already."

There *was* a guy in the picture already. But it was complicated, like this whole situation.

Even so, at the thought of SmallvilleGuy, I dropped my hands from Devin's arms.

"Stop trying to distract me," I said, partly to change the subject and partly because I was afraid the Warheads had gone after him back there. "Did those guys do anything to you, before?"

"What do you mean?" he said. He made a mini-shrug. "I'm the king. What could they do?"

I didn't believe him.

But cluing Devin in on my suspicions that the Warheads were involved in some sort of unsavory top-secret research *and* that he might be in danger of becoming the next target of their group consciousness—well, that would take a little more time than we had before first period. And a lot more evidence.

Unlike Anavi, he wasn't volunteering any details beyond the ordinary. It was possible the Warheads were messing with me. Possible they hadn't done anything to Devin to make him so subdued. I wanted him to open up, though.

"Why'd you make your character a fantasy guy, not a mercenary or a soldier or an alien?" I asked.

He ducked his head in—unless I was misreading him—embarrassment. The first time I'd ever seen him less than confident.

"Spill it," I said, twisting the screws.

"I like reading that stuff, okay?" he said. "Big novels with elves and orcs and dragons . . . If you tell anyone, I'll—"

"Sic your dragon on me? Noted. Promise I won't tell a soul. But really, these days, isn't it okay to just let your fantasy freak flag fly?" I stroked my chin. "Oh, wait, you already did. And you put your head on it."

He laughed, and the remaining tension was broken, any embarrassment gone. But I stayed with him all the way to his first period study hall, only going to my own geometry class afterward.

I'd feel much better when I saw Anavi, and confirmed that she was doing all right. This time, my skill at conspiracy theorizing might be getting the best of me.

Come on, SmallvilleGuy, dig up something else on this company that I can use.

★

The morning was a long one, filled with geometry (teachers would seemingly never learn that hard-selling that we'd need a subject later in life only made it sound more like we wouldn't) and AP lit (I considered appropriating SmallvilleGuy's take on *Macbeth*, for I too liked the witches best). I got a few more thumbs-up and high fives, which I wanted to enjoy, but I hadn't been able to find Anavi. It was possible her parents had kept her home, but the day before she'd seemed so certain that she *wanted* me to mention her by name.

That had been before. Before her lunchtime revelations of the desire to slaughter and lay waste to all the worlds in *Worlds War Three*.

Before the mid-day break, I waited by Anavi's locker. But if she was here, then she'd gone straight to lunch, so I headed that way.

I had wanted to enter the cafeteria together, in case the Warheads tried anything. I was still in Anavi's corner.

The Warheads might have been taken to pretentious-officeville by Principal Rumpled Shark, but they were free now, ensconced at their usual table by the doors. Whatever wrist slapping had occurred, you'd never know it to watch them.

They wore their holosets. I figured there was no danger in crossing close by them on my search for Anavi, given that they were deep in the game.

But they began laughing as I passed, without even turning off the glowing scenes in front of them. A chill passed over me, and I felt that shove against my mind, pushing me away. But more insistent. The pressure lingered.

Not so long, but long enough to make me want to get away from them. And fast.

I sped up, almost careening through the cafeteria. I garnered some "what's with her?" looks as I half-ran, but I ignored them and went for the back corner and Anavi's usual table.

She was sitting there, alone, and I was surprised that Maddy and Devin weren't with her. I'd expected them to be.

But then the two of them rose from a table along my route, and Maddy grabbed my arm. "Don't," she said.

"Don't what?" I asked.

"Go over there," Devin said.

He still seemed less energetic than normal. But maybe I was imagining it, seeing something that wasn't there through the lens of my worry.

"She ran us off," Maddy said. "She was *rude* about it. I even gave her a word to spell, thinking she was joking at first."

"Let me try," I said. "You guys stay here."

"Your funeral," Maddy said.

"But I was so young and full of life," I deadpanned.

I knew the whole deal and they didn't.

Anavi might not be up to talking to people yet. So I moved

toward her slowly, concerned about full troll-slaying mode. Why would Anavi be nasty with Maddy and Devin?

It didn't make sense. And it wasn't like her.

I pulled out the chair next to Anavi, who kept staring straight ahead. Sitting down, I put my hand on her arm. "Everything all right?"

"You can't sit here," Anavi said, flat, toneless. "Go away."

"Anavi, talk to me. Are they still bothering you?"

Anavi threw off my hand, kicking back her chair as she stood. "*You* are the one bothering me."

She stalked away while I watched her go, gaping.

Devin and Maddy walked the rest of the way over. "Told you," Maddy said, without a hint of smug.

As Anavi went through the cafeteria, people were pointing and noticing her. Maybe that was all it was. Maybe she hadn't counted on so much attention.

But another thing I hated was trying to convince myself of something that I felt in my gut was a lie.

CHAPTER 14

I entered the Morgue alone after school, feeling like I'd swallowed the kind of giant boulder that might be used to landscape Devin's castle. A giant boulder that remained stuck in my throat. I wasn't in trouble, but I was *troubled.*

The rest of the day had been more of the same.

I hadn't been able to return the smiles and high fives, and even the continued posting of testimonials and supportive comments on the *Scoop* site didn't break the spell of the worry that weighed me down. I *was* proud of the story, and I stood behind it, but the point had been to help Anavi out of the dark place she'd been in. Not to isolate her further.

I wished Anavi would talk to me.

The others were already at the office, chattering away and gathered around one of Devin's giant monitors.

The *Scoop* site was up on it and visible from all the way across the room.

"Listen to this one," Devin said, and read aloud from the screen. "'I could never tell anyone, until I read this story. I thought I was the only one who stopped playing because I was too weak to fight back.'"

He paused before adding his own commentary. "Dude, if I recruited this guy and all the others who mention gaming, I could have the biggest kingdom in *Worlds*."

Maddy laughed. "You hide it well, but you are such a nerd."

"I am not," Devin countered. But as he spotted me, he amended, "I'm the coolest nerd you know."

"That's probably true," James said, then turned his head in the same direction as Devin, catching sight of me too. "There she is, the girl of the hour." He raised his voice and called, "Perry, Lois is finally here."

I hadn't even noticed that there was a door back in the most dismal corner of the office. But today it was propped open by an old cardboard box and darkened by the shadows around it like the entrance to some missile-toting dragon's cave. Why did everything in real life suddenly feel as dangerous as in the war game?

"Get in here, Lane!" The shout rang loud and clear from the gaping black maw. Er, door.

The metaphorical boulder lodged in my throat, I didn't say anything to the others. I answered the boss by walking past them, ready to get reamed.

Perry was a pro. He didn't read our stories before we filed

and posted them, but he did select which ones got linked to on the *Daily Planet* website. He must have believed the facts were good when he gave the go-ahead for my story to be featured. He might not have had Anavi blow him off, but I suspected that by now he'd sense something was wrong, that the entire story wasn't known yet.

Or not. When I reached the threshold of the dungeon-like office where Perry waited for me, he was grinning—hardly scary dragon-esque or even intimidating editor-esque. His feet were propped up on a desk as ancient as the ones out front, contrasted by the lightweight laptop open on top of it.

"The newsroom gets noisy," he said. "Sometimes I come down here, where I can hear myself think. When I'm figuring out a tough story, the quiet helps."

Like we were equals. Like we were going to swap techniques or something.

Me? Oh, I use my friend from a fringe message board to help me out when I'm up against a tough problem . . . like mind control. Do you believe in mind control? Wait, silly me, I mean psychological coercion. Or it could be a hive mind thing, hard to say.

"Sit." Perry's well-shined shoes swung down to the floor, and he waved me forward.

"I've been waiting for the other shoe to drop," I said, relieved to discover my throat was functional.

I took a seat in an oversized wooden chair in front of the desk. The back and arms were coated with dust, but I wasn't about to complain.

Perry's grin slipped when he registered what I'd said. "Well, it's not going to drop right now. I wanted to give you my 'atta girl, way to go, cub reporter' speech. You should be riding high on your first story. What's wrong?"

I ran my index fingers through the film of dust on the chair arms, not meeting his eyes. If I couldn't tell Devin and Maddy about my suspicions related to the Warheads—and the real reason for my continued worry about Anavi—then I definitely couldn't tell Perry.

I settled on, "Just . . . today was a little overwhelming. That's all."

Perry's eyes narrowed, and he leaned forward.

Great, I just lied to my editor, a man who's been nominated for a Pulitzer. Smart.

"Get used to it," he said. "Your story was solid work, but it's only a start. You need more. We need more, if the *Scoop*'s going to prove viable."

"Yes, sir." I rubbed the dusty fingertips of each of my hands together.

"Sir? Now I *know* something's wrong. But hey, I'm familiar with the type who doesn't go in for praise. I don't care that much for it myself. Go. Get back to work. That's the only thing for reporters like us."

Like us. I wanted to accept that as the truth, but I'd never been gladder to be dismissed from anyone's presence. I practically jumped out of the chair.

When I reached the door, Perry said, "Good job, though, Lane. I knew my instincts about you were right."

Uh-huh. And I'm pretty sure my instincts are also right.

The others had migrated back to their own desks. Devin appeared to be hard at work moderating the ever-lengthening comment thread, but he looked up when I reached him. "Don't let Anavi's reaction get you down. I'm sure she'll be fine tomorrow."

I grunted in response.

"And don't worry that we're feeling lazy," James said. "Perry already told us we need to pull in another half-dozen stories like that in the next few weeks. No pressure."

I sat back down at my own desk, nodding. Why did I feel like the firing squad was still waiting? I survived my encounter with Perry. Devin might be right about Anavi—maybe she did just need time, space.

This sense of foreboding wasn't logical.

But it *was* real and I couldn't seem to shake it.

I considered asking Devin to borrow his holoset, see if I could find Anavi in the game right now. That might make me feel better, to see her behaving normally. But he was busy, and I had James's game set up at home waiting. I could try later, see if SmallvilleGuy would meet me so I didn't have to go in alone.

Maybe he could help me figure out why I was so uneasy.

But I made no move to log on to the computer or take out my phone to ping him. I sat, waiting, for what I couldn't have said.

I didn't have to wait long.

A burst of screeching guitars blared from Maddy's general direction. Of course she'd have an old punk song for a ringtone. It stopped when she answered her phone. "Mom, what is it? . . . Um, I don't know what you're . . . Mom, no. I'm sorry, I . . ."

Maddy stopped talking to listen. I could hear the voice she was listening to from five feet away, because Maddy's mom was shouting.

I couldn't make out the words, but no parent called to yell like that without a reason.

Next came a loud buzzing from James's vicinity—he took out his phone, the latest model, the same he'd whipped out at us earlier. He glanced down at the screen and frowned, answered quietly. "Mom, is everything okay?"

"Weird," Devin said to me, reaching into his pocket and pulling out his own vibrating phone.

"Your mom too?" I asked him.

"Nah, Mom's on a big case this week. She's a public defender." He gaped a little, then set the phone on the desk. "A text here from my grandma, tipping me off to a message on the machine. She says I have detention. Because I work here."

I swiveled back to James and Maddy, who were both talking on their phones. They wore expressions that could be classed as Unhappy. Extremely Unhappy.

James said, "But I didn't even participate in the article."

My own phone trilled then, the word **HOME** popping up on the screen. I'd saved the number the night before. The Lanes had to be the only household in America that kept a landline, but my dad insisted backup communications were essential, even for a family.

Not in a case like this.

I hit ignore, postponing the inevitable.

"Nothing about the reason except that it involves the *Scoop*?" I asked Devin.

But before he could answer, Perry interrupted, shouting, "Lane, get back in here now!"

Right. The firing squad. Here it is.

Maddy was fast-talking back at her mom, and James continued to argue innocence to his. Devin watched the unfolding drama like he was in a theater and missing only the popcorn.

I stood to walk into the verbal hail of bullets that surely awaited me. But Perry didn't wait for me to come to him. He stormed out of the back office toward me, gesturing for quiet. Maddy and James used it as an excuse to say goodbye and hung up on their mothers. "Lois," he said.

So I *was* in big trouble. Definitively. He'd called me Lane earlier when we were talking. And he was speaking softly. Something I'd never heard him do before.

My phone rang again on my desk, **HOME** flashing. I reached over to hit ignore. Then I turned back to Perry.

He stared at me, pressing his hands together like he was praying. Maybe I should be—for divine intervention. Because he took a few menacing steps closer to our desks. Closer to mine. I resisted the urge to flee.

"You did vet all your quotes in the story . . . The sources are all confirmed, correct?"

That wasn't what I expected him to ask. I went through the piece mentally before I answered.

"Lois?" he prompted.

"Well, Principal Butler might not have known he was going to be quoted . . . exactly." I didn't know what Perry was getting at. "But he did provide the responses to direct questions. They weren't out of context."

"And the girl? This Anavi Singh, she corroborated all the allegations?"

The boulder returned to my throat, growing in size. I swallowed, my foreboding transforming into fear. "Is she okay?"

Perry didn't answer for a long moment. "If by okay you mean requesting a retraction of the entire article, saying that she hasn't been bullied a day in her entire life, then yes, she's fine. We here at the *Scoop*, however, are on life support if you can't make this story stick."

"A retraction?" I was choking again. "But it's true. You saw Butler dismiss her. All the rest is true too. I saw it myself. She told me to use her name."

Perry stalked toward the door. "The paper has a strict correction policy. No request hangs out there for longer than three business days, not unless Legal gives the thumbs up. Tomorrow's Friday, so I'll give you until Monday after school—at the very latest—to get her to withdraw the request. Or we'll probably be shutting this whole thing down. The *Daily Planet*'s reputation is too important to risk." He stopped in the door's threshold, not bothering to turn and look at us. "Maybe the Morgue was too symbolic a place to house this little experiment." The way he spat the word "experiment" made me cringe. And then he slammed the door behind him.

So much for me being a reporter like him. At least he and his accusations were gone.

But the silence that he left in his wake didn't last long.

"We have detention!" Maddy said.

Devin said, "So it is all of us."

James nodded. "Assuming Lois has it too."

"I'm sorry I got you all caught up in this." I tugged on my lip. Trying to think. But there wasn't an easy way out. I gave up. "Please blame me. It's my fault."

Why would Anavi lie like this?

"It *is* your fault," James said. "I wasn't even credited on your apparently way overblown story. This job is important to me. You better fix this."

"I will," I said.

If I can.

The last remnants of the plan were falling apart all around me. My promise to Anavi wasn't working out that well either. I should have known better than to hope things would be different—be better—here.

"You have to," James said. "I don't want my reputation to take a beating like my—"

I could have finished the sentence: like his dad's. But I didn't. I'd done enough damage for one day.

Instead I went to my desk to collect my things. Gathering up my messenger bag, I slung the strap over my neck and proceeded to the door.

"Where are you going?" Maddy asked.

"Home," I said, "to face the General's music."

CHAPTER 15

And that angry music was already cranked to maximum volume when I crept through the front door, attempting to sneak past the real firing squad, aka my parents. I barely noted the garlic-infused smell of lasagna—my favorite—because dinner was going to be the opposite of fun.

"You do not ignore calls from me," Dad said, meeting me. He was decked out in his full dress uniform. Which meant he'd left work earlier than he planned, almost certainly because Mom had called him to tell him about the detention.

He waved me toward the kitchen.

Oh no.

"Now, get in here," he said. "We need to have a talk over dinner."

I'd been crossing my fingers, if weakly, for actual yelling

when I got home. Talks over dinner were what my dad used for serious business. Every move we'd ever made was announced at a "talk over dinner." Every grounding I had endured, every phone privilege lost, every punishment that had ever been meted out to me had started this way. The situation had already been bad and now it was getting worse.

I couldn't afford to be punished. I had to do my job—or it would no longer exist. I wouldn't have just wrecked things for me, but for Maddy, Devin, even James.

I barely had time for dinner.

But I didn't argue. I dropped my bag, not bothering to avoid Lucy's trap when I reached the arch of the kitchen, but instead reaching around the wall and pulling her out, gently.

"Not now, brat," I said. "I'm about to get a talking to."

"I know," Lucy said, eyes big, interested, and a touch sympathetic.

Mom was waiting at the kitchen table, the perfect lasagna sitting in the center of it, along with a bowl of salad and a plate of garlic bread. Her expression was neutral, which gave me no hint of whether she might be in my corner. Sometimes she was, when Dad reacted unreasonably.

But my fear was that a big reaction was merited this time around, from their perspectives. My history of getting in trouble would not do me any favors.

I sat down at my usual place like I'd been sentenced to. I wasn't hungry—a first.

Dad took his own place at the head of the table. "Your principal called here," he said.

"You should know he's a world-class jerk." I couldn't help pointing it out. "The kind of fawning fake you usually can't stand."

None of this helped my case.

"Mom gave him my number," Dad said, "so we could speak about you. I talked to him before you started school and he was very nice. He told me he legitimately cares about his students' futures." I bet he had—and my dad, who was normally decent at spotting fakes, had bought the line. "Everyone I asked said East Metropolis is the best public school around, one of the best in the country."

And the best schools in the country always loooove me.

I was smart enough not to say it.

"You promised me you'd try to make things work here. But it might be time for us to discuss military school again," Dad said.

Mom frowned at him but didn't say anything. She half-rose and began serving the food. A quiet way of communicating that she wouldn't be on board with that.

Or that's what I hoped, anyway.

So I did not counter with the argument I had the first few times Dad had raised the specter of military school: that I was confident I could—and would—get myself kicked out in twenty-four hours or less.

"Now," Dad went on, "I don't know what possessed you to write a false story accusing the principal himself of running a lax operation and not protecting students from bullies, but he assures me that's what you've done. This . . . newspaper business may not be the best fit for you, Lois. We can compromise. No military school, but no more news either."

He stopped to let that rest, as if it was a completely rational solution, and began to eat. Lucy was gaping at both of us. I reached over and picked up a piece of garlic bread. I took a bite of it, trying to be casual.

It tasted like nothing. Like cardboard.

I knew that my mom's garlic bread was delicious.

I wasn't even able to fool myself that I wasn't freaking out. If I let my dad see how much I wanted to work at the *Scoop*, I'd be showing a vulnerability. He could then use it against me.

But there was no other way.

"Dad," I said, setting down the bread, "do you think bullying isn't a big deal? What if Lucy or I were being tormented by people at school? If it was bad enough that we couldn't do anything without being afraid?"

His fork hovered in the air. "I've taught you how to handle yourselves. That wouldn't be a concern."

"But what about for people who don't know? People like the girl I wrote about, Dad. She's a former spelling bee champion. She plays videogames, but she doesn't know self-defense—and anyway, they weren't bothering her in that way. I think maybe you don't understand what it's like now. It's not like in your day."

"In my day?" he asked.

Whoops. "You know, like jocks stuffing nerds into lockers."

"You know what she means, Sam," Mom said, entering the conversational fray. "Things are different now."

"At any rate," Dad said, "the principal says that you made this up. That this girl denies any of it ever happened."

My hands formed into fists. I shifted them to my lap. "Because she's being bullied. I am going to prove the story is factual. Just watch me. I have until the end of the day Monday."

"That was not the compromise I put on the table."

"I reject that compromise."

We sat in silence, me staring at Dad and him staring back.

He hadn't even asked for my side of the story.

"Lois—" he started.

But that was enough. "I did nothing wrong. I'm trying to help a girl who is being preyed upon and needs my help because the so-called 'adult' in question, your precious humanitarian Principal Butler, doesn't want to get involved. But he *is* involved. The kids I wrote about—the Warheads—are bullying Anavi, and Butler's a part of it. This is bigger than just the story I wrote. Can't you see that? Why can't you ever trust me? I'm doing the right thing. The trouble will blow over, like always."

Dad fumed at me from the end of the table. He set down his fork.

"Now, Sam, you know that Lois's heart is always in the right place," Mom said. "She just has trouble making others see that sometimes."

"Sorry, Mom," I said. "I have to leave the table."

She looked at me, and I managed a weak smile for her. I could read Dad well enough to know he was preparing to give me a lecture. Before he could start, I pushed my chair back from the table. "I'm not hungry. So I'm going upstairs to work. And I'm *not* leaving the *Scoop*."

"Go to your room," Dad said.

"I just said that I was." I tossed my napkin onto my plate, shaking my head when Mom started to protest.

Blood rushed to my face, my ears pounding with it as I raced upstairs. I automatically locked the door and prepared to log in to my computer, still so mad I could barely talk. Or type.

But I managed the passwords.

SmallvilleGuy: *Where have you been? I've been dying here, waiting for hours. I was afraid I missed you when I had to step out for chores. The story was great. How did your day go? What did Butler do? The Warheads?*

SmallvilleGuy: *I want to know everything.*

I took a few calming breaths, which did nothing to make me feel calmer. I almost felt sorry for him. All the things that happened to me today . . . I didn't know where to start.

SkepticGirl1: *I have detention.*

SkepticGirl1: *My dad is bringing up military school again.*

SkepticGirl1: *I just stormed away from the dinner table.*

SkepticGirl1: *The* Scoop *is going bye-bye if I can't fix everything.*

SmallvilleGuy was typing. My breathing steadied. A little.

SmallvilleGuy: *Wait—why is all this happening? The story was good.*

SmallvilleGuy: *Great. It was great.*

SkepticGirl1: *Oh, right.*

I didn't want to even type the words, they were so inexplicable. So mystifying to me. But I had to tell him the rest so he'd be able to understand.

SkepticGirl1: *Anavi claims everything is a lie, and requested a retraction from Perry. I only have a few days to get her to take it back.*

SkepticGirl1: *She won't even talk to me.*

For a long moment there was nothing—not even an alert that he'd started to type a response. That he had to take a pause almost made me feel better. He must have been as shocked as I was.

Finally, words came.

SmallvilleGuy: *Lois, I'm so sorry.*

SmallvilleGuy: *But you know what this means? You're right about everything. And you can't stop now. We'll dig deeper. I already found out that ARLabs donated bunch of computers to the school this year. And that the main guy behind the real-sim tech had some interesting ideas back in the day about group play and neural pathways that I'm looking into.*

The story—the real one—he was right. We had to keep chasing it.

SkepticGirl1: *Really? I'll do some looking too.*

I heard steps on the stairs.

SkepticGirl1: *Someone's coming. Catch you tomorrow?*

SkepticGirl1: *And thank you. Talking to you helped, more than you know.*

SmallvilleGuy: *Wait, don't forget!*

But I had to shut the laptop then. It was the first time I'd ever closed one of our regular nightly chats without asking who he was, in one way or another. I wondered if that was what he'd wanted to remind me of, unable to believe I would disappear again without it.

I lunged over to the door and unlocked it, just as the knock sounded. I opened it ready for round two of my battle with Dad.

Lucy stood outside, holding a plate of lasagna.

"You really did it this time," she said. "But you seem to be off the hook for now. Mom sent this up. Dad let her."

"Thanks, Deathmetal," I said, accepting the plate. My stomach rumbled its approval. I hadn't been hungry before, but I was starving now. "You're a good sister."

"I hope they don't send you away," Lucy said. Then, "Night," as if she'd said too much.

We were so alike, the two of us, battered by too many moves and too much change. I ducked inside to set down the plate on my desk, holding a finger up so she wouldn't leave. I crossed back to the door and folded her into a hug. "I'm not going anywhere. Promise."

"Okay," she said, and extricated herself from my grip, faking cool. "Better go check in with my unis."

I waited until Lucy went into her room, then shut my door on the rest of the world again. Talking to SmallvilleGuy *had* helped, but I needed to think. To try to figure out how victory had turned so quickly into such resounding defeat. So I didn't go back to chat when I reopened my computer while wolfing down the lukewarm lasagna. I went to Strange Skies instead, clicking through new threads.

There was a hot topic, the little flame beside it indicating lots of conversation, and it had only been posted that evening.

Posted by **SPNscholar** *at 7:15 p.m.*: I have a very interesting report of seismic activity in central Kansas to share. It occurred earlier this evening, nowhere near a fault line. You won't hear anything about this on the news, because the tremors were deep enough that they barely registered on the surface. But a seismograph in our lab here at the university picked it up, and we can only assume it was an earthquake with subterranean origins. The oddity is that there was no hint of prior activity that might cause such a quake or any obvious explanation for its occurrence at this particular time.

At least I wasn't the only one who'd had a day filled with weird upheaval.

The poster was a scientist researcher type, and they tended to be among the more reliable and sane members of the boards. I was too tired to look up a map to see if the quake was anywhere near Smallville.

I would have to try to remember to ask SmallvilleGuy if he'd felt anything.

CHAPTER 16

The next morning I kept my head down as I scanned the faces of everyone I passed in the halls before first bell, looking for Anavi. I had used the entrance at the far end of the building in order to elude Butler—who I knew would be waiting to gloat about sentencing us to detention. His slick front of false charisma would be back in place along with his pricey silk tie.

My strategy of avoidance was working so far. Sadly, my attempt to locate Anavi was proving less successful. I'd been all over and there was no sign of her.

After sleeping on it, I was sure that if we talked all of this could be resolved quickly and relatively painlessly. Assuming Anavi had calmed down enough to hear me out.

I was many things, but I wasn't a quitter. I didn't give up, and I wasn't going to start.

Anavi *had* trusted me. I needed to know what caused that to change.

Dad was already gone for the day when I left for school, but I had no illusions that fight was over.

He was regrouping too. I wouldn't be surprised to find a stack of glossy military academy brochures on my bed, all shiny patches and medals and horses and smiling teenagers who looked like they'd begged to be there but who were last-resort delinquents.

I caught sight of a familiar cluster of black-clad students up ahead, near the front entrance, but I refused to turn back. There was the possibility that the Warheads had done something to Anavi. Something more. Something worse.

So I forced my posture straight and my steps steady. When I reached them, I stopped and crossed my arms, casual but demanding. "Have you seen Anavi?"

The group turned to face me, slowly and in even smoother sync, somehow, than they had been before. Their heads tilted slightly to the right, and the looks they gave me were pitying.

"Where—" My arms dropped, my throat dried up.

Anavi was right there. In front of me.

She was wearing head-to-toe black and had her head tilted slightly to the right and she was pitying me just like the others.

She was with *them*.

I had prepared many arguments. I had anticipated various scenarios. None of them were anything like this.

"Anavi, why?" I realized, too late, that I shouldn't have spoken, that if ever there was a time to retreat and do more licking of wounds and reconsidering of strategy, this was probably it. I waited for that mental shove, for the pressure against my mind.

Would Anavi be assisting them if it came? Would I be able to *feel* that, or would it be that same uniform push as before? Was Anavi truly one of these creeps?

No. She couldn't be. *No.* Not willingly.

I braced for their attack on my mind.

But instead Principal Butler showed up beside us. "Here she is. Lois Lane herself. I thought she was going to be late again, and that would mean another day of detention."

I never thought Butler would be the one to save me from anything, but gratitude spiked through me for his timing.

He grinned that slick shark's smile. His gloating set me back on my feet.

The others were with him—*my* others, the *Scoop* staffers. Though they didn't seem overjoyed to see me. They were frowning at me like when they got their parents' angry phone calls.

Except for Devin.

He frowned at the Warheads. And at Anavi. He looked at me and raised his eyebrows in question. I shrugged, helpless.

He recognized that something bad had happened. But he couldn't know *how* bad.

Suddenly I was less worried about any attack against me than them targeting him. I was almost certain that they had tried to the day before. Anavi had said they had to be nearby to do anything. It was a safe gamble that remained true.

I needed to get him away from here.

"Detention awaits?" I asked, striding away in the opposite direction, saying a silent prayer that they'd follow. Hoping that I picked the right way for detention.

"Yes. Time to go think about what you've done," Butler said, hurrying after me to make sure I heard. A quick glance told me that he and the others were behind me.

I slowed so they could catch up.

"You could have created unnecessary difficulties for Anavi. And for me," Principal Butler finished, drawing even with me.

"Wouldn't that be a shame?" I asked in a tone he could interpret however he wanted.

As we walked away, a chorus of voices raised to follow us:

"Yes, think."

"About how you lost."

"And about how we won."

"We told you we would."

The last voice, unmistakable, belonged to Anavi.

⋆

An hour into detention, I realized I should have asked Butler what it was we had supposedly done wrong. I didn't even know how he'd justified this detention. You couldn't sentence students to punishment because they worked somewhere you didn't like or for publishing negative things about you.

Unless you run your school like Butler does. Then you probably can.

Detention was living up to the grim reputation the word

conjured. We'd had to hike through the patriotic blaze of a gym that looked recently renovated to a decidedly less spruced up area in the hallway beyond. The large open space had been outfitted for detention with rows of desks, but I suspected it was a former locker room from the few cubbies remaining around the edges of the walls and what I imagined was the lingering odor of stale sweat and gym socks, the hollow echo of a thousand dirty jokes.

We were shown to desks, and told there was no talking or studying, just quiet reflection on whatever had landed us here. It was going to be hard to stay awake.

And we had to stay awake. That was another rule of detention.

One that became even harder to follow when the instructor, a small man with a widow's peak, announced he had "something to aid your reflection," and switched on a small stereo on the corner of his desk. The low music that came out was sleepy classical.

I was convinced Maddy would start to weep. Her T-shirt today was for a band called Fatal Retraction. Coincidence?

Maddy looked miserable. So did James, but I was trying not to care about that. He scowled at me whenever he caught me looking, and I shrugged that off with only a moderate amount of guilt. He hadn't taken me up on being listed as a contributor to the story. Technically, he didn't deserve to be punished with the rest of us.

Not that any of us deserved this.

Devin alone seemed not to be harboring any hard feelings

toward me, but he wasn't into this scene either. There were a handful of hipsters in the back row who had waved and called to him in greeting when the four of us entered. These must be the cool kids Maddy had mentioned in the cafeteria. Being seen with the likes of preppy James, misfit-by-choice Maddy, and unknown quantity me wouldn't help Devin's reputation. I couldn't help wondering again if the hipster crowd knew about his kingdom in the game or his love of big fat fantasy novels.

Basically, what it boiled down to was that I was ruining the lives of the people I wanted to be my new friends.

And then there was Anavi. Anavi, who was—it seemed—one of *them*.

SmallvilleGuy could and would help me, but there was only so much he could do from far away. If I was going to get to the bottom of this and have that retraction request retracted and find some way to rescue Anavi, then I needed more allies.

Needed allies, and wanted friends. I wanted to earn their trust back. But if I told them everything, about my growing suspicions of hive mind control experiments, they'd think I was crazy.

Evidence of what was going on at the lab might be enough to seal the deal. Prove it. But first, I needed them willing to listen to me again.

We'd been stripped of our phones outside the door, taken by Butler himself with another slick grin, and would only be returned at the end of the day.

But then there was a positive development. The teacher

stopped following the rules (or maybe he didn't have to), and succumbed to a nap. His widow's peak fell forward as his weak chin dipped down to his chest.

Someone spoke in the back of the room, and I said, "Shhh."

To my surprise, whoever it was did. Who knew how long this opportunity would last? I didn't want to risk waking the teacher up by talking.

I needed this time to get a message across. So I took a piece of paper from the reporter's notebook in my backpack and wrote fast. I copied the same message—more or less—three times. Then I tore the paper into pieces as quietly as I could and tossed them to Maddy, Devin, and James.

I'd apologized and asked them to please meet me at the *Scoop* after school to discuss our next move, that I had something important to tell them.

I would have to figure out something not insane-sounding to say—*if* they agreed.

James's note was the only one that landed on the floor instead of his desk. He considered it, next to his expensive sneakers, making no move to pick it up.

Maddy and Devin opened theirs, and I could barely stand to look at them to see what their reactions were.

Devin gave me a small thumbs-up and a nod. Okay, I figured he'd be the easiest.

Maddy stared down at the paper for a long time. Finally, she looked up and solemnly nodded.

The teacher coughed, and I shifted back to face front. He

sat bolt upright as if he hadn't been asleep, though the way he was blinking himself awake confirmed that he had.

I yawned, turning my neck so I could see if James had moved yet.

He quietly sighed and bent over his desk to retrieve his own note. He read it and put it in his pocket, with no indication whatsoever whether he was in or not.

Fine. Two out of three was better than no one.

CHAPTER 17

The others might have agreed to meet me, but they hadn't completely forgotten and forgiven. After Butler showed to redistribute our phones at the end of the day and told us (well, me mostly) that he "hoped you've learned a valuable lesson," we went our separate ways.

I risked taking the subway, since the other day's cab tipping bonanza had left me cash-poorer for the moment, and I might need what remained for some unavoidable expense of the investigative variety. I could only cross my fingers that Maddy and Devin would be waiting at the *Scoop* office when I got there. Possibly even James.

But I wasn't holding my breath. Or at least I wasn't admitting that I was.

As I crossed the lobby of the Daily Planet Building, my

phone buzzed and I took it from my bag. I'd signed into the messenger app as soon as I got my phone back, so SmallvilleGuy could reach me if he'd learned something else while I was busy with the day's punishment.

SmallvilleGuy: *Out of dentist?*

I tapped out a short reply.

SkepticGirl1: *Huh?*

His next message came fast.

SmallvilleGuy: *Autocorrect. You out of detention?*

I snorted.

SkepticGirl1: *Yes. On way 2 work.*

SmallvilleGuy: *Do you have your holoset?*

SkepticGirl1: *I have James's.*

SmallvilleGuy: *Something going on in the game. I'll meet you in there.*

I hurried past the security guard. I almost hoped the others hadn't gotten to the office yet, because I wanted no delay in finding out what had red-alerted SmallvilleGuy.

So obviously that meant Maddy and Devin *and* James were waiting when I got to the Morgue. They'd wheeled their chairs out from behind their desks, making a tidy row across from mine. Waiting for me to explain.

I had to. Maybe SmallvilleGuy wouldn't get too antsy in *Worlds*.

"You're here," I said, not quite able to keep the surprise out of my voice.

"You said you had something important to tell us," Maddy said. "And we know you didn't lie about Anavi. I don't understand what's going on, but . . . something is."

I took a seat on the corner of my desk. "You really should be in news instead of style," I said.

Maddy shrugged one shoulder. "I've been told I'm stylish. So, what's up?"

"Yeah," Devin said, leaning forward with his elbows on his knees. "Anavi never got along with those guys and all of a sudden they're hanging out and she doesn't even sound like herself. I don't get it. Is it about whatever Project Hydra is?"

"You remember Project Hydra," I said. "Yes, I think that's exactly what it's about."

"What is it?" Maddy was frowning again. "Did you find out and keep it from us?"

"I don't know everything." *And I can't even tell you all of what I suspect.* "But I did, sort of—well, okay I followed the Warheads. The other day when they left school after lunch, I caught a taxi. I didn't want to risk getting you guys in trouble."

"Given today's jail sentence, that's ironic with extra sprinkles," said Maddy.

I went on. "Anyway, Ms. Johnson, from our comp sci class—"

Devin raised his eyebrows. "*Our?*"

I would never get through this if they kept interrupting. Then again, they had every right to give me a hard time.

I'd endure it.

"You knew I wasn't staying in that class forever. I didn't

want to get too attached to Ms. Johnson and make our parting too much sweet sorrow."

"Continue," Devin said, with a flowery, regal flourish of his fingers.

"They all loaded up in a van and Ms. Johnson drove them across town . . . to the headquarters of Advanced Research Laboratories. I think Butler has them hooked up with some sort of experiment there. He freaked when I asked him about Hydra. We all know he's letting them get away with whatever they feel like, and it must be because of this. And now Anavi's involved too."

"What kind of experiment?" Devin asked.

The kind that apparently makes you lose your personality and start finishing the sentences of creeps. The kind that has no positive application I can think of.

"That," I said, carefully, "I don't know. Yet. But I figure if we can uncover it, then we have a bargaining chip with Butler. We can make the retraction stuff all go away, and end whatever they're doing too. No way this is all above board. Butler's too determined to keep it hidden."

"Huh. Okay." Devin leaned back. "Apology accepted. I'm in."

"Why didn't you tell us about this before?" Maddy asked.

"I told you, I didn't want to get you in trouble. With or without extra sprinkles. I wanted to know more before I brought you guys in. But we've run out of time for that . . . and I'm not sure I can do this on my own."

James still hadn't said anything.

Finally, he did. "Corporate donations to the school have increased big time in the last couple years. Butler's brought in a whole bunch of companies to form research partnerships. I've met some of the senior execs from Advanced Research at fundraisers for Dad, and I'd believe they're into anything, as long as it's something they aren't supposed to be into."

"I heard Butler got a whole bunch of new computers from them early this year," I agreed.

"Could that be a bribe? Or a pay-off, at least?" James asked.

I wouldn't have banked on anything James had to say being helpful. But he was surprising me. "Could be. At least, a pay-off of a sort. You know Butler well enough to know he wants to shoot foxes or skeet shoot or whatever the nouveau riche do to pretend they're your kind, with generations of money. I think he wants the connections. The power."

James didn't disagree, though he shifted in his seat when I mentioned his kind of rich people.

"Is there any way for us to figure out when Hydra started taking up the Warheads' afternoons?" he asked. "We could see if it matches up with the donation."

Devin considered. "I looked back at last semester on a couple of their records the other day and it wasn't there. Looked like a new thing, this semester only, so can't be longer than a few weeks? They could have been going over the summer, I guess—but if they were, it didn't show up on their transcripts."

"Whether it coincides exactly or not, it's probably *not* a coincidence," I said, throwing James a bone.

I didn't need to bust his chops about his family all the time.

It's not like anyone got to choose who they were related to, not really.

"How *are* we going to find out what they're doing in time?" Devin said. "I could try hacking into Advanced Research's system, but it'll be way tougher than the school's firewall. It would take me days. *If* I could do it, it would be after Monday."

Monday was Perry's deadline. We couldn't risk waiting that long. "And if you got busted, you could be in real trouble," I pointed out.

Not that a little thing like that would stop me, but I didn't intend to get these guys in any more trouble if I could avoid it.

So I decided on a course of action. I would get into the lab, but not quite yet. I wanted a better idea of what was happening once the Warheads arrived there. And if my luck didn't screw things up, what I had in mind would be enough evidence to convince Perry why the retraction request had been made. Enough to save the *Scoop*.

"Don't worry," I said. "We'll bug them."

"With killer bees, or . . . ?" Devin trailed off.

"No, not with killer bees." I rolled my eyes. "With a small unlikely-to-be-detected sound-and-heat-signature-capturing device. A bug. I figure Anavi will be the easiest to slip one onto. She always carries her backpack. If we do it first thing Monday morning, we should have enough for Perry by the end of the day. I'll be the responsible party and take the heat if someone has to, so don't worry about getting caught."

Assuming we wouldn't get enough information from this method, I was working up a plan B . . . or was it a plan C?

But the rest of them *really* didn't need to be involved in that. I had learned my lesson, though probably not the one Butler intended: don't get people in trouble if you want them to be your friends.

The plan, plan A, my original plan when I arrived in Metropolis—well, that was toast. My dad and I would have to work something else out. Because I had no choice but to get in trouble. To not fit in. To make enemies and rock the boat so hard it might capsize with me in it.

No choice but to do what was right.

"A bug." James was shaking his head, the old disbelief back. "Where would you get one?"

Just when I was feeling like James might be all right. "Doubting me? Have a little faith. I'll bring it to school."

I happened to know that Dad had a stockpile of all sorts of handy tools in a locked cabinet in his office. Finding the key would be a challenge, but I was up for it. And once I did I'd have access to all kinds of things, like the latest generation of listening devices and spy gear.

I focused on Maddy. "You think you're up to helping me plant the bug?"

"Oh, yes, definitely," Maddy answered instantly. "Are there videos I can watch to get ready? Research I can do?"

"You'll be a natural," I said.

"You better be right about this," James said. "Because if we don't nail Butler, *this* is all over." He swept a hand around us, indicating the office.

"It's so sweet of you to act like you care about that," I said.

I didn't miss how James's attention gravitated to his shoes, as if they were fascinating objects he'd never seen before. That was interesting.

"What do we do now?" Devin asked. "Please don't say 'nothing.' I don't want to just sit around all weekend."

Right. SmallvilleGuy was waiting. "Now you and I are going into the game. A . . . friend tipped me off that something's happening in there. We should probably be careful when we go in."

"I'm a *King*," Devin said. "I don't do caution."

"Your secret is out," I said.

"They don't play, so they don't even know what that means," Devin countered with a grin. But I didn't miss his worried glance over at James.

Would James recognize his holoset? There was a little red dot on one side, but it seemed like it had come that way.

I rummaged in my bag and pulled it out, sat down in my chair and slipped it over my ear. My shoulder ached with phantom pain like when I'd been shot. Devin already had his holoset on, but hadn't powered up yet.

Maddy said, "We just sit here and watch you guys? Boring."

James's eyes narrowed, and he said, "Or I could ask Lois for my holoset back and go in with Devin instead."

Devin and I exchanged a guilty look. "I need to do this," I said, "and I was just borrowing it." Devin didn't say anything, so I went on. "And Devin said you've never even used it since he set it up. Is that true?"

James nodded, annoyed again.

I said, "*And* you'd be playing as an elvish princess named Lo."

James blinked. I thought for a second he'd take me up on it to be testy. But he said, "Go on, use it."

"Um . . . thanks?" I was tentative. Thanking James felt weird. But he didn't even exert himself to toss back a "you're welcome," so I wouldn't be doing it again anytime soon.

Devin reached up to tap the button on his holoset, but waited with his finger poised. "Ready?" he asked.

I nodded, and we pressed our holosets on at the same time. I started, "Remember, be care—"

But as the gamescape replaced the dim Morgue, the words died in my throat.

Worlds War Three was on fire. I felt the ground tremble, then shake, under my still-bare elf feet.

I looked frantically around to find Devin, and there he was, a few feet away from me. Wearing a royal purple tunic with chainmail and plate armor, and an ornate, if tastefully small, crown. He stood, regally gaping.

I gaped too. It wasn't the whole world that was burning.

It was only Devin's kingdom.

His castle lay in ruins, flames licking from the openings along the tower walls, and much of the rest nothing but rubble. The proud flag that bore Devin's likeness had been ripped and burned almost to shreds. I could barely make out his image on it.

All that was left was an impression of his silhouette, like he was a ghost.

A hand touched my arm, and Devin stopped staring and sprang into motion. He drew a long sword from a sheath covered in scrolled metalwork. It was augmented with a gun barrel on top of the blade.

"Stop right there!" he ordered, leveling the sword gun at the newcomer.

Devin made a kingly presence, defending his castle and me.

Unfortunately he was pointing his sword-gun at SmallvilleGuy, who wasn't the source of the devastation.

"Devin, this is my friend," I choked out through the growing haze of smoke that surrounded us. Funny how my throat was so easily convinced it was real. "He's not responsible."

Devin hesitated a second before lowering the sword. "He's the one who told you about this? Asked us to meet him?"

SmallvilleGuy came closer, not intimidated by the monarch who'd threatened him, though in the game he was a gawky alien who should have been. He reached up to resettle his rectangular glasses, a tiny giveaway that maybe he was nervous beneath his cool. "That's me. And I'm the one who was with her the other night when we ran interference with the Warheads. Good call on making her elvish royalty."

I felt like I should be blushing, and then realized with horror that my elvish princess cheeks might be reddening. "Did you see who did this? It was them, wasn't it?"

Because who else would have? And it was more evidence they might turn on Devin next.

It was as if SmallvilleGuy read my mind and saw the concerns there.

"Yes, they were single-minded about it," SmallvilleGuy said. "Eyes only for Devin's property, even when other characters showed up to loot the ruins."

"They'd have to be, to manage this in such a short amount of time," Devin said, and the words were fainter than when he'd spoken before. Shell-shocked, like he was beginning to understand the extent of the destruction.

"It wasn't like anything I thought possible in here. They were so much stronger, working in better coordination with each other than the other night, even," SmallvilleGuy said. "I did manage to talk one of your dragons into chasing them off. That's where the fire came from."

Devin squinted, no doubt reading SmallvilleGuy's stats.

Good luck. You'll never figure out who he is.

"Since when can friendly aliens talk to dragons?" Devin asked.

SmallvilleGuy rubbed his chin, looking embarrassed. "Since one found a cache of uber-secret cheat codes buried in threads on a private developer forum for game architects and workers."

I knew what that meant. He'd managed to do some more research. His friend from the boards had come through. Nice. "You find anything else usefully cheat-y?"

"Just more of the same type of . . . thing we talked about the other night. R&D project rumors."

Devin wasn't paying attention to us, though. He was wandering toward the remains of his castle. SmallvilleGuy and I trailed after him more slowly.

My cheeks still felt warm and I decided it must be from the fact that everything around us was on fire. Yes, that was it. Definitely.

SmallvilleGuy was my friend. We were *just friends.*

"So I guess they're talking to you again? That's a good sign," he said. "I'm glad you have backup out there. The Warheads . . . they really were in rare form when I saw them. And there's something else. I hate to be the one to tell you. But did you happen to see Anavi today?"

"She was with them, wasn't she? I know already. They got to her. I saw her with them this morning. I failed her, and I think we both know who's likely to be next."

We gazed at the wreck in front of us. Devin stood in front of the tower, his head craned back to take in the flag, his posture resounding with defeat.

"They were strong and they'll be back," SmallvilleGuy said. "I doubt Daisy can hold them off for long."

"Daisy?" I asked.

"The dragon. She did say Devin didn't like other people to know he named her that, so maybe keep it to yourself."

I found that I was smiling at him, without even intending to. Despite the fact that the world was literally burning around us and everything was awful. I couldn't help it.

"I'm a vault," I said. "What other secrets do you have?"

I regretted it as soon as the words left my lips, knew he'd misinterpreted them by the way his expression changed. A subtle closing down and shutting me out. The graphics in this game were *too* good, sometimes.

Did he look like that every night when I asked who he was?

"That's not what I meant," I said, but my smile was gone. "Anything else about our bad guys?"

"Oh," he said, kicking aside a piece of rubble. "**TheInventor,** my buddy I told you about, vouched to get me registered on that private site for developers so I could see any relevant discussions—lucky for me they didn't require the same kind of proof you did. He pointed me to some chatter about a project at Advanced Research Labs, a study of team dynamics and how to enhance them using real-sim technology."

"Signs point to Project Hydra," I said.

"Seems likely. The results so far are getting high marks from the boss, but one of the researcher guys actually running it came from the game company and was talking about it with some of his former co-workers from there on the site. All in vague terms, but it was clear that he doesn't think it's a good idea. He won't say why out in the open though. I did gather that their boss has the research team gearing up for a presentation soon to some sort of potential buyer. I still don't know exactly what it is." He paused. "Lois, are you going after them alone?"

My heart kicked in my chest, and I felt ridiculous again.

"I won't do anything I don't have to."

It was the best I could do.

"Fair enough," he said. "Though I guess this means you're giving up on staying out of trouble."

I stopped walking. We were almost to Devin, and he was looking for a clear path into the wreckage.

I turned to SmallvilleGuy. "What can I say? Every time I try to walk away, I run right into it instead."

But he would see through that, wouldn't he? Me playing it off like it didn't bother me.

Yes, he would. He did.

"Lois, you haven't done anything wrong."

"I know. I think this is just who I am. I'm never going to fit in anywhere. I'll always be . . . different."

"Is that so bad?" he asked.

And he waited for the answer, like it mattered to him too. Through his glasses, I saw that his eyes were blue. Kind and blue. These graphics were good, but were they accurate? Of course his skin wasn't green outside the game, but were his eyes that same blue?

I'd be more than okay with it, if they were.

"No," I said, finally, "I don't guess it's such a bad thing to be different."

His lips tilted up in a smile, a small one, like another secret between us. He was about to say something else, and I wanted to know what it was so badly I was afraid to breathe, afraid I might miss it. I leaned in toward him, so I could hear better, squinting against the smoke.

But whatever it was got lost. His smile dropped away, and what he said instead was: "They're back."

CHAPTER 18

Anavi wasn't just one of the pack. She was at the front of the loping formation. But even in here there wasn't anything else to distinguish her from the rest. Gone were her camouflage and grenades with words on them—she was in black and armed beyond all reason, like the squadron arrayed around and behind her.

An angry red dragon flew over their heads, screeching bloodiest murder. Missiles were mounted under the sprawl of her wings.

That must be the famous Daisy.

SmallvilleGuy called up to her. "Good girl, Daisy! Let them have it!"

So much for keeping the name quiet.

Devin stalked out of the crumbled arch that used to be the

entrance to his castle. He wasn't alone. He brought a small-in-number but large-in-size army with him.

Two elephants, draped in robes printed with his silhouette, lifted their massive trunks to trumpet loud displeasure. Behind them came some sort of winged creatures, part eagle and part lion, with fearsome talons that hovered a few feet off the ground as their feathered wings beat to hold them aloft. Baby trolls—they were much smaller than the one Anavi had taken down, so I assumed these were babies—rode on top of the beasts and swung clubs or strung bows.

"They didn't find the hidden entrance to the mine tunnels beneath the tower," Devin said. "That's where I keep most of my troops." He looked smug as the ground shook again, but this time under the weight of the feet of his soldiers.

I would never understand all the ins and outs of this game.

Daisy landed on Devin's other side and breathed a fresh round of fire at the attackers.

"The flying things that aren't dragons are . . . ?" I asked.

Devin blinked. "Oh, my griffins. Awesome, right?"

The prospect of battle seemed to have revived him from his earlier defeat. For the moment.

But the Warheads had gathered extra gear and munitions of their own while they were gone. A shimmering white force field popped into existence around them.

"Enchanted ice barrier," SmallvilleGuy said. "This is bad. It's probably the only thing besides a fortified alien aircraft that your army can't penetrate."

"Crap," Devin said. "You're right."

Devin waved his arm to indicate to his troops that they should retreat. The creatures milled around us, the dragon screeching in protest. But he was still their royal commander-in-chief. Devin raised his other arm and waved once more for them to go, and that did it.

Even if they didn't want to, the trolls fell back, taking their mounts with them. The elephants lumbered along last, one looking back and trumpeting a final threat.

I realized something. When the Warheads had come after Anavi in the game, the only thing they bothered with was stealth and brute strength. There had been little finesse to the attack. But if they'd managed to bring the only weapon Devin couldn't stand up to, that indicated a more, well, *strategic* kind of strategy.

"They're smarter, aren't they?" I asked. "It must be because they have Anavi."

"Maybe," SmallvilleGuy said, nodding. "More brainpower."

"They can share resources. Not brains," Devin said. "I don't know what you guys are talking about, but we need to get out of here. Retreat's the only option for now."

It was clear that behind the ice barrier, the Warheads were prepping some sort of new weapons. Weapons that undoubtedly would hurt as bad as or worse than that screaming bullet wound to my shoulder the other day. SmallvilleGuy never had said if or where he'd been hit.

Painful memory or not, I didn't like the idea of fleeing the scene. "We can't just let them win. If we leave your castle undefended, they'll destroy it completely."

"We have to," Devin said.

The certainty in his voice killed me. I didn't want him to give up so quickly. It was my fault this was happening. Mine and the Warheads and whoever had made them this way.

"Any cheat codes?" I asked SmallvilleGuy.

"I'm out of any that would help here." He said it with regret. Like disappointing me was as much a disappointment to him as anything else could be.

And that's when I knew we were out of options. Officially.

"Then we have to go," I said. "If there's no chance of winning. I don't want to get shot again for kicks."

The Warheads' ice barrier collapsed and Daisy breathed another round of fire. That bought the three of us a few final moments to close our eyes, ground back into our actual bodies, and reach up to turn off our holosets.

The last thing I saw in the game was SmallvilleGuy, moving his body to shield mine from whatever the bad guys were about to lob our way, as he lifted his own hand to his ear—no doubt in and outside the game. Somehow I knew he wouldn't stick around there once Devin and I were gone, and out of harm's way.

Back in the real world, it took a few moments—I couldn't have said how many—to feel like I was here instead of there. The same seemed to be true for Devin. He blinked at me without quite focusing.

Maddy laid her hands on my shoulders, giving me a little shake. "What was happening? We're dying in here. We could only hear your sides of the conversation."

"We're okay, I think." I lightly shrugged Maddy's hands off and stood. "Devin, I'm so sorry for what they did. I can't believe . . ."

"Yeah," he said, dazed, "me either. That was two years of work. Gone."

"You still have your troll army and the griffins and the elephants," I said.

"For now."

"I am not following any of this," Maddy said.

"Neither am I," James put in.

"Anavi and the Warheads attacked us, but they'd done way worse before we got there," I said. "They took Devin's castle apart brick by brick."

"Ancient stone by ancient stone," Devin corrected. "They must have used explosives."

"Devin has a castle? What kind?" Maddy asked.

"Never mind," Devin said, and I stayed quiet. "It's no big thing. I'll rebuild later."

He didn't sound so convinced. And I knew it *was* a big thing. Two years was a long time to spend building something to have it torn down in an afternoon with no warning.

Then there was Anavi, her personality gone.

But not for good. I won't let any of this be for good.

Devin said, "Thank your friend for me. It would have been worse if he hadn't helped out."

"What friend?" James asked. "Is that the other person you were talking to? The one you told you'd never . . ."

My cheeks were definitely burning, and not the elvish ones.

They'd heard my side of the conversation with SmallvilleGuy. About how I'd never fit in. About how being different wasn't so bad.

"Never. Mind." I examined my desk so I wouldn't have to face them. "We have a plan for Monday. This weekend we'll use for intel and lying low. Let them think they have the upper hand."

The Warheads probably did have it, but I expected someone to respond to me and agree. When no one did, I looked up to see why. The others were staring at the door to the Morgue.

I turned and discovered that Perry was standing there.

Next to my father.

Dad was in his full regalia. He stuck out in the dim, dusty cavern of the office like a heroically sore thumb.

"You won't be doing anything this weekend, Lois," he said. "You're grounded."

My hand went to my hip. "What are you doing here?"

The others were gawking at me like I might be crazy.

Oh, right. He was in full intimidation mode, wasn't he? Even Perry was subdued.

"Your dad wanted to chat, make sure I was aware of the situation," Perry said. "He wanted to discuss the timeline for following up on Principal Butler and Anavi Singh's complaints."

"I bet he did."

"Lois," Dad said. He was using his warning tone.

Fine, I had one of those too. "Dad."

"You can get your things together. Perry assured me that he takes this all seriously, and that if the allegations are true that this—" he glanced around, searching for a word, and I had to admit the office probably made the *Scoop* look like it wasn't much. But it *was*. Appearances were deceptive. "—this *outfit* will be disbanded."

So he'd settled on outfit. As if my job was a dress or some random clothes I picked up on a shopping spree at the mall.

He went on, "You'll spend the weekend thinking about that instead of trying to get the upper hand at whatever you're up to."

Aha. Bingo. Eureka. What he was doing became as clear as the crystal James's family no doubt used at the dinner table.

This was his next move in our battle.

"You're shortening my timeline. You know the less time I have to do legwork, the less likely I am to prove my story was right." I whirled to my desk and picked up my phone, taking the time to text *Grounded* in the app with my right hand while I fumbled around with my left to cover what I was doing. Then I logged out. I never knew how snoopy my parents were going to get when they were mad at me.

And I wasn't sure Dad had ever been this mad before.

Picking up my bag, I jammed in some random papers before heading his way. "This is very nice of you, Dad. Very supportive."

He sighed, a sound of pure frustration. "Lois, I *am* supportive . . . of you making a fresh start here. We talked about you staying out of trouble. It sounds like you're using this job to do what you always do."

Yeah, we had talked about it. But it wasn't my fault

that I wasn't willing to stand by and let bad things happen unchecked. *He* should understand that as well as anyone.

Why couldn't he seem to?

I ignored him, stopping in front of Perry. "Mr. White . . . Perry . . . sir, don't worry. I take the *Daily Planet*'s reputation seriously and I know the *Scoop* reflects on it. It won't be damaged, not by me. Even if he seals me up in a closet all weekend."

So the last part was a little grumbly. Sue me.

Perry's eyes widened with alarm. But when he spoke, the words were simple. And oh-so-important to me.

"I believe you," he said.

This was more than progress, after how he'd flipped the day before. It was enough to carry me out of the office with my dad.

Dad could try to shackle me all he wanted. It wouldn't work.

★

Or maybe it would.

As soon as we walked through the front door at home, he held out his hand and said, "Phone," waiting until I placed mine in his palm. This was after a long, tense, silent car ride home.

Mom was coming off the bottom of the stairs into the living room. She carried my laptop with her.

I bit my lip against a protest that would give away how much I didn't want them anywhere near my computer. The passwords should be uncrackable, even if they tried to get on it. But this would mean no chats with SmallvilleGuy all weekend long.

No intel. No nothing.

Good thing I had proposed lying low until Monday. "You're seriously taking all my stuff? How am I supposed to get anything done?"

Dad said, "You can do your homework in longhand. You can't have that much to do after just a week. Grounded means no contact with the outside world. It means thinking about what kind of life you should be making for yourself. Lois, I know at sixteen it seems like you have all the time in the world, but before you know it—before your mom and I do—you'll be in college. You'll be out on your own."

"Right now I'm counting the seconds until that sweet, sweet freedom is mine."

"We only want what's best for you," he said.

"No," I said, "I think you just want me to be someone else. Someone I can't be."

I started for the stairs, slipping past my mom. I turned back to them. "If you really think what I've done is so bad . . . Dad, go read the comments. On the story at the *Scoop* page. Read the comments and see if you think that it didn't need to be told, that there was no merit to it. I did not lie. Perry believes me. It's too bad you can't bring yourself to."

I pounded the rest of the way up the steps, only slowing when Lucy peeked out of her bedroom door, making puppy-dog eyes. I paused to brush my hand across the top of her head. “I’m not going anywhere—really, I’m grounded, not being sent away,” I reassured her. “Don’t worry.”

And I finished the journey to my room across the hall, shut and locked my door.

My parents might be able to prevent me from reaching the outside world, but I would also keep them out of mine.

One way or another.

*

I had plenty to keep me busy. Plotting, worrying, planning, more worrying.

First, I plugged Maddy’s tiny MP3 player into my docking station, and I listened to the playlist she’d put together. She really did have excellent taste. It proved to be a nice mix of arty ballads that captured my frustration at being trapped in my room along with punk and hip-hop influenced anthems I jumped around to, raging against the injustice of same.

Then I spent more time plotting. I might have been forbidden access to my phone and outside assistance, but giving a girl time to think . . . that was turning out to be useful after all. As had the stationery set my parents gave me for my eleventh birthday, in case I wanted to write any of my old friends. Was it a coincidence that year had been my first foray into calls home from school because I was in trouble?

Not likely. Even back then, I’d been fighting for someone else. The first time the school had called home to complain about my behavior was when a teacher mispronounced the word “massacre” as if it ended “cree” and a straight-A student named Angie corrected her. The teacher had flipped out and sentenced Angie to lose her recess time for a week. I knew massacre was pronounced "mass-a-ker" from the military history shows Dad loved to watch, and so added my voice of support to Angie's.

That had gone over well.

Anyway, now I used the pastel pink stationery that had been given to me soon after to write a heartwarming note of apology to deliver to Principal Butler on Monday—something I projected would come in handy at getting him off my back. If only temporarily.

Lucy had been bringing food and drink to my cell, and she even offered to lend me *Unicorn University*. Though she'd looked vaguely terrified that I might take her up on it and ruin her reputation.

But by Saturday night, I was out of productive distractions. I needed to get the bug for Monday.

I waited until midnight to make a jailbreak from my room to seek it out, banking that my parents would be sleeping soundly by then. I'd avoided them since the heated discussion the night before.

They were being unreasonable.

I crept down the stairs barefoot—channeling my inner elf—and into my dad's home study where the contraband was stored. I crossed the threshold and the glowing lamp he always left on at night rewarded me with the sight of both my phone *and* my laptop stacked in a chair across from Dad's desk.

Tempting, but only after I'd gotten what I came for.

Although not being able to lock the office door wasn't ideal for the search. I was afraid to even close it, in case someone made a trip downstairs to the kitchen for a glass of water.

Wait. Dad wasn't paranoid enough to have added a nanny cam, stashed away in some hollowed-out volume of military history or embedded in a statuette of a Civil War soldier, was he?

I hadn't even considered that. Then again, those were the spots I had to check, the kind of places where he sometimes hid the key to the heavy lock on the tall wooden cabinet in the corner of the office. The cabinet where he stored the cache of high-tech toys and gear I planned to raid.

Well, not *raid*. Borrow from.

I went to a bookshelf and checked inside a volume about President Ulysses S. Grant, or more importantly in Dad's view, the great General Grant, which was actually a hollowed-out box. Nada.

Given that we'd just moved to Metropolis, he could be homesick for places with a base closer by. So next I went to an end table with a model tank one of his soldiers had made for him years before and undid the hatch on top. Empty.

"Argh," I muttered, looking around.

My attention landed on a framed photo on the short bookshelf beside his desk. It was us, our family decked out in our finest, with me and Lucy in front of Dad and Mom, the three of them smiling happily and me not. My black hair fell over my shoulders in soft waves that Mom had labored over, but I was scowling at the camera. We'd had it taken last year, and

Dad and I had a big argument that day. I remembered slamming doors, but not what we fought about. Thinking back, though, he'd first mentioned requesting a permanent assignment right after that.

I walked over and picked up the picture frame. And . . . felt a shape along the back. I turned it around.

The key was stuck to the back of the frame with a small dollop of putty. I pulled it free and, setting the frame down, beelined for the cabinet. The key slid into the brass lock and the cabinet door gave up the treasures inside with a click.

Row upon row of Dad's goodies awaited. Directly in front of me were a tiny camera, a few small laser pointers, and some sleek black cylinders that might have been actual handheld lasers. Below was a line of close-quarters prism flares and other gadgets; the flares we were allowed to use on the Fourth of July, a more exciting alternative to sparklers, as long as you called for everyone to squeeze their eyes shut before you let them off.

Finding the bug I needed was easy. I closed my palm around the ink-pen-shaped infrared video and listening device on the second to bottom shelf, complete with a pen-cap receiver. I stowed both inside the pocket of my fuzzy robe.

I closed the cabinet, glad I didn't need directions on how to use the bug. One of the military scientists who liked Lucy and me best had let us observe when he demoed it for Dad. I'd kind of hoped to find an even newer generation with fresh improvements in Dad's stockpile, but this would do nicely.

I relocked the door, crossed to the picture frame, and

restored the key to the putty. I should go back upstairs, but I paused.

My laptop and phone were right there.

I scurried across the thick rug toward the chair. I was willing to risk booting up down here, instead of lugging the computer all the way upstairs where I might get caught on the way. And I rationalized that I'd risk only a few more minutes to attempt a check-in with SmallvilleGuy, make sure nothing else had happened in the game, tell him about my plan for Monday, see if he had any new info to share.

Maybe he'd have a new picture of Nellie the baby cow or Shelby the dog to lift my spirits.

If Dad caught me, I'd tell him I was looking at email. Lifting the laptop, I sat down and opened it, letting my phone drop down beside me in the chair.

"If I wanted you to use that this weekend, then I wouldn't have taken it away."

I flinched.

Dad stood in the doorway. He flipped on the brighter overhead light. "I am surprised it took you this long to sneak down here, though. Now put that down and go back to bed."

Good thing you didn't show up two minutes earlier. I closed the laptop, but hesitated for a split second, considering my odds of success if I tried to slip the phone into the pocket of my robe along with the bug.

"Leave the phone too."

I scowled at him, imitating my expression in the family photo. But I did as he commanded. It was only one more day of this unnecessary captivity. One more day until I'd be able to take action.

When I reached the door, he stopped me with a hand on my arm. Now it was his turn to hesitate, but then he said, "I did what you told me to, read all those comments . . . Look, I get the point. Maybe the job isn't all bad. I hope you get things straightened out. All we want is for you to be happy, Lois."

I hadn't expected him to take me up on the suggestion, or say anything remotely like that. I owed him an honest response.

"I don't know if happy is what I want. I may want more."

He nodded, fatherly, and I remembered that he wasn't all tyrant. And even when he was, he was still my dad. He sighed and said, "Honey, that's what we're afraid of."

I returned to my room, and my sentence. Sure, I could do my dad the favor of thinking about what I wanted my life to be like for one more day. But I didn't need to.

I was beginning to think I'd figured out exactly what I wanted to do with it.

CHAPTER 19

On Monday morning, Maddy caught up with me at my locker, practically bouncing with excitement. "You ready?" I asked her.

"Are you kidding? I couldn't think about anything else all weekend," she said, sweeping a hand down to indicate her leather jacket. "I tried to dress the part."

"Excellent." I extended my hand to her with the pen-shaped bug across my palm. "You're on planting detail."

She put out her hand and accepted the bug. She stared at it, like she was memorizing every detail.

"Just don't let her see you with it, okay?" I said.

Maddy frowned. "But how do I . . . "

I bent and untied the left one of her heavy-soled, swirly-colored shoes. "You'll notice your shoe's untied, and while you're fixing it, you'll stash the pen wherever is handiest. Her backpack would be best, in an outer pocket. Somewhere she's less likely to notice it."

"Oh, okay," Maddy nodded. "What will you be doing?"

"Me? I'm the distraction." I shut my locker. "Let's go."

"But what if . . . " Maddy was worrying.

I couldn't blame her. I'd spent a fair amount of the weekend doing the same. "You're going to pull this off with no problem. *We* are. Girl power, right?"

"Girl power," Maddy agreed. "Though it sounds really dorky when you say it like that."

We went up the hall together, slowing when we got close to Anavi, like we were approaching a strange dog that might attack us.

Anavi might. Or if not her, then the Warheads around her, lounging against nearby lockers with no concern for whether they were blocking access. Anavi hadn't seen us yet, busy putting books into her locker almost mechanically. Her backpack was slumped on the floor beside her feet, unzipped and open.

That was a lucky break. Maddy's eyes widened as she noted the fact too.

The restrained quality to Anavi's movements as she swapped out books was disturbing to witness. Not that she had been magically self-assured and the smoothest of smooth before the Warheads stole her soul, but she'd been . . . *herself.*

"Steady," I said to Maddy.

Who rolled her eyes. Under the leather jacket, she wore yet another band T-shirt—King Wrong. My curiosity about it flared. About all of her shirts. Everything on Maddy's playlist had been great, but *none* of the thirty bands on it were ones I'd seen advertised on her T-shirts, and that seemed odd. I'd ask her about it later.

Right now, Maddy was doing her best to be casual and would convince anyone except me with the act. She had her right hand in the pocket of her jeans, probably gripping the pen so hard her knuckles were straining.

"Anavi," I said, clearing a path through a couple of Warheads by ignoring and ducking around them. Maddy stuck with me.

Anavi turned from her locker so that she was facing me, and the rest of the Warheads subtly shifted so they were too.

I muscled my way closer without touching any of them, so that Maddy could get into position right beside the lockers. And the backpack. But I didn't check to make sure Maddy was where she should be. That might give us away.

"I wanted to apologize to you, to all of you," I said, and I felt like a pretty good spy not to choke on the words. They practically flowed off my tongue, a necessary lie coated in warm honey.

"Really?" said a Warhead.

And the chorus chimed in: "That doesn't . . ."

". . . seem like you."

Anavi's head tilted to one side, her eyes narrowing a bit behind her glasses.

"No, it doesn't seem like you," she said.

I glanced around to confirm that the others had mirrored her posture. Could they be any creepier?

Probably shouldn't try to answer that question.

"I am sorry, whether you believe it or not. So sorry that I felt like I had to tell you. We can call the whole thing done." It was risky, but I couldn't help adding, "You can leave Devin alone now too. Since this is over."

"Can we?"

"I don't know . . ."

". . . if we can."

"Or if we want to."

"Look, I'm moving on and you should do the same," I said, careful not to grit my teeth. "I just wanted to make things right with you. I want us to be friends." And I went in for a hug for the capper.

If Maddy hadn't already completed her task, then this was her moment. Her last chance to get the bug in place in the backpack.

Anavi took a few long moments to react to the hug. The Warheads weren't used to random embraces.

I made sure my grip was firm. "I am sorry," I said, lower.

I meant it. Just like I meant the part about being friends. I was determined to discover what Project Hydra was and end it—to find a way to bring Anavi back to herself.

Finally, Anavi grunted and the Warheads started talking.

"Let her go."

"What are you thinking?"

"Get out of here."

"Now."

A press against my mind underscored the command, and I

tightened my hold on Anavi in reflex. Thrown off balance, I needed something to hang on to. I'd forgotten about the threat of this.

But the pressure increased in response, shoving against my mind, longer than either of the previous times. I fought to think of the game, of teasing SmallvilleGuy, of that night in Kansas, of anything I could latch onto to try to ignore the pressure until I could get clear of them.

The problem was thinking at all. But I managed. Barely.

I was beyond grateful when Anavi's hands came up between us and shoved me away. Anavi gave her head a shake, almost like she had in the classroom when she was fighting the Warheads' intrusions in her own mind.

"Next time you will regret the consequences of your actions," Anavi said.

"Yes, there'd . . ."

". . . better not be . . ."

". . . a next time."

Anavi's phrasing—"regret the consequences of your actions"—was like how she'd put things before she went all hive mind. The slip gave me hope she was in there somewhere, reachable.

But whatever of her had returned was gone again as quickly. Her face smoothed into a mask, and she shut the door to her locker. Without turning, she bent to pick up her backpack. And then she was moving away, down the hall with her pack animals, all of them in perfect sync once again.

I put my hand against the locker. "Did you get it in there?"

Maddy lifted her hands to dust them. "Yes, I got it in there. I thought you were about to ask her to run away with you, you took so long with the hugging."

"Nice work," I said, pasting on a smile in return.

"I don't get that way they talk." Maddy was watching the Warheads disappear up the hall. "How they always know what the other ones are going to say. What's the deal with it, do you think?"

I shrugged. I didn't want to lie to Maddy. And it wasn't like I could explain everything yet.

Here was hoping the bug got us enough answers to end this.

*

By the time lunch period finally ended, I felt like my blood had been replaced with electricity. Over the course of the morning, the word had been circulated from Maddy to Devin to James that all of us would meet up in the library, in independent research room A, which Maddy had booked during her study period under the guise of watching a video about women factory workers in World War II for AP history.

If the others wanted to see and hear the bug show, they had to skip their first afternoon classes. I had the same study slot as Maddy, but I was supposed to stay in a different area of the library.

That was easy enough to deal with. The librarian only had us sign a sheet as we came in, and then got busy with the million other tasks that were her real job.

I rapped my knuckles on the door of room A, and it cracked a sliver. "Password?" came the whispered reply.

Maddy's eyelinered eye was silhouetted in the shadow, a flickering black and white movie visible behind her projected on the wall.

"Let me in?" I had completely spaced the fact that Maddy had come up with a password code. She was getting into Independent Study: Cloak-and-Dagger in a major way.

"Password," the reply came.

Over at her desk, the librarian was helping someone check out a stack of books, and the last thing I wanted was to draw her attention. I needed to activate the bug. But I couldn't point this out to Maddy without prolonging the torture and exposure. Squinting, I recalled our earlier conversation about this.

My head hurt, which probably meant I didn't remember right away because I'd been shaking off the sensation of having a bunch of hands—er, minds—pushing against mine. Maddy would make it something to do with the cover story, wouldn't she? She'd been proud of it . . .

"Rosie," I said, too loud with triumph. I verified the librarian was still busy. And she was, but two other boys in a stack nearby were looking over at me.

"The Riveter," Maddy said in a softer tone, and swung the door the rest of the way open. "Enter."

"Remind me never to cross you, Mata Hari," I said.

"She was World War One, not Two," Maddy said coolly.

"Then remind me to copy your history notes."

Devin was already there, his feet propped on a table in front of the muted movie displaying on the wall. And so was James. Though he sat as stiffly as if he'd been marched in at gunpoint.

"Relax, James," I said. "No one will ever know you're a sleeper agent."

I paused next to Devin. I hadn't seen him yet today. He was staring up at the flickering footage, filmed on an old factory floor and filled with industrious women. Only he wasn't really watching it. His eyes were simply pointed in that direction.

That was odd.

I nudged his shoulder with my hand. "You okay? Your loyal subjects were still on your side when you made your triumphant return, I bet."

He shook his head side to side, and then blinked up at me.

"Oh," he said, "yeah, fine. I didn't stay in long."

I wanted to question why he was acting so weird, but we were out of time. A look at the wall clock confirmed it.

"They should have arrived at the Advanced Research headquarters by now," I said, tossing my bag onto one of the tables and rummaging for the cap that activated the bug and served as receiver. "And be through security, which means we're on. You want to do the honors?" I asked Maddy, lifting the pen top.

"Go ahead," Maddy said, though I got the impression part of her wanted to say yes. Playing it cool in front of James, I bet. Someday he'd kick himself for not noticing her.

I shrugged and pushed the little depression on the end of the pen cap, and a red light blinked, a soft beep following. "That door locked?" I asked.

"Yes," Maddy responded immediately. Which was good,

because we would have a tough time explaining this to anyone who happened to klutz into the room.

I set the cap down on the table, positioning it so we would all have a good view. The audio crackled to life first, tinny with footsteps shuffling along a hallway, and to accompany a projection that popped into being, showing the infrared heat signatures detectable by the bug. Walking bodies, beating hearts, shuffling feet . . . Then they were all standing close together. They were in an elevator. Yes, definitely, because a few seconds later a series of regular beeps sounded and right after the last one, they were filing out of the tight space and along another hallway.

James stood and leaned in close to examine it. "Where did you—did you steal this from your dad? Your dad, the very important general who already hates the *Scoop*?"

"No, I didn't," I said. "I borrowed it."

James might have been skeptical, but he didn't call me a liar. Which was good, because I wasn't. I had every intention of putting the bug back where it belonged.

"What is it doing?" Maddy asked.

Devin hadn't said anything. I'd thought he'd be the one interested in the tech.

"Devin, you can probably guess how it works. You want to explain?" I tried to drag his personality out. Maybe he was depressed about losing the castle? But I didn't want to make the mistake of assuming he wasn't in the Warheads' mental crosshairs like Anavi had been.

"That's all right," he said, "you go on."

"Pretty simple, really," I said. "An audio-only bug is great for conversations, but useless if you might be looking to visit a place later or find something that the target has put in a safe or some other hiding spot in an office. This gen of infrared camera can shoot through fabric and let you see where your target goes within a location, how many bodies are in a room, stuff like that, not just what they say when they get there."

The Warheads appeared to be filing into a room, and so I was able to avoid any more questions from James by pointing to my ear and then the image. Now we'd discover how Advanced Research Laboratories was molding young minds every afternoon.

"This must be our newest recruit," a man's voice said.

The audio was as crisp as if he was in the library study room with us. The tinny quality had vanished. Another feature of this particular bug model: it compensated for noise impurities. Too bad the latest iteration hadn't been in Dad's cabinet, because it boasted clearer visuals.

"Sir, yes, sir," a chorus of voices said in sync.

"The Warheads?" Maddy said.

I nodded, frowning. I'd never heard them speak at the same time before, no overlapping.

"You don't have to do that," the man's voice said, in a sympathetic way. "Or call me sir. Sorry, but it's time to get you linked for real and into the sim. Hop up." Given his gentle tone and that he sounded like he dreaded the next step, he might be the researcher expressing doubts on the private forum SmallvilleGuy had gained access to.

The heat signatures that were gathered around the man spread into a wide circle around him, then sat down one by one in a coordinated way. If I was right, they were facing the center of a large room.

The sympathetic man was joined by a trio of other people, who went by each of the seated Warheads in turn. The heat signatures didn't make movements crystal clear, but they were plain enough that we could see that the man's helpers appeared to be leaning in as they stopped at each Warhead, touching the sides of their heads. It was easy to guess they were hooking holosets over the Warheads' ears.

"Why would they use regular holosets?" I asked.

No one answered, though Maddy shrugged.

The lab couldn't *just* want them playing the game? They could do that anywhere. Anytime. There had to be some twist on the tech happening.

The hues of the splotchy forms were growing brighter around the circle. Heating up. Like they were nervous.

No, not nervous—excited.

Like they were excited for whatever was about to happen.

Three of the standing heat signatures left the room. From the slightly tilted angle, I could tell Anavi's backpack was on the floor, presumably next to her seat. Maybe she was a softer hue than the others? But it didn't last. Soon, she was the brightest of all. A red so vivid it might have burned to the touch.

The first man had remained in the room, and he said, "Get ready, guys." And then, "Linking subjects now."

A series of tones sounded—an eerie pattern that

repeated—and each of the Warheads' heads seemed to lean forward, like there was something they wanted to see better.

Whatever they were looking at must have been inside the real-sim their holos projected, though, because the center of the floor remained empty of any heat signatures. No one besides the Warheads was in the room except the man off to one side. I noticed that he had raised his hands to cover his ears.

The tones that sounded were almost familiar. Almost, but not quite, and they finally concluded, replaced by several moments of quiet.

The man said, "Cue up today's test scenario. In three, two, one."

CHAPTER 20

When the countdown ended, the man strode over to Anavi and crouched in front of her. "You're safe here. Don't worry. The link gets easier."

"I'm fine," was the murmured response in her familiar voice, a suggestion of irritation in it.

The others echoed it around the room, magnifying the irritated tone. "We're fine."

"No need to pretend. You're not that closely linked." The man chided them, still sounding sympathetic. "We need to be able to record accurate results. The boss will notice if we don't."

He muttered afterward, purposely muffled in his elbow, so they wouldn't hear him. But the bug picked it up: "Wish I could pretend I didn't need this job."

He thought they were pretending to be more closely linked than they were? Ha.

"He doesn't know," I said.

"Doesn't know what?" Maddy asked.

Oops. I hadn't meant to say that out loud. Not yet. Not when it would only lead to a discussion of mad science, and me possibly losing them as friends.

"What were those sounds?" James asked.

"Don't know. We should listen," I said to cover my slip-up. I was as curious about the tones as he was. But I knew one thing. It was becoming obvious that the experiment was having more of an effect on the Warheads than even the people running it were aware. And that at least this worker was troubled by the results, despite being ignorant of the full extent.

The Warheads weren't just recruiting and toying with fellow students.

They were toying with the people running the experiment.

The next fifteen minutes should have been dull but instead were riveting. We watched as the Warheads remained motionless in their seats, while the man running the experiment gave them verbal cues about moving through a landscape.

"Figure out a way into the compound," he'd say, and then clap reluctant encouragement a few moments later, at their apparent proficiency in doing so.

Then, "Now find the third floor and defuse the bomb. With no—or, wait, the prompt says with minimal civilian casualties." He watched what we couldn't, shaking his head occasionally.

It did sound like they were running them through a real-sim environment. But it wouldn't make sense to go to all this effort if it was only the game.

"Devin?" I asked.

After a lag, he said, "Yeah?"

"You ever play in the afternoon, sneak in a session?" I asked.

He seemed more like his normal self when he answered. "Sure. Excellent time to accumulate loot. Not as many people in our area on then."

"Did you ever see the Warheads in the game at this time of day?"

"Not in a long time," he said. "And I would have noticed."

"If they're not in the game, then what are they doing?" James asked.

I didn't have an answer.

In the projection from the lab, the man asked, "How are you guys so much better today? Is it the new recruit? Whatever it is, the control room says this is going to affect the demo schedule."

The Warheads were still playing—or whatever they were doing—as far as the heat signatures showed. None of them moved.

But they did answer him:

"We're stronger. We're going to keep getting stronger."

The man held a hand up to his own forehead, as if he'd been struck by a sudden, shooting headache.

I had a suspicion what that might be. My hand pressed against my own temple in semi-sympathetic memory.

"Okay," he said, subdued, "time to bring them out of the link. Nice and easy, guys."

The eerie tones sounded again, repeating over and over, and once more the Warheads leaned forward like they were trying to get a closer look at something . . .

The overhead light popped on above us and I wasn't the only one who jolted in surprise. The *brrrring* of the bell that signaled the end of the period followed.

Good timing, as far as I was concerned.

"Someone else has the room now," Maddy said. She turned to me. "What were they doing? Did you find out what we needed to know?"

I reached out to turn off the receiver, considering how to answer. I'd wanted this to make everything clear. But there was no way they'd interpret what we witnessed—strange though it might be—as something more-than-strange. Strange Skies' brand of strange. This wasn't like what I had seen in Kansas. If I was in their place, I'd cling to the most normal explanation available.

And so I still couldn't reveal my suspicions without them deciding that I was crazy. But I did know what *I* had to do next. *I* had to scheme my way inside the shiny headquarters of Advanced Research Labs.

SmallvilleGuy could have snooped out more details about the nature of the experiment over the weekend. I should get him the recording from the bug too.

Plus, I missed him. This was the longest we'd gone without chatting since we met.

"Almost," I said. "I just need to talk to Perry later. Get him to give us a little more time."

"Well, that's no big deal then," James said, not going light on the sarcasm.

Devin was staring where the receiver's projection had been. I nudged his shoulder again as I stowed it. "Wake up, sleepy king. Time to go to class."

"Oh, right." He shot me a weak grin.

I wasn't nearly far enough ahead of my bad luck. I was going to have to run faster, or I was afraid it would catch up with me.

With all of us.

*

When we left the library, I waved and hurried away . . . and then found a spot to lurk across from the entrance to the principal's office. There was a bare blue patch of wall between a classroom door and a line of lockers that proved the perfect vantage point for my purposes. Principal Butler had a rep for not hanging around in his lair much in the afternoon, preferring to run his charm offensive in the halls.

I knew it was risky to keep skipping so much class. But, hey, I *would* go to this one, just a little late. If things worked out the way I wanted, I'd even have a note to cover it.

There were a lot of things I was worried about. Another call to my dad about problems at school was on the list, but not high enough to trump what had happened to Anavi and the experiment. Definitely not high enough to trump the possibility of me and my friends—yes, I was thinking of them that way, even James, whether they thought of me as theirs or not—losing the *Scoop*. Or Devin being targeted by the Warheads.

I waited a long, tense ten minutes, but finally Butler emerged. My bad luck kept a low profile, and he went in the opposite direction. I hadn't made a contingency plan in case he had walked toward me, and, wow, that was sloppy amateur hour, wasn't it?

Maybe I was more worried than I'd realized. Scattered.

This part I had to do exactly right. It started with nice blonde Ronda, who I turned a smile on for as I swept through the door to the reception area. I'd discovered that the other administrative staff were housed in a less centrally located office suite. Butler didn't like anyone getting too close to his laurels.

"Is the principal around?" I asked, as if I didn't have a clue.

Ronda was a smiler by nature, and returned mine automatically. But hers faltered at the question. "You set him off the other day."

Poor Ronda had been the one who called me to the office, and the one who'd had to summon the Warheads after.

I took a few more steps toward her desk, leaned in and spoke softer, conspiratorial. "He's kind of a bully, isn't he?"

Ronda's smile departed completely.

"Look, I just want to leave an apology note in his office." I flipped open the top of my messenger bag and pulled out the pink envelope I had prepared over the weekend.

"You can leave it with me," Ronda said.

"If you, say, stepped out to use the ladies' room, he'd never know you even saw me. I'll be quick. I just want to leave this. It'll put him in a good mood. I swear."

For a moment I was sure Ronda's Stockholm syndrome was about to kick in and she'd say no. But she shrugged, gathered her purse and said, "I like you, so fine. I take a break every day about now. Need a little afternoon sugar fix. Powdered white donuts are my favorite, if you ever need to know."

She crooked her head as she passed me on her way to the door. I didn't disrupt her momentum with a thanks. I sailed up the hall to Butler's office with my envelope.

The apology inside was a cover—and more. I hoped it'd do its job and I could do mine in the time it bought and paid for. Even if I was also worried about pulling off the rest of my plan. It was risky to take on Advanced Research Laboratories on my own. Dangerous even to contemplate it. That didn't change the fact it was my logical next step.

Butler's office was still stuffy and over-decorated. I hoped his password was the same too.

Of course I could always flip to the page in his leather notebook to get the new one, if he'd changed it. I pushed his chair back, not willing to grace the same seat as him, and bent to the keyboard. I typed in the word *Macho* (seriously) and the numerals 1 and 2. And I was in.

His inbox was open, and I searched through his contacts for ARLabs.com, the company's domain. I recognized the CEO's name.

"Why, I think I will create a new message to my good friend, Mr. Steve Dirtbag Jenkins, aka the boss," I murmured as I pulled up a blank email and started typing.

The subject line read: Interview with Student (puff piece).

The email itself was a thing of beauty. I figured Butler would have done his due diligence to make sure his pals at ARL weren't surprised by the story about Anavi and the Warheads in the *Scoop*. And so I informed Mr. Jenkins, CEO, that trouble-some new student reporter Lois Lane had seen the light—as had her extremely powerful father—and that she'd agreed to make it up to the Principal by doing a story that very week on the charitable relationship the company had with the school, their largesse in mentoring students with new computers, nau-seatingly kiss-up-y, etc. I provided my own email address and said the student would be in contact directly that afternoon to confirm the appointment tomorrow at 12:45. I added a grace note about racquetball, because it seemed like the kind of non-sport Principal Butler would think rich people were into.

After that, what remained was a satisfying click on Send and then quickly setting a new rule that instructed the principal's inbox to forward any replies—or emails at all, actually—from Mr. Jenkins, CEO, or anyone else at the ARLabs.com domain straight to me and delete the originals unread.

"Now, that is a job well done," I said, signing out and prop-ping the envelope on his keyboard.

I helped myself to an excused tardy slip off Ronda's desk on my way out. That would buy me the extra time to duck back into the library and send SmallvilleGuy an update on what we'd seen and heard, along with a file of the bug's recording in case he wanted to check it out. My parents had given my computer back that morning as I had left for school, but they still had my phone.

Other than that, making my appointment with the CEO was all I had to deal with.

Well, and Perry.

CHAPTER 21

I shouldn't have been so cavalier about Perry. When I arrived in the Morgue, he was waiting in that coffin cave of an office at the back of the room.

I didn't bother stopping to chat, because I had no idea how I should answer the questions my *Scoop* colleagues were bound to ask about the things we'd seen and heard from the lab and what *our* next move should be. I didn't want them making any move that put them in danger or would get them in trouble again. And I didn't want them deciding I was too nuts to be friends with.

My reckoning with Perry gave me a brief stay on talking to them. As I entered the cave, the first thing he said was, "I haven't gotten a withdrawal of the retraction request."

Not wanting to spill everything in a heartbeat, I shut the

door behind me so the others couldn't eavesdrop. I made my way over to the dusty chair and sat.

Remember how he treated you like an equal? Act like one, Lane. Don't wuss out.

"I need more time," I said. "Not much, but a little. A day?"

"What can you do in a day that you haven't in the last few?" Perry sat back in his chair, skeptical. "Legal will have my head if her parents sue. Or if Butler makes too much noise about the story being inaccurate. *Or* if your dad registers a complaint. In fact, tell me a way this doesn't go wrong."

"I will. There's more going on here, Perry," I said, noting how his eyebrows ticked up at my use of his name. He'd *told* me to use it. "I have—well, we have, all of us—uncovered evidence that Butler is in bed—figuratively, not literally, because I do not want that image in my brain—with a company called Advanced Research Laboratories. And that Anavi is only asking for the retraction because she's been added to an experiment they're doing with the students who were bullying her. It's why Butler lets the Warheads get away with . . . murder."

"What kind of experiment?" he asked. "It better not be another charity thing the company is doing if you're asking for more time."

"Did I say experiment with? I meant experiment *on*."

His eyebrows rose. "Keep talking."

"I don't have all the details yet, but I can tell you that I'm sure it's not harmless. And it's not the kind of thing that should be happening, with or without the principal's support. Give me one more day."

"Listen," Perry said, "my dad wasn't a fan of my decision to become a journalist either. But this is a calling."

"I know. I hear it. Loud and clear."

"One more day?"

I nodded.

"I'll smooth it over with Legal. But at the end of tomorrow—no, by *this* time tomorrow—we'd better have something to cover us. The retraction must be gone *or* we have to present proof that the request came in on illegitimate grounds. A new related story like the one you're working on would do it."

I was smart enough to get out while I was ahead. I stood. "Thank you, Perry."

"Good luck, Lane."

The one thing I could never count on. Oh well.

"How'd it go?" Maddy asked in a loud whisper when I neared the desks. Her space-age quality headphones hung around her neck, faint music audible from them. James was waiting for my answer too.

"He's giving us a little more time. A day."

Devin said nothing, staring at his monitor. I wanted to believe there was something on it. I was afraid if I checked and there wasn't, I'd lose my nerve. That would mean they had Devin too. Or that they were close to it.

All the more important for me to finish this.

So I went to my desk and pulled out my laptop instead of logging onto the *Scoop*'s.

"What's the plan?" Maddy asked.

James was watching me, his eyes narrowed speculatively,

like he wondered what I was up to. He might be a decent reporter after all.

"Wait and see what they do tomorrow at school," I said, knowing it was weak. "What else can we do?"

Neither of them looked convinced. I needed to change the subject and go back on distraction detail. "I forgot to tell you that I really liked your playlist, Maddy. But how come the bands on it weren't the ones whose shirts you wear? Were the bands on the playlist your favorites or are those different and you didn't think I'd like them?"

Maddy said, "Oh yeah, they're different," and mumbled something that might have been "you're welcome," then slipped her headphones back on. She went back to typing away.

I had meant to distract Maddy, maybe get her talking about bands. I hadn't thought that she'd be *that* thrown off by the question. It worked out, though.

James glanced from me over to where Devin remained lost in his own little world. "Lois," James said, pitching his voice low, and looking back at me, "I'm not here because of my dad. At least, not because he wants me to be. I'm here because the journalists who took him down were the heroes of the piece. And I need the paycheck. There was a reason he was embezzling. He made a lot of bad investments, and it didn't leave much left for Mom and me. I need this to last, so *you* need to keep your promises."

I blinked at him. James was here because he *wanted* to be here? He needed the money?

(We were getting paid?)

My mind was officially blown.

He didn't say anything more and didn't seem to expect me to answer. He returned to working at his computer, typing away. Leaving me free to write Dirtbag Jenkins, CEO, a lovely email and send it, telling him that I'd be at his offices at 12:45 the next day as promised by Principal Butler, and I looked forward to meeting him.

I required a slight lead on the Warheads for what I had in mind—at a minimum, getting proof of what was going on in that lab. Whatever it turned out to be.

Then I turned on my email auto-reply to be safe. If he couldn't reach me or Butler, I'd be able to play dumbbell if anyone at the offices said the appointment had been canceled when I showed up. Not that I expected he would cancel. He'd been assured it was a puff piece and that I had an important father.

Next I signed in to chat to see if SmallvilleGuy had listened to the recording yet. I couldn't wait until later.

I only had one day. Desperate times called for chatting in front of the others and trying not to make any goofy faces.

SkepticGirl1: *You around? Get my message?*

The little italicized script popped up that indicated SmallvilleGuy was there and typing.

SmallvilleGuy: *Missed you too.*

I smiled.

SkepticGirl1: *I didn't say I missed you.*

SkepticGirl1: *But I did.*

SmallvilleGuy: *Good, because I was about to feel dumb.*

SkepticGirl1: *Why?*

SmallvilleGuy: *For staging a picture of Shelby and Nellie Bly in jail—like you were all weekend.*

He sent across the photo and I cracked up. He'd staged it in a barn, through a gate so that metal bars were like a jail cell (sort of), and the black and white baby calf was standing on the other side, a cranky-looking giant cow behind her (Bess, no doubt), and Shelby gazing up at her adoringly with a big dog grin.

I shouldn't be laughing. A glance around told me the others thought I'd lost it. There was nothing to laugh about. We were down to the wire.

My heart beat quicker.

Because SmallvilleGuy was trying to lighten things for me. He'd thought of this over the weekend, assuming I'd be driven mad by being stuck in lockup, knowing that Monday would bring its own drama after what had happened in the game.

It was the sweetest thing. I tried to come up with a clever way to say that, but I couldn't, so I stuck with the truth.

SkepticGirl1: *That might be the sweetest thing anyone's ever done for me.*

SmallvilleGuy: *I figured you'd need something to smile about. And you're a sucker for cute animals. (Don't worry, I won't tell anyone. You're still the toughest person I know.)*

Before I could answer *that* . . .

SmallvilleGuy: *Anavi hasn't withdrawn her request?*

SkepticGirl1: *No, not yet. You have any bright ideas about what they're up to at the lab?*

SmallvilleGuy: *Did you tell the others everything? About how they can mess with other people's heads?*

I sighed. If only.

SkepticGirl1: *I couldn't. There was nothing that tipped over the line that would make them believe in mad science.*

SmallvilleGuy: *Lois . . .*

He was typing, and then typing, and then typing some more. But when he posted his message, it was short. More deleted things I'd never see.

SmallvilleGuy: *I hate the idea of you going up against these guys alone.*

I gnawed my lip, tapping a finger on the edge of the keyboard.

I hated it too.

But I would do it anyway. The next day, in fact.

SkepticGirl1: *I need to get in there.*

SmallvilleGuy: *If they're willing to experiment on human beings . . .*

SkepticGirl1: *This could be dangerous? I know, which is why I'm not taking anyone else along. I can handle it.*

SkepticGirl1: *You and me, remember? We protect people. We do what we have to do.*

SkepticGirl1: *At least, that's what I think. You going to tell me it's not true? That you'd do anything different in my place?*

SmallvilleGuy: *I don't like it. Just wait. Give it time.*

I shook my head before I remembered he couldn't actually see me.

SkepticGirl1: *Time's up. They said they're getting stronger and the lab guy seemed to agree.*

SmallvilleGuy: *Right, about that. What you sent helped. I did some more article searches. I'm willing to bet that Project Hydra is a new application of the real-sim tech. The original creator of Worlds had all these theories that were considered "out there" around group gaming and remapping neural pathways. He believed that the right auditory stimulus paired with the right real-sim imagery could do it. He gave a speech once saying he believed people's brains could be rewired to work together and create a whole new, smarter consciousness during the game. And then disconnected just as easily with a different set of audiovisual cues.*

SkepticGirl1: *Those tones we heard. They leaned forward during them both times. They weren't just listening, it was like they were looking at something too.*

SmallvilleGuy: *Exactly. We can't see what they were seeing, but I think it's probably a special sandbox real-sim environment not all that different than the game, and there's a visual cue in there that goes with those tones. But the tones were the same both times. I checked. If he was right, every time they see and hear the cue, it's making the connection stronger. From what I can tell, the lab guys don't even realize they aren't disconnecting the link. They have no idea they're connecting it more strongly at the end of the session.*

SkepticGirl1: *Strong enough to stick outside the lab by accident? That makes sense. The guy obviously didn't believe they were linked before they got there. The Warheads must be able to keep the new minds in line until the real link is put in place at the lab. That would mean it—this group consciousness—is growing on its own, right? That's why the Warheads are recruiting. That's what they called Anavi. A recruit.*

SmallvilleGuy: *The creator thought it was possible to maintain the link, but that there were ways around it. He didn't think people would want to live as part of a hive mind outside the game. He also theorized that the mind protects itself—that if a linked group was disconnected during the* *audiovisual cue by a hard interruption then the neural pathways would seal themselves back up permanently.*

If I understood it right, this was the best news of the day.

SkepticGirl1: *Then there's a way to stop it.*

SmallvilleGuy: *I hope so. What they're doing isn't right. And I got the sense on the forum that at least the one researcher doesn't want to be doing any of this, that he knows it's wrong.*

SkepticGirl1: *Agreed. It seems like it's got to be the guy in the audio on the bug, Mr. Sympathetic. Is the creator involved in this too, do you think? Could he be using the same tones on purpose?*

SmallvilleGuy: *No, he died last year. My guess is they were only able to get their hands on his research after that. What's available publicly is just theories, no details.*

SkepticGirl1: *Then the boss they report to has to be the CEO of ARL. We were on the right path all along. They're taking ARL's old ideas about syncing up a unit and mashing them up with the new tech. I can't figure out how they think they can use the Warheads this way and get away with it . . . There's still a missing piece.*

SkepticGirl1: *But I'll find it. I'm going in there tomorrow.*

SmallvilleGuy: *Promise me you won't go alone. If they're your friends then you can trust them to have your back.*

SkepticGirl1: *And they can trust me to have theirs.*

SmallvilleGuy: *Lois, it's not safe.*

SkepticGirl1: *The only one who signed up for this is me. End of story. (Well, a whole new story, hopefully.)*

I jumped in my chair when Maddy cleared her throat. Loudly.

James and Maddy—and even Devin—sat in their tribunal formation, a straight line together watching me.

SkepticGirl1: *Gotta go.*

I signed off and said, "What?"

"Who were you arguing with?" James asked.

"And don't say nobody or that you weren't, because you were," Maddy said. "Or at least starting to. I know argument face when I see it. And you were flirting before. Don't deny that either." She gave me a look that let me know there would be a private interrogation about that later.

Which was okay with me. I'd love to have someone I could talk things over with. See if she thought SmallvilleGuy and I were just friends . . . or something more.

But when I opened my mouth to speak, Maddy went on before I could get a word out: "Was the argument about what we heard and saw today in the study room?"

Devin said, "Lois, it's time to stop keeping secrets from us. The Warheads . . . they can do things, can't they? Things they shouldn't be able to."

It was nice to see Devin acting more like himself, asking questions again. But I gathered my hands in my lap, my palms gone ice cold.

There was no good move here. If I lied, didn't tell them anything, sure, they'd be safe—probably—but they'd never trust me again. If I told them the truth, they'd—almost certainly—believe that I was a full-time resident of crazytown.

I knew what I wanted to do. Sometimes you just had to be brave.

CHAPTER 22

I faced them without blinking. If I wasn't going to hide the truth anymore, I might as well see the moment they started to doubt me.

"You're going to think I'm completely crazy," I said.

"No," Maddy said, "we're not. Don't you get it?"

No matter how animated James got, his glossy brown hair stayed perfectly in place. "We're not stupid, Lois. Gamers don't read each other's minds. Not normally."

They were willing to listen. They were receptive to hearing what I'd been so certain would make me an outcast of the highest order.

"That's it," I said. "Sounds like you were figuring it out already. They might not be mind readers, not exactly, but they are sharing a consciousness. They're connected to each other."

I paused, then finished, "What we saw and heard from the lab is an experiment using real-sim tech to link the Warheads into one many-headed mind. Project Hydra in action."

"To what end?" James asked with a frown.

"Now *that* part I'm going to have to get a little more up close and personal to find out." *And to stop.*

I waited, expecting that even though they'd said they would believe me, hearing it out loud would prove too much. That they'd tell me to hold on a sec, while they called my parents and informed them that I'd lost my mind.

Devin said, "I hope you have a plan."

It took me a moment to figure out what to say.

"I always have a plan." And I started to modify mine, which had been in the early stages. Having backup when I went into Advanced Research Laboratories would be better. SmallvilleGuy was right about that. "You guys are sure about this?"

They agreed, nodding without even looking at each other.

"We have to save the *Scoop*," James said.

I was more than on board with that sentiment. "Agreed. So—"

"Wait," Devin said. "Before you start, I'm volunteering."

I didn't like the sound of where this was going. "I thought you all were."

He took a breath and said, "Yeah, but you're going to need a man on the inside."

"I can't let you do that."

The response came in reflex. But even as I said it, I

remembered what I'd thought about Devin before. That he was the one on the staff most like me.

He set his chin and shoulders. "Not your call," he said.

There was no point in arguing. "I don't like it."

"Noted," he said. He hesitated.

His face changed and I recognized the expression on it. It was close to the one Anavi had been wearing the first day I met her, like he was about to tell us something he'd rather not, but had no choice.

"And you should be aware that I know what I'm probably agreeing to here," he said. "The Warheads have been . . . I think they're trying to . . . "

He didn't want to say it, and so I said it for him. "They've been messing with your mind. Inside your head, right?"

He didn't respond, just looked at me. A long, hard look.

"I'm so sorry," I said. "I couldn't be sure. The guys at the lab didn't seem to notice that their little experiment is hungry to grow. That the new people are being *forcibly* recruited. Not that it's likely they'd care if they did know." With the possible exception of the sympathetic man. "First Anavi. And now you. I never wanted anything bad to happen to either of you, not because of me."

"They've been bothering me since the other morning," Devin said. "After we ran the story. And then that attack on my castle—they told me they were coming after me. And they did. But it wasn't your fault. It's because I play *Worlds* and I work here."

I shook my head. "I hate these guys so much."

"But Anavi's one of them now," Maddy pointed out.

"You're right," I said. "And she said one was a friend of hers before. Maybe they're all decent enough and it's just the experiment. I don't know." I caught Devin's eye. "You ready for the plan?"

"You knowing about what's been happening makes me feel less like I'm losing my neurons," Devin said. "I'm ready."

"So, you'll be our man on the inside. It *will* be useful to throw them off and to have you there. But only as long as you're sure that you still want to volunteer to infiltrate them?" I asked.

"I am."

"And Maddy, you and James will be our backup," I said. "That okay?"

Maddy shrugged one shoulder, casting a shy glance toward James. Who didn't even catch it. James said, "Tell me what that means."

"It means you two are going to have one of the most important jobs of all. You're going to be the ones who bail us out if things go sideways, off the rails. You'll show up at—" I paused. "Devin, I don't think you should hear me explain this part. Just in case."

"You mean just in case I turn actual traitor?" he asked.

There was a tense silence. That was exactly what I was worried about. I shouldn't let him do this.

The Warheads were getting stronger, and they wanted Devin. Did he understand what it would mean if they succeeded in getting him?

But he must have. He was nodding. "I've felt what they can do. Okay. Just in case."

"Just in case." I didn't even like to contemplate the "in case" we were talking about. "Best if we keep all the elements separate anyway, so that I'm the only one who can really go down for this. I'll know the full picture, no reason for you guys to. Plausible deniability—you can claim I told you to do something you thought was innocent if we get caught. Devin, you and I can debrief after I talk to these guys."

Devin didn't protest, but he gave a lost look around, like he wasn't sure what to do. "Should I leave?"

Maddy rolled her chair over to her desk and grabbed her fancy headphones, handed them to Devin. "Noise canceling," she said. "Now you can stay."

He dutifully put them on and went back to his desk. I worked out with Maddy and James what their jobs would be the next day.

I had one more partner in crime left to convince. And he was the only person besides me who would get to know everything.

★

One of my top five favorite smells greeted me when I got home, still worried but feeling better. A plan always made me feel better. As did pizza.

"What happened to merit a pizza night on a Monday?" I called, heading for the kitchen. Hopefully, it wasn't to celebrate my imminent departure for military school. I was feeling cautious optimism that Dad and I might have reached an understanding in his office the other night.

Two delivery boxes were open on the counter and Mom had broken out the paper plates. No dishes to wash was a part of the pizza night tradition. Lucy sat at the table tucking into what was probably her fourth slice. She had the metabolism of a hummingbird on an energy drink. Dad was there too, already home and out of uniform in jeans and a T-shirt.

"We hadn't had one since we got here," he answered. "Everything go all right today?"

He meant had I met the deadline for proving the story was true.

Not yet, but almost. If everything went like it was supposed to.

But I didn't feel like explaining about Perry agreeing to an extension. And it wasn't like I *could* explain the rest: *Oh, yeah, tomorrow I'm going to bluff my way into a fancy lab under false pretenses to expose a secret experiment. And later I have to sneak the bug I borrowed from you back into your office. Nothing for you to worry your pretty little genius military mind about.*

"Everything's fine," I said. "You guys mind if I take mine up to my room?"

Mom and Dad exchanged one of those inscrutable parent looks they should patent to torture criminals. Finally, Mom said, "Figured you'd be sick of the four walls of your room after the weekend . . . but if that's what you want. You shouldn't hold a grudge, hon. We're your parents and we love you."

"I know, and that's not it. Just a lot of work to do. Swear." I hesitated, then asked, "Can I have my phone back too?"

After another long, silent consult with Dad, my mom said, "It's in your room, on your desk."

"Thanks," I said, and loaded up a plate with two—better make it three—slices before they could change their minds about letting me skip family time.

I had to move slower than I wanted on my way upstairs in order to keep the plate level. SmallvilleGuy and I had left things in an unsettled state that afternoon. But I'd caved on letting the others in on things, so maybe he'd approve. Maybe he'd agree to pitch in more.

My plan needed him. I was afraid that what I had in mind might not work for him, though.

After I locked my bedroom door, I deposited the plate on my desk, removed my laptop from my bag, and slid into my chair. My palms were slightly damp—nerves—but I ignored them. I opened the laptop and keyed in my passwords, pulled up the chat window, saw his name, and only then took a giant bite of pepperoni pizza.

SkepticGirl1: *Metropolis has been holding out on me.*

SkepticGirl1: *Their pizza is amaaaaazing.*

In the chat window, there was no typing message, no nothing, for half a slice. Then . . .

SmallvilleGuy: *You're not mad at me for fixating on the not going in alone thing?*

SkepticGirl1: *Nope.*

SkepticGirl1: *You were right. I told them and they believed me. We have a plan.*

SmallvilleGuy: *That's good.*

SkepticGirl1: *They don't know my whole plan, though.*

SmallvilleGuy: *Why not?*

I inhaled, let the breath out with a sigh. I reminded myself again: sometimes you had to be brave.

SkepticGirl1: *Do you think you could figure out a way into the real-sim sandbox environment where they're running the experiment? Get a character version of you into it, I mean. Who could then interfere with the visual part of the cue. You do already have a way to contact the guy we think is most likely to help us disrupt the experiment. He might be willing to steer you in the right direction.*

I stared at the screen so hard my eyes felt like they were burning. Waiting and waiting. He wasn't typing for the longest time, and then he was.

SmallvilleGuy: *Maybe.*

The unenthusiastic reaction was what I'd warned myself about. So why did it make a disappointed pang shoot through my chest? I couldn't pretend it was the pepperoni.

SkepticGirl1: *Devin's going in as one of the Warheads—acting like he is one—but if what you said before is true . . . I don't want to just get pictures and expose what they're doing. I want to stop it. Break the link. Set the Warheads free.*

SkepticGirl1: *And it seems by the founder guy's logic, what we have to do is disrupt the linking process during the visual and audio sequence that is the cue. The one that's been strengthening them would probably be best—so we need to disrupt it at the end of the session.*

SmallvilleGuy: *Inside and outside the environment, you mean. That's why you were asking if I can find a way inside?*

SkepticGirl1: *Seems like the best bet to cover all bases. I can handle the outside. But I need someone inside the sim environment to work with me, and you're the only one I think can do it. This might be Anavi's only chance to not be one of them forever. Maybe some of the rest of them deserve saving too.*

I didn't give him time to respond.

SkepticGirl1: *So . . . can you help me?*

There was nothing to do but wait and see if he'd come through.

SmallvilleGuy: *Lois.*

SmallvilleGuy: *I can't risk getting caught in there. Even as a character.*

SmallvilleGuy: *If they traced me somehow and came here . . .*

He wasn't going to help.

I knew this was a possibility. But it didn't hurt any less because of that. It might have hurt more.

I'd wanted to be wrong.

SkepticGirl1: *I'm not going to bother asking who you are this time.*

SmallvilleGuy: *You don't know what I'd give to be there for you. To tell you the truth.*

I thought back to what he'd said earlier, when he was trying to convince me to do what he just said he'd love to—to tell the others the truth. He'd said my friends would have my back.

He was right. Any real friend would.

Were we real friends? I had always believed that we were. I *felt* like we were that, at a minimum. He knew more about me—and knew me better—than anyone else in the world. The idea that my sense of what we meant to each other could be fake, that it wasn't true . . . I was not prepared for that.

SmallvilleGuy: *I can't. I can't risk it. Lois, I wish I could.*

I set down the pizza slice. My eyes were burning, but I took a deep breath. I wouldn't cry.

SkepticGirl1: *If it's too much of a risk then it's too much.*

SkepticGirl1: *I'll send you the details anyway, just so you have them. You'll be the only one besides me who knows everything. Maybe what I can do on my own disrupting on the outside will be enough. I'll just have to go big.*

I visualized the inside of Dad's cabinet. I'd return the bug, but there was something else I'd have to borrow from his stockpile of goodies this time around. I could put it back after all this was over.

SkepticGirl1: *I'm taking along a prism flare.*

SmallvilleGuy: *You'll be careful, though?*

The hits kept on coming. He hadn't changed his mind, even though he must have known how disappointed I was, and how much I needed him to come through.

But I had to pretend that it didn't hurt. When bravery didn't turn out like you wanted, there was always that option. The fact he couldn't see me would make it easier. Besides, sometimes it felt like I'd been playing pretend my whole life.

SkepticGirl1: *I will. I promise . . .*

SmallvilleGuy: *What?*

SkepticGirl1: *That I'll be as careful as I can.*

SmallvilleGuy: *Not comforting.*

SkepticGirl1: *We all have our flaws. Yours is being a mystery. And a worrier. By tomorrow night everything will be back to normal.*

Except I didn't know what our chats would be like after this. This situation might change everything between us. And Dad probably still had those military school brochures handy, if the plan crashed and burned.

But SmallvilleGuy couldn't see any of that.

I had to keep pretending. Everything was fine between us. Just fine.

SkepticGirl1: *Unless, of course, I'm a brainless hive mind zombie hooked up to some kind of devil robotron in the basement of a secret lab. Then I'll have to take a rain check.*

SmallvilleGuy: *Not funny.*

SkepticGirl1: *Hilarious, right? Talk tomorrow. Wish us luck.*

But he didn't. He didn't have time to. I logged off first, not able to fake it anymore.

He'd declined to lend his hand and come to my aid. That meant I didn't know exactly how tomorrow would play out, how the plan would go. If it would work.

Operation Save the *Scoop* and Destroy the Hydra.

I finished my pizza and typed SmallvilleGuy the message that I'd said I would—another just in case—describing how I envisioned the disruption inside and outside the simulation. I did it understanding that he wouldn't risk showing up in whatever the real-sim was the lab guys were running. Understanding that he wouldn't, but hoping that he would.

No one would ever know I had that hope but the two of us. It seemed harmless enough to hold on to it. In the meantime, I'd have to make my disruption outside the real-sim that much more effective.

I waited until Mom and Dad would be sound asleep and dreaming before I tiptoed downstairs to the study. The key was still hidden behind the picture frame with our family photo. I slipped the bug back into its spot, then removed the small cylinder of a prism flare.

I crept back upstairs and went to bed, but I didn't sleep much more than a wink. I couldn't stop thinking.

The problem with having friends was that you might lose them. Or they might get hurt.

CHAPTER 23

I hid behind my locker door to swap out my history book and notebook the next morning. Part one of the new plan wasn't so different than the one I had on my first day. Sort of. If I squinted and looked at it sideways.

I was supposed to keep a low profile at school, faithfully attending morning classes—so I wasn't risking a call home that would screw things up.

My intention was to fly so far under the radar that I avoided anyone's detection until after my trip to the lab. I was making like a stealth student (instead of a stealth bomber), and would try to keep my distance from the other *Scoop*ers as much as possible too. I'd purposely structured the plan so that if it failed—*please don't let it fail*—any blame would rest squarely with me.

So in one of the brief moments when I was at an easily-pinned-down-and-accosted location like my locker, Maddy showed up right next to me, vibrating with nervous energy. Her band T-shirt today was even more meta than the norm. The hot pink graffiti font on the gray shirt proclaimed My New Band Name.

They hadn't been on the playlist either.

Before I could ask about it or Maddy could so much as say hello, Principal Butler oozed over and stopped beside us. He was wearing the most self-satisfied version of his oily smile that I had seen yet. His suit today must have cost a month's salary, a faint blue pinstripe and a salmon tie, both in fabrics that shouted designer label.

"Miss Lane," he said, "I was surprised to get your note. Apology accepted. With this change of heart, I think you may do all right here after all."

Maddy's jaw dropped open, but thankfully she didn't say anything. I had neglected to fill the crew in on my apologetic smoke screen.

"Me too. Thanks for . . . " I swallowed. *Got to get out the words. Don't want him to suspect you're up to something.* "Thanks for being willing to do the bygones thing."

"The slate is clean," he said.

It seemed like the conversation should be over, but he lingered, unfortunately.

Maddy continued to gape at our exchange, although there was no indication he noticed she was there.

Good. Better if he forgot Maddy was associated with me.

This truce was destined to be short-lived, whether by implosion or explosion.

But I needed it to hold for now.

"Was there something else?" I asked, chipper.

"Your dad wasn't angry at me that you got in trouble, was he?" he asked.

"Only at me, so you're safe," I said. "You really sold him on the school. And how much you care about the students."

A soft snort came from Maddy's general vicinity.

"Glad to hear it," Principal Butler said. He meant it too. His self-satisfaction spiked, his shark-like quality in full effect. "I'd love to take him out for dinner—your whole family—to welcome you to Metropolis."

Nightmare.

"I'll tell Dad. But we better get to class now," I said, shutting my locker door on the conversation. "Don't want to be late."

"Now that's model student behavior," Butler said, beaming.

ARGH, no. Don't say anything, don't say anything.

The bell for first period rang and I pasted on a frozen smile and grabbed Maddy's arm, towing her away.

My smile stayed frozen when we ran smack into the Warheads. This time it was Maddy who did the pulling, tugging me over by the lockers to give them plenty of room to pass.

Anavi was in the middle of the pack, her face as smoothly blank as the rest, and . . . and . . . and . . .

Devin was behind her. Wearing black. Facial expression schooled into submission.

He gave every appearance of being assimilated. It was his role in the plan.

That didn't make it any easier to watch.

Especially since I was no longer convinced that my attempt would succeed at breaking the Hydra's neural bonds—not without SmallvilleGuy's participation. Devin was in real danger. We all were.

I couldn't wave away a surge of doubt. What if Devin's bland expression wasn't an act, but legitimately blank like the rest because they had him? Brain, line, and sinker. We should have worked out a signal.

He didn't even seem to notice Maddy and me. If the other Warheads did, they didn't bother to stop and mock. They glided past like slimy eels swimming toward their shark master, stopping only to greet Butler by lifting their hands in small waves as they moved by him too.

Even Butler looked uncomfortable at the sight of them.

They couldn't really get Devin so quickly, right? Part of the reason I hadn't fought harder against his suggestion was because with Anavi it had taken days.

Before Butler could turn and come after us for more awkward chitchat, I said, "Let's go," and started walking.

"I hope gamer boy knows what he's doing with them," Maddy said.

"Me too," I said. There was no way to determine if Devin was acting or not, not without blowing our entire plan.

And the plan *had* to work. I had to make sure it worked. Not just for Anavi's sake, but to protect Devin too.

*

I rattled through my morning classes like a runaway subway train, the same worries rumbling through my mind again and again. And again.

First Anavi, and now Devin? I needed to know if he was faking it or not.

No matter what Devin said last night about it not being my fault, he would never have gotten involved, never have become a target in the first place, if it wasn't for me.

You don't know that. That was what SmallvilleGuy would say, and he might be right. Devin was smart, into tech, a skilled *Worlds* player, *and* in the Warheads' comp sci class. Just like Anavi. Maybe he would have become a target for them anyway.

But, even so, I sped things along. And I'd allowed him to volunteer to take this risk.

It's my fault, one way or another. I can't fail.

I waited outside the cafeteria before lunch to catch Devin. If I could, I wanted to go into the next few hours comforted by the knowledge that he *was* faking, that they hadn't managed to steal into his mind. To steal his mind.

When I spotted him, he wasn't alone, but with Anavi and another boy who was one of them. This was the best shot I'd get to talk to him.

"Devin, got a sec?" I asked.

All three angled their heads to regard me at the same moment, and the stranger's face split into a slow, mocking grin. Anavi's did too.

But Devin's reaction was delayed. He shook his head before smirking.

"Devin?" I asked.

He took a step toward me. Anavi and the boy were frowning, and I saw a few more Warheads coming toward us from up the hall. The trio and I were also blocking the entrance to the cafeteria, but I stayed put and ignored the grumbles of the students around us.

"Devin, you good?" I asked softly.

He blinked, and for a single moment, he was there with me. It was the difference between someone looking past you and someone *seeing* you. "I can't fight," he said. "Too strong. You can't help." But he added a wink. That gave me hope that he was still fooling them.

For his ears only, I said, "Oh, I'm definitely helping. Hang on."

The other Warheads reached us, a small army in black that was more intimidating than Devin's inhuman troops in the game.

"Don't worry," I said, raising my voice. "He's all yours."

"Maybe you are . . ."

". . . wising up."

"He is ours."

"You're just lucky we don't want you."

"You are persistent at bothering us," Anavi said, but there was something in her tone that almost sounded like it could be regret.

The telltale push against my mind began, but Devin tossed

a dark "Learn to fear us" at me and turned to the cafeteria doors. The others snicker-laughed, but they followed him.

I had to assume he was still sticking with the plan.

I migrated through the cafeteria to the back corner, and Anavi's old table. A shy boy with floppy hair had taken my spot, so I sat at the end closest to the sprawling main floor—where I could keep an eye on the Warheads until it was time to leave. While I was sending a text to the taxi service, the chair beside mine scraped back and Maddy joined me.

If I was going to be a master of stealth, I'd have to get way better at hiding out in the open.

"Devin's creeping me out," Maddy said. "He is acting, right?"

"I think so," I said.

We watched the Warheads' table. Each member of the group, Devin included, had on a holoset and made the same barely visible movements of their heads or shoulders, the same occasional slight murmurs from their lips.

"Don't worry," I said, and I didn't know if I was trying to convince Maddy or myself. "Everything will be back to normal soon. The plan will work." Not that I believed in normal, strictly speaking. And I'd be a whole lot more confident if SmallvilleGuy wasn't going to be MIA.

"So . . ." Maddy lifted her hand to brush back a crimson strand of hair from her cheek, ducking her chin. "About what you asked me before?"

"Before?" I tried my best to focus on Maddy, but the Warheads were powering down and removing their holosets.

Their hands rose to pluck them off, and they placed the earpieces in front of themselves along the table.

Their eyelids fluttered, then closed. Devin's shut last.

Maddy was focused on the surface of our table, not seeing any of the holoset drama play out.

She said, "You know, when you asked about the bands, my shirts . . . why none of them were on the playlist?"

"Uh-huh," I said.

I looked back across the room. The Warheads had gone completely silent, a table-wide point of stillness in the bustling cafeteria. Like they were engaging in some bizarre exercise in lunch-table meditation.

"I make them," Maddy said. "The shirts. I make up the band names. They're bands I wish I could be in."

I wanted to respond to her, but I couldn't manage to speak. Because, surrounded by the meditating Warheads, Devin rose to his feet with a jerking motion, as if his limbs were outside his own control.

His hand jerked in that same way, his fingers rising until they were at his temple. I'd seen enough salutes to recognize one in progress.

I was looking dead at him, and he at me. But instead of lowering it after the mocking salute, he moved his hand and pointed from his eyes to me.

The threat was obvious. As was the fact that he hadn't been controlling his own motions.

The Warheads' eyes popped open again, and those slow grins crept over their faces. Devin's included.

So they knew I was watching. They couldn't know the whole plan—no one except SmallvilleGuy and I did. For this very reason.

I shifted to face Maddy.

Maddy, who made up her own fake bands every day and designed shirts for them, because she wanted to be in one.

"I am so sorry that I can't talk to you right now about what you just told me. I definitely will not tell anyone else, and I think you're amazing," I said. "But I have to get out of here. Try to stay away from the Warheads. We will talk later. After. Promise."

Maddy said, "Go."

James intercepted me halfway to the cafeteria doors. I had to pass the Warheads to get out, so I waved him closer.

"You're my cover," I said to James.

"All right," he said, and I gave him credit for not arguing.

Suddenly, I *was* afraid of them. I was afraid my plan might not be enough, not if they could do what I was sure I'd just witnessed, reach out to minds *and* control bodies. Not if they had Devin. What kind of experiment was this going to turn out to be?

Witnessing the details of their interactions at the lab would reveal all. What was the lab boss planning to use this linked consciousness for? Why was the researcher so disturbed by it?

James must have seen my attention flick to the Warheads' table—or been a good enough journalist to figure out it was them I was avoiding, even if he'd missed Devin's salute—because he moved so that he was between them and me.

"Now what?" he asked.

"We walk fast," I said.

And we did. I didn't even risk a backward look to see if they'd noticed me leaving.

Only when James and I were outside the cafeteria did I stop and breathe again.

"What's going on with Devin?" James asked. "I didn't really believe what you said about Anavi. Or what he said they'd been doing. Not completely. But now he . . . doesn't seem like himself."

It was more important than ever that I do this next part alone, without compromising any of the others more than I already had. The plan was in motion, and I had to stick with it.

Next stop, Advanced Research Laboratories for my meeting with Dirtbag Jenkins, CEO. Or, more precisely, to skip out on it and find Project Hydra.

"You should learn not to doubt, James. I'm sure Maddy will explain everything to you."

"Why can't you?"

I was already striding toward the exit at the end of the hall. "Me? Because I have to go. You know I've got somewhere to be."

I'd see them again later.

Depending, that was, on how things unfolded from here on out.

CHAPTER 24

I made tracks as fast as I could, striding with purpose and a jaunty wave past the security guard and off school grounds. And when I stopped to open the taxi door up the block, at the same spot where I'd met it the first time, I was surprised to find the same driver.

He waggled his eyebrows and wriggled fingers heavy with gold rings. "If it isn't the excellent tipper. Thought it might be you, so I volunteered. Headed to the Daily Planet Building again?"

Great, a driver with a good memory who would expect me to empty my pockets to tip him. So it went. I climbed in.

"Not today—not yet, at least. I'm going back to Advanced Research Laboratories HQ." I pulled out my phone so I could give him the address, but he screeched away from the curb.

"I know the place. Where you went the other day. You going inside this time?"

"You know it."

I was prepared for a jittery ride spent staring out the window at the city gliding past.

I really did like Metropolis—all these people bustling around, so many stories waiting to be told. I logged on to the messenger app in case SmallvilleGuy reached out, and my phone immediately buzzed in my hand.

SmallvilleGuy: *You're on your way?*

I glanced around, even though that was pointless. He wasn't anywhere nearby. He was in Kansas.

He just knew where I'd be roughly now because I sent him the details of the plan.

I decided to give him another reason to rethink not participating—the best reason, today's reason.

I sent back: *Yep. And they have Devin.*

SmallvilleGuy: *Wish there was more time. That I could be there in person.*

SkepticGirl1: *Don't worry about it. I'm the cavalry or a spy. Whichever works better.*

SmallvilleGuy: *Listened to audio again, 5 beeps on elevator. Floor Hydra's on must be 5.*

And then another popped up:

SmallvilleGuy: *Been private messaging with researcher, told him we were journalists & trying to stop the experiment.*

SkepticGirl1: *Nice cover story.*

Funny that it was the truth. I was a journalist, and I was definitely trying to stop the experiment.

SmallvilleGuy: *Thought you'd like it. I think disrupting the signal how you plan will work.*

Except the disruption wouldn't be exactly how I planned. It would only be me, outside the real-sim.

The taxi screeched to a halt at the curb in front of the tall, mirrored column where ARL made its home.

"Here you are, big spender," the driver said, "safe and sound."

I tapped out a final response: *Thanks for the floor. I'll try not to get hive minded.*

SmallvilleGuy: *I'm here for you. Good luck.*

The wish for luck was what I'd asked for before I signed off without warning the night before. But when he said he was here for me—he wasn't. I was on my own for this part.

Knowing the floor did help, though. And maybe the research guy would be more likely to pitch in if he could.

"Sweetheart, you getting out?" The driver extended his hand, the other pointing at the meter.

"I'm no one's sweetheart." But I dug out the money and gave him a bigger tip than I could afford.

I got out of the cab and looked up at the sleek building. It was too bad SmallvilleGuy had wished me luck. I was going to need something more than that. We all were.

Fortune never had done me any favors. There was no reason to expect it to start today.

The building had no revolving doors, only a trio of entrances that reflected an image of me back as I approached. No preview of what waited inside.

I squared my shoulders and entered a lobby with white walls and floors and steel furniture. The entire pristine and cold effect evoked some sterile minimalist ideal of a laboratory.

A suited woman with her hair pulled back and bright red lipstick sat behind a desk that had a sign-in book on it. Beyond her was a bank of three elevators. She didn't say a word of greeting as I approached.

Two could play the brusque game. I picked up the pen and leaned over the table to sign in. "I'm here to see the CEO," I said, but as I looked at the sign-in book, I choked on my next words. Well, started to choke. I recovered with a cough.

A few lines above where I was about to write my own name was a familiar one.

A very familiar one: General Sam Lane.

My finger traced across the line. He'd signed out already. Two hours earlier.

"Whew," I exhaled.

Then I remembered that the woman had been watching me the whole time. I put on the best innocent smile in my arsenal.

"You feeling okay?" the woman asked. "I don't have any more appointments noted for Mr. Jenkins today except the one he's in now. And none with a child."

I blinked. I'd half expected this.

"Oh no," I said, letting my face fall in as exaggerated a manner as possible. If Superior Sally here wanted to think of me as a child, I could run with that. "I'm going to be in so much trouble if this doesn't happen. I emailed him to set it up. The principal got so so *so* mad at me for just a slight mistake, and I was assigned to do this article to get back in his good graces. I'm new in town. I just need to write this glowing profile. But I can't do it without interviewing Mr. Jenkins. My dad even asked him for me too, when he was here today."

The woman's eyes narrowed, and her lack of sympathy was both frustrating and—I had to grudgingly admit—impressive. "Your dad?"

Everything goes in the heat of battle. It was his own rule.

I wished I knew what he'd been doing here.

I pointed at the line with his name. "He was here earlier. General Lane?"

"Yes, he was, a meet and greet," the woman admitted, not sounding happy to have to concede the point. "And he wants you to see Mr. Jenkins?"

"I have to write this story. Then the principal and my dad will be off my back. Can you point me in the right direction?" I batted my eyelashes, keeping my expression wide open. "I'm such a screw-up. I swear I sent him an email about all this."

"Sign in," the woman said, picking up the phone. "I'll buzz his assistant to come down for you."

I didn't bother to argue that I could make it on my own. The silver roman numerals on the clock behind the woman told me that my lead on the Warheads was ticking away by the moment. I couldn't afford another delay or they'd spot me way too early. Without protest, I scribbled my name on the line, embracing a sloppy penmanship so that none of the Warheads would be able to read it if they had to sign in too.

Devin only knew that he was inside to observe and report back as an eyewitness source. I'd been counting on him to also come to my aid if needed once I found the experiment and attempted to disrupt it. But I hadn't spelled out that was what I planned to do. All Devin, James, and Maddy knew was that I had scheduled a visit with the CEO for this afternoon.

If the Warheads had Devin as completely as I suspected from the salute, the last thing I needed was for him to see me and tip them off to my presence here and now. As long as I stayed out of sight, they might not realize I was here until it was too late.

But a glance back at the entrance made it clear that I might well be discovered. No one outside could see into the mirrored entrance of the lobby, but I could see out. The van had pulled up at the curb and the Warheads were filing out, black-clad form after black-clad form.

Crappity crap crap.

Now what was I supposed to do?

"She's coming down on the elevator?" I asked the intense disapproving woman in my bubbliest ditz voice. "I can go over to meet her?"

"Knock yourself out." The woman sighed at the sight of the Warheads coming toward the building in their synchronized mass. "Little creeps are here."

Maybe the front desk lady *was* as smart as she thought she was.

The nearest elevator *bing*ed open as I approached, and I bolted for it. The doors slid apart to reveal an inside designed in the style of the high-fantasy portions of *Worlds War Three*. A dragon's wings dominated the sides, emerald green scales edged in gold, and a trio of elves with pointy ears wielded menacing weaponry along the back wall. One had a tiara banded across her forehead like some long-lost princess from my elvish royal family.

There were three elevators, so I'd have laid down my last ten bucks that the other two were done up in the alien and military motifs from *Worlds*. And the service elevator would feature sparkly unicorns.

An older woman with a lined face stood in front of the panel of buttons inside the elevator. She yawned, wrinkles deepening around her eyes, and then said, "Miss Lane?"

Looking over my shoulder, I saw the front door opening to admit my classmates—and did my best not to leap into the elevator and startle the CEO's sleepy assistant.

"That's me," I said, when the woman's eyebrows slowly rose. "I can't wait to meet Mr. Jenkins."

"About that," the woman said, reaching past me to turn a key that was inserted above the rows of numbers and punch the top button, which lit in response, showing the number 70. The doors closed and we sailed up. Fast. The low beeps that signaled each floor were the only way to track our progress. "He's in a meeting, so you'll have to wait."

"No problem. I'm just so grateful to you for fitting me in. Mr. Jenkins must be very busy—so many projects to oversee."

The woman didn't bother to respond, except to yawn again.

The elevator stopped at the top floor much sooner than I had expected, sensation of flying through the air or not. Seventy was a long way from five.

And then the assistant removed the tiny key above the rows of numbers and palmed it, and it seemed even farther.

"This way," she said, edging out, confident that I would follow.

I did. Measuring each footstep so I didn't lap the woman, and considering my options in dealing with this unexpected problem.

Using the elevator apparently required a key. Which was good to know, if more than a little inconvenient.

It was also inconvenient that the sleepy assistant had remembered to take the key with her, since I was going to need to get my hands on it pronto. While fire codes meant there'd be stairs, going from floor seventy to floor five without getting caught—yeah, that wasn't going to happen.

The woman tottered at the negative version of warp-speed until she was behind a futuristic white desk. I took a seat on a white leather couch in the waiting area opposite it. As I watched, the woman set the key right beside her desk phone. Leaving it highly visible, if too far from the edge to reach out and snatch without getting busted immediately. Even by a woman who clearly needed to develop a caffeine habit.

Behind her desk, there was a long white hall. One side was a row of silver doors. The other wall was glass and offered a view of Metropolis as stunning as my daydream version from the top of the Daily Planet Building that first day on the job. Not so much as a speck of dust or a spot from a fingerprint marred the window to the world below.

I barely spared it more than a glance. Thinking . . . Thinking . . .

"How long have you worked here?" I asked, keeping the same innocently obnoxious perky tone I used downstairs. "Have you been with Mr. Dir—" *Oops, probably shouldn't call him Dirtbag here.* "—Jenkins long?"

The woman blinked heavy lids at me. Finally, she said, "You could say that. I'm his mother."

Not chatty then. Also, not someone I could use the Ronda method on. Mothers loved their sons.

"How long do you think he'll be?" I asked.

The woman lifted one shoulder in an exaggerated shrug. "Some time."

I cannot take this.

I didn't have "some time" to waste. I didn't even need to see Mr. Dirtbag Jenkins, CEO. Not when I knew which floor was my destination. And it might be better if I didn't see him, not until I was leaving at the earliest.

The older woman blinked at me again, still giving every impression that she was a few seconds from naptime . . . or perhaps bored with life at the top of her son's world. Boredom could make anyone lazy.

That realization brought me an idea, one that could work. I snapped my fingers and said, "Oh, shoot! I'm such a dumb bunny!"

The woman looked at me like *I can't believe you just called yourself that*. I wanted to say *Me neither.* But that wouldn't get the job done.

And this was a job. If I didn't execute my part of the plan, none of the rest mattered. Devin was probably down there getting initiated into the experiment right this second.

The thought spurred me into motion. I stood and crossed to the desk, messenger bag still looped over my shoulder.

"I left my notebook downstairs in the lobby. I'll just hop down there in the elevator and get it. I'm so glad I realized now and not when I'd have to keep Mr. Jenkins waiting. Good thing he's going to be awhile. I just need that key, and I'll be right back."

Only then, so as not to appear over-eager, did I let my hand dart out to grab the key from the desk.

"I don't—" the woman started.

I brandished it. Triumphant. "I'll be right back. You stay here. Don't move a muscle. Rest. I wouldn't dream of making you go back down. I can tell this is an exhausting job."

I closed the key into my fist and backed away, going slowly at first, then speeding up and turning around to hit the call button. The elevator *bing*ed and opened in an instant, eager to please its master.

And I was inside, jamming the key into the opening above the rows of buttons and tracing my hands down the rows in tandem to push the fifth floor and the door close buttons at the same time.

The doors whisked shut and the car dropped rapidly, with

beep after beep as it flew past floors. I raised my hand to salute my fellow elvish warrior princess.

"Here comes the cavalry," I said.

The elevator came to a smooth halt, and I tried to prepare myself for whatever came next. When the doors opened onto the fifth floor, I stepped out, crossing my fingers that SmallvilleGuy had counted the beeps on the recording correctly.

Gone was the bright white and sterile air of the lobby and the top floor. This was more like the hall to the Morgue. Well, not quite *that* bad, but close enough.

Everything was clean, but the walls were a light gray and the overhead lights seemed purposefully dull, casting a low, diffuse glow that made everything look like part of a nightmare.

The question was, where on this floor were they?

I pocketed the key from the elevator and moved farther into the hallway, listening as hard as I could. I took care to keep my thick boot soles from making noise, and I swung my messenger bag around so that it was accessible.

The first room that had voices coming from inside also had an open door, and I paused outside it. From where I stood, I could see a row of techs manning a bank of flat screens and keyboards and other equipment. They were also miked with headsets that curled around in front of their lips, presumably to allow communication with whoever was on the other side of the wall of one-way glass they stared at. The men at the controls were typing or adjusting knobs, swearing excitedly and nodding their heads at what was beyond the glass. There was one woman among them, but she wasn't talking nearly as much as the others, her face pinched in disapproval.

I couldn't see through the one-way glass from this angle, but it seemed like a safe enough bet this was the control room for the experiment. And that the rest of the workers running it, with that one disapproving exception, were far more gung ho than the man from the recording, the one SmallvilleGuy had been in contact with through the developer forum.

Judging from their chatter, today's session was in full swing. There might have been things to learn from eavesdropping on them, but today wasn't only about discovery. It was about disruption.

I kept going, continuing up the hall. If I was right, the one-way glass meant the next room would be the one I needed to find. I'd see Project Hydra in full-throttle mode.

I pulled aside the flap of my messenger bag and moved to the next doorway, which was also open.

And I stopped, gaping at what I saw in front of me. Had I somehow stepped out of reality and into the game?

But it wasn't the game in any way I'd ever seen it.

CHAPTER 25

The room was dark except for an illuminated scene in the middle of it, one filled with dust and desert and rattling explosions and muted screams—or, rather, a holo-scape version of those things that looked and sounded real until I blinked.

Until I looked harder to see what was really going on, and reminded myself that I *wasn't* in the game. I was standing right here.

The floor of the hall was solid under my feet, and my hand was braced against the doorjamb. When I moved it to pinch my other arm, to be sure I was right, it *hurt*.

But I didn't let a sound escape. No one noticed I was there. Not the miked project manager in the room or the Warheads arrayed in a circle of chairs around the scene. Everyone was too riveted to the experiment underway. I edged around the room, staying in the shadows and taking it all in, doing my best to understand what this was.

The tech might be similar to the game's—the Warheads had on holosets that resembled to the ones I'd worn—but it wasn't quite the same. This was a whole new sinister fourth world brought into being. One simply about war, with a tableau of a desert battle.

The game was the clear jumping-off point, but instead of the holosets projecting the war sim directly in front of their eyes, immersing them in it the usual way, these projected out, a spray of lights coalescing into the detailed scene in the center of the floor in front of the Warheads. That projection was what had thrown me off for those first confusing moments.

The lone researcher in the room held a clipboard and appeared to be conflicted as he watched the scene. He spoke up to give reluctant orders to the Warheads.

"Unit formation B," he said. His was the voice from the other day. "Direct your avatars to infiltrate the compound to lay charges now."

Devin and Anavi were in seats next to each other, slightly reclined, their lips moving occasionally.

The battle scenario on display was what people who played videogames thought warfare was like. But I knew better. I might hate bullies, but at that moment I hated the people at Advanced Research Laboratories more.

This was what I'd come here for. This was *it*. What I had to stop.

Inside the simulation, there were black-clad figures of

soldiers, moving in a kind of sync that would be any commander's glory. Here in the room, the Warheads had placid faces, divorced from feeling any of the fear and chaos, from the hot possibility that the sand would blow up under their feet and steal their lives, from everything actual soldiers in the field coped with every day.

They weren't fighting one on one. No, that would be too easy.

The scene shifted, parts of it coming in and out of focus.

The Warheads were undertaking a group assault on a large compound. The power of them acting as individuals but part of one ingeniously strategic mind was a beautiful—and terrible—thing to witness. They raced toward the compound, and then into it, moving fearlessly throughout the scene, never a false step. A soldier's form even shooed a little girl out of the way once they were inside, pushing her back toward the exit.

The guy monitoring the results spoke into the headset mike he was wearing, not raising his voice so the Warheads would take it as a command. "There's one of the boss's selling points. Humanitarian actions."

He must be talking to the control room monitors. He didn't sound like the compassion on display in the game was anything more than a kind of currency that their overlord would turn into profit.

My plan was a risk without SmallvilleGuy to help, even if it was a calculated one. Standing here, I knew it was worth taking.

It might work.

And Devin and Anavi—and the rest of the Warheads—would be hurt more by where this clearly illegal experiment was leading, if it wasn't stopped.

You couldn't conscript a group of teenage gamers into a "research project" on team gaming dynamics and then play around with their brains until you made them into a weapon. But Advanced Research Laboratories was attempting just that.

The man watched, sad and riveted, as the forms being directed by the Warheads raced around the scene. "They're doing it—he'll try to sell the military guys on this now for sure," he said. "You can all say this is right, but it's not. You'll tell them that this group can direct the ground troops better than the best trained officers in the world could do on their own, and it'll be true. They'd never have agreed, but once he shows them this, he'll convince them to let us tech up real troops for these guys to drive in the field. He'll make us do it."

I almost gasped, but I managed to hold in the sound. Everything came together for me.

This wasn't *just* about resurrecting the company's old research into creating a fearless group consciousness, smarter and more strategic with its many minds. It was about bringing *all* the old research ideas they'd gotten in trouble for together. Reinventing it with the gaming creator's technology and theorics to make it a reality. The group mind in front of me was simply the first phase.

If what the man said was true, then the next step would be creating the capacity for the Warheads to control *actual* soldiers in the field. It was so far past wrong, so far past illegal . . .

this was playing with people's minds without bothering to give them a reason. It was stealing their lives. If the military said no, someone else would say yes. Other people with tasks that required intense planning, bad people with deep pockets who would want to be able to control the bodies they sent into the line of fire, or into a building to steal some priceless target.

Someone would always say yes.

I had to try to destroy this here, now, in its infancy, before it could go any further.

I slid my hands into my messenger bag and grappled gently to find the prism flare I'd brought with me, a treasure from Dad's cache I hoped was significant enough to get this job done solo. At close quarters, it would be bright enough to blind everyone in the room temporarily.

A vibration distracted me.

My phone. I grabbed for it, looking up to make sure no one had spotted me.

The Warheads being in the sim continued to buy me cover, as it had kept any of them from noticing me lurking in the shadows. They were running a complicated formation in the first floor of the building—one soldier shot an enemy combatant wearing civilian clothes but wielding a rifle, and then the squad went into the room past him and planted small cylindrical objects in the corners.

"Now clear out of there," Mr. Sympathetic commanded them. His attention was trained on the test subjects and their actions in the scene.

So I took a chance and checked my phone

SmallvilleGuy: *Ready? The researcher decided to help. Backup's coming to cover you.*

My knees went briefly weak with relief. He had my back after all.

I sent back: *When the tones start.*

The two of us *had* to disrupt the audiovisual cue that synced the Warheads' minds together and allowed the group link to occur in the real-sim—and, unbeknownst to those running the experiment, outside it. Doing it at the right time inside *and* outside the sim should break the bond as their neural pathways resealed to protect their minds. According to the game creator's theory, at least.

That theory had better be right.

I deleted my messages with SmallvilleGuy so that no one could find them if I got caught, and then put my hands back in position on the fist-sized faceted cylinder of the flare. I continued to skirt the edges of the illuminated scene, waiting for our moment.

I watched as the black-clad troops left the compound and gathered together on the far side of a stretch of desert—cauterized by chaos, running civilians and commandos that were enemies in the simulation. They faced the large complex they'd been creeping around in, setting explosive charges.

They were about to make a successful strike in a zone that was the kind of populated area the military tried not to drop bombs on these days. And a series of charges set on-site, not just where it was convenient, but in the best possible places? That was an all-new level of accuracy, and would be far less controversial than drone strikes.

I stopped when I was right behind Sympathetic Experiment Man. This was all about to go down, for better or for worse.

A soldier in the simulation had a detonator in hand, waiting. Once the explosives went off, today's simulation would likely end. We would have only the length of the audiovisual cue to get this done. It should be like the shock of coming out of the game too quickly, but magnified in effect. But if we missed the sync signal window, our chances were over.

"You guys seeing this?" the man said into his headset, low. He put his hand to his forehead and said solemnly, like it was the worst development imaginable, "This is it. Success. What are we doing?"

There must have been a response from the control room, because he lowered his hand from his head and raised his voice: "Blow the charges."

I guess I'd see what kind of assistance the research man was willing to give to make this right.

The avatar in the scene who was holding the detonator pushed down on the top, and the compound exploded in a series of jarring booms.

My heart pounded, seeming as loud in my ears as the fake explosions. But it was as if I could hear the pitch they apparently planned to give the military—maybe even my dad? It would be all about saving civilian lives, with minimal risk to high-value assets (aka Project Hydra), because on-ground soldiers could take it all, at a much lower chance for human error.

There'd be no worries about soldiers not following orders to the letter, if their minds and bodies were being controlled—driven, the man had said—from afar. No more weaknesses in on-the-ground strategy and behavior. Not when the people making the decisions were safe in a suite like this. They might well be convinced.

But would anyone be asked to consent? Anavi and Devin hadn't been. Anavi's friend, the one the rest of the group had taken first when it started to expand, hadn't been. In fact, from what I could tell none of the Warheads had ever been asked to do anything more than use real-sim tech, without the truth about what this experiment was intended to produce. The soldiers definitely wouldn't be.

I'd done my homework for the story I wanted to write. Experiments of this nature, with zero informed consent? International law came down on them hard after World War II.

I looked at Anavi and Devin, beside each other, being forced to participate in this, whether they *knew* they were being forced or not. Their lives would be over if this experiment went forward. Their minds would never be their own.

"Get ready to bring them out," the man said into his headset. He raised his voice, scrubbing a hand at the back of his neck. "Coming back in three . . . two . . . one . . ."

He started to turn around, and did a double take when he finally saw me standing there. "Who are you?"

"Me? I'm an interested party." I steadied my hands on the flare. I was ready. But where was SmallvilleGuy? He'd said there would be help with the inside-the-sim part. "I'm here to stop this. Maybe you're expecting me?"

The guy didn't make a move, but something shifted in his face. It might have been approval. "You're young," he said, voice low. "I did what I told him I would in the sim, left the door wide open. He just had to put in the code I gave him, send the character to the right place. She'll do the job."

Before I had time to take in what that meant, the first of the tones sounded. The man stepped aside, clearing my way to the edge of the projection.

In the simulation, a round flying ship ringed with lights flew into place, the pattern cycling over and over. The Warheads began to lean forward, the eerie tones playing in sync with the lights' visual music.

But the Warheads gasped and cringed back in their seats as Daisy the dragon flew wildly into the scene with a horrifying screech that drowned the tones, before shooting a missile directly into the ship.

Which exploded.

SmallvilleGuy had sent the cavalry, all right. He'd convinced the man to insert Daisy into the research scenario.

He hadn't risked coming himself, but he'd gotten the help we needed. He'd completed his part in the plan.

The tones were still audible out here, cycling toward the end of the tune. The Warheads were recoiling from the fire in the real-sim, but they were watching it, trying to find the pattern they needed. The neural link must be fighting to stay alive.

Too bad.

I closed my eyes, because it was my turn.

I held the cylinder high overhead and yanked the pin free from the top, reveling in the dull boom that signaled the prism flare was activated and the extended flash of brighter-than-bright pinpoints of light on the backs of my eyelids as it blinded the room.

We'd disrupted the all-important signal, inside the game and out. *Please let the theory be right.*

For Anavi and Devin's sake.

Replacing the pin, I stashed the prism flare and stumbled in their direction, waiting until the pinpricks of light were gone before opening my eyes. When I did, I saw chaos nearly as impressive as that on the fake battlefield had been.

How much worse would this be if I was coming out of a shock—like when I'd been shot on my way out of the game?

"Devin? Anavi?" I asked, grabbing their hands. "I know that had to hurt, but you have to come with me. Breathe."

I tugged and they rose to their feet, both of them wobbly. Devin blinked, and blinked some more, focusing on me as well as he could.

"Go! Security will be here any second," the man said, his hands over his eyes.

Annddd sure enough, an alarm began to sound, ringing and ringing and ringing.

"That's our signal to get out of here," I said.

"I'll be okay . . . " Devin shook his head once more, his eyes barely open. But he was there. "I can think. Anavi?"

She leaned against him, blinking.

Two men in security guard uniforms entered the room, and

I started to steer Devin and Anavi toward the door. I shouted, "Help the kids first!"

We were close to the door by then, and staggered through it. Only to be greeted by more security guards rushing up the hall toward us.

A tall man in front slowed as he approached us. He held out a hand and said, "Everyone's on lockdown. We're going to need you to come back in with us and wait it out. "

That wasn't going to work. I had to get Anavi and Devin out of here.

Thinking fast, I fumbled in my bag and brought out the prism flare. Not that I had any intention of using it. A repeat flare that quickly after the first could cause more than temporary vision damage. My friends and I were the good guys. And what made us the good guys was acting like it.

But the security goons didn't know that. They'd assume the worst of me in this situation and I needed them to until we were clear.

The man frowned as I lifted the cylinder, Anavi and Devin shielded behind me. "Back off. Let us out or I'll set off this flare. I'm guessing you don't want your prize test subjects here getting hurt."

They wouldn't know that Anavi and Devin were useless for their CEO's evil purposes. Not yet.

The security cowboy started to surge forward, but a hand from behind pulled him back, against the wall. We were allowed to pass.

And there was the elevator, which I guided us past. I opened the stairwell door. "Sorry, we have to take the stairs. Pretty sure they can stop that elevator."

"You are kind of terrifying," Devin said, going through to the stairs.

"Thanks," I returned.

Anavi was shaking her head, her blinks slowing as her eyes recovered. She hesitated at the threshold. "Lois, I—I had no intention of collusion, I—"

I pressed her into the stairwell after Devin. "Good to have you back."

Both of them were recovering. They were going to be themselves. That was all the thanks I needed.

"Do you think the connection's severed for everyone?" I asked.

"I could still feel the others when Daisy tossed us out of the game. Weak, but there. The second shock severed us. Cleanly," Anavi said.

"She's right," Devin tossed over his shoulder. "It was like my brain made a moat, forced everything on the other side of it."

We half stumbled, half ran down the stairwell. "How did you figure it out?" Anavi asked.

"Long story, lots of research. Some help from my trusty sidekick."

"I don't think that was a game," Devin said. "It didn't feel like *Worlds*."

"It wasn't—or it wasn't going to be one forever," I said. "They were going to try to sell it to the military. "

Maybe even to my dad.

Maybe he would have liked it. Maybe he would have wanted to buy it.

No, I wouldn't believe that. Couldn't. It was plain enough that the military hadn't been told anything about this. And Dad would never have agreed to it. But soon they and the rest of the world *would* know the details—assuming the rest of the plan went smoothly.

We reached the door that opened to the first floor. Part of me was more nervous about this than any of the rest. We had to make a getaway if we were going to tell this story. That was the only way to ensure the experiment got put on permanent ice. "Follow my lead," I said, pulling open the door. "We'll move quick and hope for the best."

Or not.

The lobby was filled with more security guards. There were stun guns pointed toward us. The tightly wound, superior front desk woman held a taser that I did not doubt she'd delight in using.

It was my responsibility to get the three of us free from this place. Once we were out the front doors, everything would be fine.

That meant holding off security until our reinforcements showed. The only bluff I had was the prism flare.

So I hefted the cylinder high.

"Stay back," I said.

A tall woman in a suit wearing an earpiece stepped forward. "I'm the head of security," she said, "and you seem to be abducting two of our visitors."

"They want to go," I said. "They never wanted to be here in the first place."

She ignored that. "I also happen to have this gadget developed by our very own lab that disables that kind of flare."

The woman held up a long, slender device. It didn't look that different from the detonator the soldiers in the simulation upstairs had been about to use. "It's got a limited range, but it can kill that or anything with a signal—like your phones—from here." She pressed a button on it. "Our instruments were designed to be unaffected by this. Yours wasn't, I'm afraid."

To be on the safe side, I said, "Close your eyes," to Anavi and Devin, before I squeezed my own shut and pulled out the pin of the flare.

But as I'd suspected, nothing happened. The woman was telling the truth about her effective little gadget.

She was also coming toward us.

Which meant the commotion at the front doors was as welcome and as well-timed as it could possibly have been. Jamming the dead flare in my bag, I walked forward to meet the woman, and when I reached her, I did something I'd done plenty of times playing around with Lucy—I tripped. I grabbed her arm for balance, and she reached out to steady me. She dropped the gadget in the process, but I was still in motion, and the device made a satisfying crunch under my boot.

"Um, oops," I said.

She frowned down at it, and I released her arm and slipped away from her.

The part of Dad's self-defense lessons about evading holds had come in handy, finally, against someone other than my kid sister.

I moved back to Devin and Anavi, putting a hand around each of their waists. "We'll just be leaving now," I said.

"You're not going anywhere," the head of security countered, smiling coldly.

That was when James's shout rang out. He and Maddy stood inside the entrance, having shown right on schedule, and he had his phone raised over his head. "I have to hit one button to transmit this entire thing live, immediately. I think I'll call it Security Lady Attacks Defenseless Student Journalists."

Gadget broken, Security Lady had no way to prevent him from broadcasting. I returned her smile, just as coldly.

Or almost. My smile might have included a hint of gloating.

Maddy added a threat to James's. "In case you don't know, that feed is showcased on the *Daily Scoop*'s homepage, but that means all the visitors to the *Daily Planet* site will see it too," she said. "Live."

The nearby elevators *bing*ed and people poured off them, including the sympathetic man from the experiment and the rest of the Warheads.

They didn't look so warlike anymore. They looked . . . dazed. Best of all, when they walked into the lobby, it wasn't in any kind of sync. The man nodded to me, a thanks in it.

The head of security turned away from me to James and Maddy. "What do you want?"

I spurred Anavi and Devin forward. "They're here for us. Like I said, we'll just be leaving."

The head of security and her team growled at that, but what could they do? Nothing. Especially when the research man stepped up and said, "Let them go."

Maddy came forward to meet us, and James backed to a door and held it open, his phone still overhead until everyone else made it outside.

James shut the door, and breaking into a jog, said, "We'd better run."

"Why?" I asked.

"I was already broadcasting," James said, "the entire time. We need to get a story up fast. Might take longer if they come after us."

"Excellent point," I said, smiling.

A taxi sat at the curb and I wasn't surprised at all to see my grinning friend behind the wheel. "Need a ride, big tipper?" he asked.

I climbed in the passenger side. The others piled into the back.

Security goons were pouring out the front door, and even the CEO's mother-slash-assistant and the front desk receptionist were with them. I pressed the button to roll down the window.

"Your CEO can email me any statement of response," I called out to them. "He's got my address." Then I told the cab driver, "Earn your money. Get us out of here."

He floored it away from the curb with his typical screech, and asked, "Where to?"

"The Daily Planet Building," I said, "and make it fast."

My phone buzzed in my bag, and I bit back another grin. The message was a question mark.

Fill you in later, I tapped out, *right now I've got a story to write.*

CHAPTER 26

I already had the story half-composed in my head by the time we got to the Morgue. I banged it out as quickly as I could, while James pumped Devin and Anavi for details, and Maddy helped Devin design the graphics to go along with it.

James also edited his video to embed within the text. This time, he did want an also-contributed credit. He was going over my copy now.

We'd turned off our phones and taken the receivers for the office's dinosaur landlines off the hook, not wanting to risk any cease and desist calls. I had to admit I was a little surprised Perry hadn't been by to check in on us yet. But I could be thankful for small favors. This would be a coup for the *Daily Planet*—and an even bigger one for the *Scoop*.

The story it told was of a principal in bed with industry. Of students privileged above others because they were taking part in a secret experiment started without their consent, one that shouldn't have taken place on living subjects, or at all. Anavi hadn't yet turned in the permission form they'd sent home for her parents to sign, which only gave approval for her to leave school property and gave no details on the experiment itself, so in the story it went. Exhibit A.

The story also said that the company in question had been days away from demonstrating the entire thing to the military-industrial complex, an ethical breach its shareholders should not reward unless they supported the idea of black ops projects that violated international law and used children.

So what if my rhetoric was heated? They'd almost stolen the selves of two of my friends.

Friends.

I had *friends*, plural, friends who knew more about me than I'd ever let anyone see. Except for SmallvilleGuy.

I still couldn't believe he'd come through by finding a way to send Daisy into the sandbox in his place. He didn't break the rules and take the risk himself, but he had been there for me like he'd said he wanted to be. Maybe I should make hoping for things a habit.

"It's good," James said, when he finished going over the story. "I just cleaned up your spelling. Sending your way, Devin." He turned to me. "Really good, actually. And you can keep my holoset. I'm not much into gaming."

"Why, thank you, on both counts," I said, surprised—and at the same time, not—by the gesture.

Maddy was practically bouncing again. "Did you see the looks on their faces when they ran out of that building?" She giggled. And it wasn't even the first time she'd said it.

"You should have seen the head of security's face when Lois 'accidentally' smashed her toy," Devin said.

"I wish," Maddy said. "You do it for me. A historical reenactment."

To my surprise, Devin made an affronted gasp, his eyes going wide and his hand clasping at his chest.

We were laughing together, then. James rolled his chair over to watch as Devin formatted the story to send it live. Maddy came and sat on the corner of my desk. Anavi was in a chair beside it, where she'd been quietly observing the flurry of activity. She didn't seem to be in a hurry to go home.

"Headline request?" Devin asked. "'Queen of the Elves Clears Out Commandos.'"

"Hilarious," I said. "I don't care what it says as long as it starts with the word 'Exclusive'."

"Done," he said.

Anavi tapped her fingers on the top of the desk.

"Spit it out, Anavi. You're making me nervous," I said as gently as I could.

"I feel I must . . . Lois, I don't know how I could ever repay you. There's no adequate compensation."

"I can think of a couple ways," I said. "And I should never have let them get you in the first place."

"Is there any other crazy mad science going on that you haven't told us about?" Maddy asked.

"Way number one," I said, leaving Maddy's question aside for a second, "if you could put in writing that your retraction request was garbage—or however you'd say it—"

"Spurious," Anavi said. "My greatest pleasure. May I use your computer?"

I got up and took Maddy's arm. "You *should* be in a band, you know. If you want to."

Maddy's smile was shy. "And leave all this? Maybe someday. Mostly, I like daydreaming about it. Is that weird?"

I smiled back at her. "Yes, but only in the good way."

Maddy's gaze found its way back to James, like it always did.

I didn't tell Maddy that he wasn't worthy of her, though I still felt like he was an idiot for not noticing that she was into him. It wasn't my place to butt in, not between them. So I said, "Boys," low so only Maddy heard. "Sometimes they are so clueless."

"I know, right?" Maddy agreed enthusiastically.

Even if he was clueless, the truth was James wasn't that bad.

"We're live," Devin said, spinning his chair so he and James could high-five.

I reached over and set the receiver back on the antique phone on my desk. Which immediately vibrated, then sounded an uber-loud ring.

We all exchanged a look, and the others pointed at me.

"You answer," Devin said. So I did.

"Get up here right now. All of you," Perry barked into my ear.

*

All Perry had said was "Newsroom," with another bark that he assumed I could find it. We piled off the elevator onto a bustling upper floor.

A floor that was overcome by a rolling hush as we made our way along the open area packed with desks.

"Perry White?" I asked.

"Second office from the corner," a man in a brown suit said. "You must be the prodigies."

We kept walking.

"Prodigy's a good thing, right?" I asked Anavi, who'd insisted on tagging along in case the retraction came up.

"Usually," Anavi agreed.

"Is that them? Get in here!" Perry, from somewhere nearby. We followed the shout to an open office door.

He had an open bottle. "It's sparkling apple juice, not champagne, because A, this is a newspaper and we don't have money for that and B, contributing to the delinquency of minors is not on today's agenda. Now, I have one question for you to answer, Lane."

He called me Lane. That was a promising sign.

"Did you give the company a chance to respond?"

I lifted my chin. "I told the CEO's assistant personally that he could email me if he wanted to go on the record."

Perry burst out laughing. The rest of us exchanged looks of the "has he gone insane?" variety.

"Was that before or after you filmed the stand-off in the lobby and broadcast it live on our streaming channel?" He shook his head, picked up the bottle, and started to pour. "Don't tell me. I don't really want to know. I'm proud of you guys. You might turn into real newshounds yet."

We accepted the praise and the sweet, fizzy drinks, and I went over to have a look out Perry's window.

The view wasn't exactly what I'd imagined, but in some ways it was better. That was the real city of tomorrow out there.

And it was my city now.

"You heard from your dad?" Perry asked from behind me.

"I turned off my phone," I said, "so not yet. But I should get going."

"Good luck," he said. "I knew you'd whip these guys into shape. They just needed someone with a nose for it."

"I can smell news," I said.

"Nah," Perry said with a grin, "anybody can scratch up news. I meant for the truth."

⋆

My parents were not waiting with sparkling drinks when I got home. They were at the kitchen table, though. "Lois, get in here," Dad called when the door closed.

Lucy was sitting halfway up the stairs, and waved at me before grimacing and making a slicing motion across her neck with her hand.

CUTE, I mouthed to her, and marched in to greet the firing squad.

"You want to tell me what you were thinking writing a story like this?" Dad asked, and the coolness of his tone was troubling.

I decided to be relieved that he hadn't asked about the distraction I'd used for the disruption at the lab. Hopefully that meant the prism flare could be discreetly replaced, with him none the wiser.

"That it was my job," I said, not showing him a moment's weakness. I knew what I was doing. I had a place where I belonged. Finally.

He said, "I'm not so sure—"

"I saw your name on the sign-in book at the lab," I said, "but I do hope that our paths won't cross that often. I know you're probably grateful to me for uncovering what I did, because I also know you wouldn't want to support a company that would do something like that. Would you?"

"Lois, of course not, but this isn't about me—"

"I'm good at this. It's what I want to do. Any help you can give me with Butler would be welcome."

I didn't think the story would make the principal lose his job. He had plausible deniability about the nature of the research, and if I was honest, I doubted he had known the details. But that was one unfortunate thing about how quickly I'd had to write the story. Not enough time to find out whether he would have defended it the same way he did the Warheads when Anavi was their victim.

There was always next time. I was curious about the rest of

the companies that had made charitable donations or become research partners with the school.

"I have to go catch up with . . . my schoolwork." I walked over and planted a kiss on my mother's cheek, then on Dad's.

I'd almost slipped up and said I needed to catch up with a friend.

Somehow, when I got upstairs, I knew not to bother logging into chat, even if it did mean potentially missing a new baby cow picture.

After a day this long, I wanted to *see* him. I figured he would want the same thing, impossible as it was.

The CEO of Advanced Research Laboratories was the bad guy. There was a risk that the people running *Worlds War Three* weren't that great either, as a baddie subsidiary, but one of the workers had helped us in the end. It was a risk I was willing to take, since this was the only way we *had* to see each other.

That was how I justified going back inside *Worlds War Three* as I slipped on James's holoset. Well, mine now. I settled on the bed and turned on the holoset.

The game sprang into view around me and for once, the world wasn't on fire or in the midst of an attack.

Two suns were setting with a downright poetic mix of dark, unnatural hues tinged violet and red. In the near distance, I could see Devin's castle, rising from the rubble like a phoenix made of stone. His army was at work rebuilding it and as I went closer, I saw two figures directing them. One was King

Devin, back in his full chainmail and armor regalia. The other was a familiar female form, whose grenades were emblazoned with words.

I was about to go talk to them when a voice behind me said, "Hey."

I turned and smiled at the green-skinned alien boy—friendly—who was smiling back at me.

"We did it," I said. "Pretty nice teamwork. Did you come up with the idea?"

"I knew I couldn't stand by and not do anything," he said. "So after I told him we were trying to stop the experiment, I asked if there was any way to send fiery backup. Once I explained the plan to disrupt the signals, he wanted nothing more than to help. I'm not sure he really thought we'd manage it, though."

"Well, sending Daisy, that was . . ."

Oh, god, I was blushing again. Already.

". . . genius," I finished awkwardly.

His smile evaporated. A seriousness took over his features and I so wished I could see it in the real world. See if that expression was real.

It felt real.

"Lois," he said, "I wish I could have been there. I hate that I wasn't."

"But you were, in the way that counts. I know it's complicated."

"You have no idea," he said.

And my elf face must have looked stung, because he said, "My fault, not yours."

He waved for me to come with him, in the opposite direction of Anavi and Devin. I did.

"I told my parents about you," he said.

My heart pounded and thumped and thudded and made a general nuisance of itself.

"You did? What—what did you say?"

"I told them you were my friend, and that I wanted to tell you the truth about me. That I wanted to tell you what I've been keeping secret, who I am in real life."

"And?" I was breathless.

"And they said that I can't. That it's too dangerous."

He sighed and turned to me. His eyes were a striking blue. I wanted, more than ever, to know if that was their actual color.

"I knew they'd say no, but I wanted to try. I owed it to you to make sure. I want to tell you everything . . . I needed them to remind me why I can't. Not yet."

"Oh, okay," I said, knowing I wasn't doing a good job of hiding my disappointment.

"But, Lois, I promise you that someday I will. You'll be the first person I tell."

I kicked at the ground with my bare foot, and then started to move forward again. "It seems like you're making an awful lot of assumptions."

He caught up with me. "You mean that you'll still be here,

waiting to find out. I shouldn't assume that. But . . . we are friends, aren't we, Lois?"

"Yes, we are." I faced him again. "I meant you're assuming I won't figure your secret out on my own first."

He smiled at me. "Want to go help your friends rebuild?"

"Sure," I said, and offered him my hand. He took it.

And we walked into the violently beautiful sunset together.

GWENDA BOND is the author of the young adult novels *Girl on a Wire*, *Blackwood*, and *The Woken Gods*. She has also written for *Publishers Weekly* and the *Los Angeles Times*, among other publications, and just might have been inspired to get a journalism degree by her childhood love of Lois Lane. She has an MFA in Writing from the Vermont College of Fine Arts, and lives in a hundred-year-old house in Lexington, Kentucky, with her husband, author Christopher Rowe, and their menagerie.

Visit her online at **gwendabond.com** or **@gwenda** on Twitter.